### *Until Justice Is Done*

"What sets McGuire's novels apart from the pack is the level of realism she brings to the legal aspects of the story."

—*The Sentinel* (Santa Cruz, CA)

"[McGuire's] knowledgeable account of the procedures the police use in investigating a rape is absorbing."

—*The Practical Lawyer*

### *Until Proven Guilty*

"*Until Proven Guilty* is a tense, nerve-jangling thriller that should satisfy fans of *The Silence of the Lambs*."
—Peter Blauner, author of *The Intruder*

"Compelling. . . . A super read. . . . What sets *Until Proven Guilty* apart . . . is McGuire's experience with the criminal justice system."

—Biz Van Gelder, *Trial* magazine

"Gripping. . . . This unrelenting . . . account of a vicious serial killer all but commands readers to burn the midnight oil. . . . [The] pathological details and criminal profiles unfailingly rivet the attention."

—*Publishers Weekly*

"Strong, taut, and terrifying . . . as exciting as it is authentic. . . . With an insider's knowledge of the law and police procedures, McGuire tells a terrific story."
—Kit Craig, author of *Gone*

**Books by Christine McGuire**

FICTION

Until Proven Guilty*
Until Justice is Done*
Until Death Do Us Part*

NONFICTION

Perfect Victim (co-written with Carla Norton)

*Published by POCKET BOOKS

# UNTIL DEATH DO US PART

## Christine McGuire

**POCKET STAR BOOKS**
New York   London   Toronto   Sydney   Tokyo   Singapore

This book is a work of fiction. Names, characters, places and incidents are products of the author's imagination or are used fictitiously. Any resemblance to actual events or locales or persons, living or dead, is entirely coincidental.

An *Original* Publication of POCKET BOOKS

 A Pocket Star Book published by
POCKET BOOKS, a division of Simon & Schuster Inc.
1230 Avenue of the Americas, New York, NY 10020

Copyright © 1997 by Christine McGuire

ISBN: 0-671-53618-4

First Pocket Books printing January 1997

10  9  8  7  6  5  4  3  2  1

POCKET STAR BOOKS and colophon are registered trademarks of Simon & Schuster Inc.

Cover photo by Barros & Barros/The Image Bank

Printed in the U.S.A.

*This novel is lovingly dedicated to*
*Helene, Gayle, Danny, Cindy,*
*and*
*Elizabeth.*

# ACKNOWLEDGMENTS

With deep gratitude to Frederick Nolan.

Special thanks to my agents, Arthur and Richard Pine, and to my editor, Julie Rubenstein.

# UNTIL DEATH DO US PART

# PROLOGUE

*The CD player in the living room of Lawrence Alonzo Sutterfield's Saratoga townhouse whirred, clicked, and then sucked the silver disc into its blood-red interior. It counted the tracks, flashed a green 12 in the LED display, and then Whitney Houston's soft voice singing "I Will Always Love You" floated across the room. Candlelight from two vanilla-scented candles on end tables flanking the sofa flickered, casting fleeting shadows of the two lovers onto the opposite wall.*

*"I'll always love you, too. Always. No matter what,"* Lawrence *whispered.*

*It had been a perfect Saturday. Two glasses of Chardonnay in the elegant, sunken lobby lounge of the Fairmont Hotel with its shimmering crystal chandeliers, then a hand-in-hand stroll around the fountain in the plaza, smiling at the children running shrieking between the vertical columns of water. A two o'clock matinee presentation of* Fiddler on the Roof *at San Jose's beautiful Performing Arts Center, champagne*

1

*and truffles at intermission, and afterward an intimate seafood dinner at Scott's. Finally a sunset drive home, sweet anticipation simmering and smoldering, like a faint far-off drumbeat increasing in intensity until it became a deafening thunderous roar.*

*"Please," Lawrence pleaded. His voice was throaty as he slid his hand up his partner's smooth thigh, stroking, teasing. "I can't wait."*

*"Soon," was the whispered response. "Slowly, lover. Slowly."*

*They had been regular though not exclusive sexual partners for more than five years. Four months had passed since their last passionate encounter at the Pacific Hotel in Monterey, but now it seemed to Lawrence Sutterfield as though they had never been apart.*

*"I love the things you wear, Angel," he said. His voice was dreamy. "Everything so flimsy, so sexy."*

*Eyes closed, he slipped his fingers beneath the lacy panties, feeling the warm body half-naked beside his own on the leather sofa.*

*"Can we begin?" Lawrence whispered.*

*"First, you have to say how much you want me. Say it."*

*"I want you, Angel. I've wanted you all day. I want to make love to you."*

*"What would you like, Lorenzo? The same game as last time?"*

*"Yes. Yes. I love it when you call me that."*

*"If that's what you want. But you know the rules."*

*"Please," Lawrence said. "Yes. Do it. Use me. Like you did in Monterey."*

*"Oh, you're so bad. Shameless."*

"Yes," Lawrence said. "Yes, shameless."

"I thought so." The tone was harder, sterner. Lawrence quaked with pleasure. "The truth now. Have you been bad? Have you?"

"Yes," Lawrence said. "Oh, yes, bad."

"I want to know. Tell me the truth. Have there been others?"

"They were just faces. Nothing."

"You are wicked. I hate it that I can't trust you. Why do you do such wicked things?"

"You weren't . . . I always wanted you, but you . . . I couldn't get you. I called and called. I needed someone. I missed you so terribly."

"Well. Perhaps I'll forgive you. If you're good."

Their mouths met, hot and hard. Lawrence's hand caressed and explored. Lust engorged him. He moaned, burying his face in the blond hair falling across his face.

"Please," he said thickly. "Oh, God, please, can we go in the bedroom now?"

"You promise to do exactly what I tell you?"

"Yes." Lawrence panted. "Yes, anything, anything."

"Come, then."

They went together into the bedroom. A huge four-poster bed with pale yellow silk sheets dominated the room, its head against the wall opposite the door. The heavy drapes were drawn. Lawrence switched on a small red bedside light, then lay down on the bed. Drowning in anticipation, he watched the slim figure cross the room, blond hair gleaming in the half-light. A drawer slid open; he heard the metallic jingle of the handcuffs, and he groaned aloud with pleasure.

"Are these what you want?"

*"Yes," he said. "Yes, hurry, yes."*

*"You know what's going to happen? You know you have to be punished?"*

*"Yes, yes."*

*"Until you cry for mercy?"*

*"Please." His voice was thick, his breathing ragged.*

*"First things first." Severity in the voice now. A touch of anger. He loved that. He lay naked, legs apart, shivering with anticipation as his wrists were manacled to the bedposts.*

*"Now," he said. "Please, now."*

*Slim, cool fingers caressed him. Warm lips touched him, sliding, soft. He shivered with delight, but he knew he must not speak until he was spoken to.*

*"Do you like that, you wicked thing? Do you want more?"*

*"Yes, oh, yes. More, more."*

*"First your punishment. For being bad."*

*Leather thongs, mysteriously produced, whispered through the air and cracked against his naked skin, streaking his face, neck, chest, and belly with angry red welts. His body convulsed, subsided. The salt taste of blood touched his tongue. He whimpered again with pain and ecstasy.*

*"Shall we go on?"*

*He moved his head in assent, unable to speak, eyes shut tight in anticipation. His body trembled like an aspen leaf in a summer breeze as the leather thongs were used to bind his feet to the opposite posts at the foot of the bed. The next part was the biting. Delicious pain.*

*"Please, Angel," he whispered. "Oh, God, please, now."*

*"Wait. Something new first."*

*Light caught the blade of a black bone-handled Buck knife. Unease chilled his skin, raising goose bumps.*

*"Angel?"*

*"Shhhhh, my sweet."*

*The cold touch of the knife blade made him flinch. Lawrence moaned aloud. This was new, dangerously exciting. They had never gone anything like this far together before. Somewhere in the far reaches of his mind, an urgent whispered warning sounded, but he suppressed its urgency and ignored it. Lust roared through his head like a runaway freight train. When the need became unbearable, he would whisper "enough" the way they always did.*

*"More," he said. A soft hiss, a cool sensation. He felt the soft scrape of the blade. The touch of a soft weight on his body made him open his eyes. He looked down and saw something that looked like a sausage lying on his belly.*

*"What's . . . what are you doing?"*

*"All part of the game, lover. Close your eyes."*

*He closed his eyes, surrendering again to sensation.*

*"You were bad. Say it, Lawrence."*

*"I was bad." He moaned softly. "I'm sorry, I was bad. Oh, Jesus, enough. Enough, Angel. Come to me now, come to me."*

*"No." Angel's voice was hard, cold. "You haven't been punished enough yet."*

*"Please, Angel," Lawrence begged. "Please, stop, enough."*

*Lawrence Sutterfield moaned again. This wasn't how he'd planned it. Nothing like this. He heard the click of the lighter, smelled the sharp tang of cigarette* smoke, and the excitement inside him faltered. Something was wrong. Something was terribly, awfully wrong.

"That's . . . enough," he said. "I don't want this—"

"What you want, my dear Lawrence, is no longer relevant."

"Unfasten me!" Lawrence screeched, writhing against the restraining handcuffs, eyes fixed in horror and disbelief on the smoke coming from the thing on his belly.

"Jesus Christ, stop this!" he screeched. "Angel, are you crazy? Stop this!"

The bedroom door opened, and a shaft of candlelight from the adjacent living room touched the blond hair and bare shoulders of the slender figure standing in the doorway.

"By fire shalt thou be cleansed. Lover."

The voice was cold and hating. The words hung in the air like the frozen breath of death. The bound man screamed and screamed again, his voice drowning the faint hiss made by the thing on his belly. He screamed for another thirty seconds, then, with a sputtering roar, a merciless hard white blinding light erupted, and Lawrence Sutterfield's body was engulfed by hell.

# 1

Kathryn Mackay, Deputy District Attorney and head of the Special Prosecutions Unit of the Santa Rita County District Attorney's office, parked her new red Audi on a side street three blocks from the County Building. She unloaded her briefcase and laptop from the backseat, strapped them onto her luggage cart, and headed for court.

Normally, she would have parked in her own assigned parking space, just a few steps from the courts building, but this morning she knew her space—and every other available empty spot—would already be occupied by the reporters, attorneys, and spectators descending upon the courtroom where her trial was about to begin.

Today would be the first time a District Attorney's office in California had charged a defendant with attempted murder by intentional infliction of HIV. The trial of Richard Hudson was hot news and high-profile, and, predictably, courtroom groupies and media from all over the state had descended on Santa Rita like locusts on a Kansas wheat field. And they were just about as welcome, at least among county workers who suddenly had no place to park and couldn't squeeze into the basement cafeteria for their morning cups of coffee.

Someone said there wasn't a motel room to be had within twenty miles, and when she saw the parking lot surrounding the front and west side of the Government Center and Courts Building, Kathryn believed it. During pretrial proceedings, Judge Woods had denied the defense motion to bar television cameras in the courtroom for this trial, ruling that TV coverage was merely the twentieth- and soon-to-be twenty-first-century means of affording more citizens the right to observe firsthand the American judicial process in action. As a result, radio and television station vans with satellite dishes on their roofs squatted by the dozen like waiting beasts of prey, their entangled tentacles of electrical wires and cables creating an electrician's nightmare to which the county's safety inspectors turned wisely indulgent blind eyes. Like everyone else associated with the trial, they knew it was going to be a damned three-ring circus, and there was nothing anyone could do to stop it.

"Morning, Kathryn."

She looked around to see DA's Inspector James Field smiling down at her. Tall and well built, with sandy-brown hair and alert brown eyes that always seemed to have a hint of amusement in them, Field had boyish good looks that were deceptive: he had well over ten years of law enforcement experience.

"Thought I better warn you, it's a madhouse inside," Field told her as he swung open the door to the courthouse. He was right. A wall of noise from the crowded hallway hit them, TV camera crews setting up, sound technicians adjusting booms, floor managers shouting instructions, reporters and spectators jostling for places near the courtroom doors.

As Field pushed the crowd aside to make way for the two of them to enter the courtroom, Kathryn glanced at her watch and saw it was already twenty before ten. Any moment now, the sheriff's deputies would escort the defendant into the courtroom.

She piled her files and laptop on the counsel table slightly to her left and sat down. Her opening statement, on five loose pages of notes, was placed directly in front of her. Those five pages of notes—and nothing else—would be carried to the podium as she began her first direct communication with the jurors since jury selection.

Kathryn subscribed to a few hard-and-fast rules with respect to opening statements: just her printed notes, everything else made to look extemporaneous, although she knew spontaneity was not her strong suit. She never left anything as crucial as opening statements or closing argument to chance: they were carefully constructed and rehearsed.

"This ours?" Field asked Kathryn, pointing to a package. Wrapped in brown paper and sealed with Scotch tape, it was flat and rectangular, about the size of a videotape. Kathryn glanced at the label and shook her head.

"It's addressed to Marty Belker. Would you mind taking it over to him?" She looked up and noticed that defense attorney Martin Belker had wandered over toward the door through which his client would appear. His investigator had not yet arrived. "Just lay it on his table—he'll spot it when he sits down."

"Sure." Field picked up the package, pushed his chair back, and stood up. He had taken no more than a step or two toward the defense table when there was a huge flat explosion accompanied by an orange and white flash that seemed to emanate from the front of his body.

In the same instant but in what seemed like eerie slow motion, the blast blew Marty Belker's briefcase off the counsel table, then the table and the three chairs intended for defense counsel, investigator, and defendant were propelled across the open space, landing in a heap against the east wall of the courtroom.

Shocked and disoriented, but aware now that a bomb had exploded, Kathryn discovered she was lying on her side against the restraining wall separating the well of the courtroom from the spectator seats. Her counsel table was on its side; papers, files, and laptop dumped on the floor. Orange smoke and a sharp, acrid odor filled the courtroom. Papers spiraled lazily down, like strange wounded birds. Everywhere alarms were going off.

Kathryn looked up to see James Field tottering on shaking legs as blood spurted out of the mangled mess of tissue and bone dangling from strips of sinew and flesh that had been his hand.

"Oh, my God, help me," he groaned. He took two faltering steps, then collapsed like a bundle of dropped laundry.

Brushing back the hair from her face, she ran across the floor to where Field lay unconscious on his back in a widening pool of blood. The end of his right arm was a mass of shredded flesh. There were deep cuts on his face, and he was breathing in stertorous gasps. The front of his jacket was a frizz of crisped wool, and there was a black patch on his shirt the size of a dinner plate. She ripped off the sleeve from her blouse and fashioned a tourniquet on his upper arm, using a splinter of wood from the demolished table to tighten the knot, ignoring the spurting arterial blood spraying her clothes and hands.

She stood up, coughing as the acrid smoke bit at her throat. In the drifting murk, she could hear people screaming and shouting in panic. Above her head, shattered strip lights hung by their exposed wires from the ceiling. Broken glass and plastic ceiling tiles crunched beneath her as she worked furiously to stem the flow of blood from Inspector Field's ruined arm. Tears rolled down her cheeks, and they were not for herself.

"Damnit, Jim, stay with me," she urged the unconscious figure. "You hear me, Jim? I'm here. Stay with me. Everything's going to be okay, I promise."

Through the thinning smoke, she heard the sound of voices shouting hoarsely.

"Over here!" she yelled at the figures she could see moving toward her. "For God's sake, hurry!"


"Kathryn, are you all right?"

She looked up from the bench where she was sitting outside the courtroom to see the familiar face of Walt Earheart, lieutenant in charge of detectives in the sheriff's office. Nearly six feet tall and weighing in around 240 pounds, Earheart looked more like a heavyweight boxer than a cop. There was concern in his eyes.

"Yes, okay, I'm fine," she said absently.

"You sure?" Earheart said. "You're covered in blood."

Probing and searching with her fingers for blood, or worse, Kathryn located only a sore spot on her left thigh. Checking further, she discovered a bruise on her leg the size of a grapefruit. *I must have jumped when the bomb went off,* she thought. *Probably hit my leg and knocked the table over.*

"No, I'm all right. Shaken up is all. What about Jim?"

"On his way to County Hospital," Earheart said. "You sure you're okay?"

"Has someone told Rochelle?"

Jim Field's wife, Rochelle, was like family. Everyone in law enforcement knew her. Before her marriage, she had been a dispatcher for County Communications.

"I sent a car to take her over to the hospital."

"Anyone else hurt?" Kathryn asked.

"We got quite a few people in shock, maybe half a dozen with minor injuries. One of the TV people broke his arm. Tripped over a camera cable when he bolted from the courthouse. Marty Belker got hit by debris or flying glass. Nothing serious. He's at the hospital being looked at, too. Must have scared the hell out of him, just like the rest of us. It could've been a whole lot worse, though."

Unless you were James Field, Kathryn thought.

As she stood up, she felt a mild whirl of vertigo, and then it was gone. Looking around, she saw there was machinery and movement everywhere. Fire engines, ambulances, and patrol cars were parked in front of the court building. She saw the familiar white van of the Crime Scene Investigation Unit—CSI to everyone in law enforcement—off to one side of the parking lot. Deputies were looping long strands of yellow crime-scene tape around the perimeters of the building, and other officers were waving away curious citizens drawn to the courtroom by the explosion.

"You have any idea what happened in there, Kathryn?" Earheart asked her.

"It was a bomb," she said. "Some kind of letter bomb."

His expression changed. "You saw it?"

When Kathryn nodded, he told her to wait and hurried across to speak rapidly to a tall, hatchet-faced man standing near the entrance to the courtroom. He looked over at Kathryn, nodded, and came back with Earheart.

"George Purington." He introduced himself. "I'm commander of the bomb squad. We've met before, but it's been a while. Don't feel bad if you don't remember me." His words were measured, precise, his dark-eyed gaze direct and steady.

"I remember you. I'm glad you're here."

"You saw the device?"

"It was a package about the size of a videotape," Kathryn said. "Brown paper, Scotch-taped at the ends."

"How heavy?"

Kathryn frowned. "I don't know. It didn't look heavy."

"Did it have a name, an address on it?"

"I only got a glance at it. I think it just said, 'Martin Belker, Esq.' And it was marked 'Personal.'"

"Who's Belker?"

"Defense attorney. He works for the Public Defender's office."

Purington made a note. "Stamps?"

"I didn't see any."

"Binding tape? String?"

"No."

"Where was it?"

"On the counsel table."

"See anyone put it there?"

"No."

"Did you handle it?"

Kathryn shook her head. "My Inspector, James Field, noticed it and drew it to my attention. I told him it was for the defense attorney."

"He'd already picked it up?"

"That's right."

Purington frowned. "And then?"

"He started across the room, and it went—it exploded."

"Do you have any idea how long it was on the table before Field saw it?"

"No. But it can't have been there long," Kathryn said.

"Why is that?"

"We were supposed to start at ten o'clock. Usually, the bailiff unlocks the courtroom early, so the lawyers can bring in files and get set up," Kathryn told him. "The package was already on the prosecution table when we got here."

"So someone put it there . . . when?"

Kathryn shrugged. "Probably sometime between about nine o'clock and about nine forty-five, when

Inspector Field and I got here. You could narrow that down a bit by asking the bailiff exactly when he unlocked the doors."

"Name?"

"Chris Taylor," Kathryn said.

"How do you feel?" Purington asked. "Can you walk?"

"Sure," Kathryn said, then winced as the bruise on her leg gave a warning throb.

"You want to grab on to me, Kathryn?" Walt Earheart said.

"I'll be fine, Walt." Kathryn smiled. "Where are we going, George?"

"Take a look inside," he said.

Kathryn followed Purington and Earhart into the damaged courtroom. The smoke had cleared now, and the place was literally crawling with criminalists in white jumpsuits, moving in a line across the floor on their hands and knees.

"They're searching for fragments of the bomb," Purington said. "Metal, paint, glass, anything that might have a residue of the explosive."

Traces of residue would be sorted by mass spectrometers which added an electric charge to molecule fragments and accelerated them through a magnetic field, separating them by mass and energy, he told Kathryn, and also by columns of absorbent material through which molecule mixtures were forced, separating them by type. Criminalists would look for telltale molecular debris that could be used to link the bomb materials to specific subjects.

"Going by what you say about the size of the package and the damage here, I'd say it might have been some kind of plastic explosive," he added. "I have to tell you, though, identifying any explosive, or determining how and where it was made, is pretty difficult."

"My jacket is in here someplace," Kathryn said.

"Kiss it good-bye," Purington told her. "They'll have already bagged it to send to the lab. Point out to me where you were when the bomb went off."

"I was sitting at the table, there," Kathryn said, pointing. "Jim was sitting beside me, then he picked up the package and starting walking toward—"

There was no need to point out where the device had exploded. A coagulated pool of blood marked the spot.

"What kind of fuckin' psychos do such shit, anyway?" Earheart growled, then caught himself. "Sorry, Kathryn."

She shrugged. It was a rhetorical question, but Purington answered anyway.

"Take your pick," he said. "There's plenty of nuts out there to go around. Loners who send letter bombs to talk-show hosts or the telephone company. Ticked-off relatives who want to wipe out their entire families. Environmentalist wackos who think the way to save the redwoods is to blow up some logger's truck. Goddamn extremists like the ones who blew up the Federal Building in Oklahoma City."

"Do you need me for anything else?" Kathryn asked. "If not, I'm going up to the hospital to see my inspector."

"Fine with me," Purington told her. "I know where to find you if I need you."

As she turned to go, Kathryn heard someone call

her name. She looked around and saw court bailiff Chris Taylor coming toward her. His face was pale and his uniform dust-stained and disheveled. A thin trickle of blood from a cut on his forehead had dried in an elongated S above his right eyebrow.

"Any news about Jim Field?" he asked urgently.

"They've taken him to County," Kathryn replied. "I'm just on my way up there."

"Do they think—is he going to be okay?"

"Who are you?" George Purington interrupted.

"Sorry, George," Walt Earheart said. "This is Chris Taylor, the court bailiff we were talking about. Chris, this is Commander Purington, bomb squad."

Purington nodded briskly. "Where were you when the bomb went off, Deputy?"

"Up there," Taylor said, pointing to a spot behind and to the right of the judge's bench.

"What time did you get to the courtroom this morning?"

Taylor stuck out his lower lip. "Must have been about eight-forty, give or take five minutes."

"Did you see anyone anywhere near the prosecutor's table at any time?"

Taylor's boyish face creased into a frown of concentration.

"There are a lot of people coming and going before a trial begins, Commander," he said. "We can't keep tabs on all of them all of the time."

"No one's blaming you, Deputy," Purington said. "I'm just trying to find out what happened in here."

"Do they—do you have any idea who did it? Why?"

Purington shook his head. "Not yet."

"You ought to get that cut looked at, Chris," Kathryn said. Taylor smiled and touched his forehead almost apologetically.

"It's nothing," he said, and paused awkwardly. "I'm just so sorry about what happened to Jim Field."

"Which reminds me, I'd better get going," Kathryn said. "I'll tell him you were asking about him, Chris."

"Would you do that? Thank you."

"Keep me posted, Kathryn," Walt Earheart said. "I'd come with you, but—" He made a gesture that encompassed the whole scene.

"I'll check with you later," Kathryn called over her shoulder as she headed toward her car.

Ten minutes later, she swung the Audi off Cabrillo Drive and took the rising road that led up to the hospital standing on the crest of the hill. They said the view of Santa Rita and Monterey Bay from the CEO's office on the top floor was spectacular, but Kathryn had never seen it. Her visits to County General usually involved either the morgue in the basement or the special suite set aside for the examination of rape victims; there weren't too many opportunities to admire the view. Occasionally, she visited her friend, who was head of the hospital's mental health unit, but Margaret's office wasn't on the fifth floor.

As Kathryn walked into the emergency room, the image of James Field walking across toward the defense table, the sudden orange and white detonation, flashed through her mind with appalling clarity. A doctor in bloodstained surgical garb appeared in front of her.

"Inspector Field," she said urgently. "How is he?"

The doctor looked uncomfortable. "Most of his injuries were superficial," he said, looking away, and she realized how young he was. "Burns, shock. But . . . his hand was . . . there was nothing left. We . . . they had to amputate."

"He lost his hand?"

"Yes," the doctor said. "His right hand."

"Shit," Kathryn said.

# 2

Out beyond Shelter Island, bright golden light played on the ocean. It seemed almost sinful to be enjoying such a beautiful Sunday morning while Jim Field was lying in a hospital room with his right hand gone. It was hard to believe only three days had elapsed since the explosion at the courthouse. To Kathryn, it had been an eternity.

Friday morning, the day after the bombing, she had filed a motion with the court to continue the trial until the following month. The judge had scheduled arguments for tomorrow, Monday. If he denied Kathryn's request to postpone, opening statements would commence the next day, which meant that at ten o'clock on Tuesday morning, she might well have to stand up in Department 8 of the Santa Rita Superior Court and explain to the jury what the case was about.

The trouble was, circumstances had altered; she knew now the opening statement she had so meticu-

20

lously composed was no longer appropriate and must be rewritten. She looked at the computer screen and sighed.

She could hear Emma practicing Handel's *Gavotte,* one of the two pieces her nine-year-old daughter had chosen to play for her violin examination in two and a half weeks' time. Not perfect, but pretty good, Kathryn thought. Emma worked as hard at her violin examination as she did for English, history, or math exams. If only practice and hard work could always make everything come out perfectly.

Back to work, she told herself, aware that she would rather be listening to Emma's violin than preparing for trial. She relegated Handel to her subconscious, forcing herself to concentrate. She was Senior Trial Attorney for Santa Rita County, and most high-profile cases landed on her desk—murders, rapes, and politically sensitive prosecutions requiring a responsive yet aggressive and single-minded prosecutor. She couldn't recall a case with a higher profile than this one. There was no room for distractions.

Kathryn looked up from the dining-room table where she was working, papers fanned out before her like cards to be played in a poker hand. Outside in the sunshine, a cup of coffee on the table at his elbow, Dave Granz slouched in a lounge chair on the deck reading the Sunday paper. They usually spent their weekends together now; in the year since her ex-husband, Jack, Emma's father, had been killed in a Los Angeles courtroom shooting, Dave had quietly taken on the role of surrogate father. He didn't make any kind of big deal out of it; that wasn't his way. He was just there when he was needed, strong and reliable. Almost as if he could feel the weight of Kathryn's gaze, he raised his eyes and looked her way.

"Need some help?"

She shook her head. Dave's presence was another distraction. It was always good to have him around, yet at the same time . . .

She sighed and glared at the small bright screen of her laptop as if she could make it do her bidding by willpower alone. It was no use; she lacked inspiration. The words were just words. *Maybe if I came back to it later,* she thought. She saved and exited the file, switched off the computer, then stood up and went across to the sliding glass door. She was dressed in her usual Sunday uniform: open-neck casual shirt and blue jeans. She was barefoot.

"More coffee?" she asked.

Granz looked up and grinned his familiar, lopsided grin. The faint white hairline scars that ran from his ear to his throat were a permanent reminder of how near death he had come when a serial killer called the Gingerbread Man had tried to cut him to pieces with a scalpel just a couple of years earlier.

"No thanks. Finished?" he said.

"For now," Kathryn admitted. "I can't get a handle on it. And this sunshine isn't helping."

"Looks like the Princess is through fiddling, too," Dave said as Emma sauntered onto the deck and plunked herself into a chair. Emma never simply sat; she sort of hovered over the chair, then collapsed into it, settling into whatever position she landed. Sam, her golden Lab, padded onto the deck behind her and stretched out at her feet. Another ball of Sunday morning energy.

"Are we just going to sit around here *all day?*" Emma said, frowning. "Mom, are we?"

"How about we drive down to Mooney's Landing?" Dave suggested. "Browse some antique stores. Get frozen yogurt. Play your cards right, I might even spring for an early dinner. Great Mexican food at La Comida Familia."

"Come on, Mom, can we go?" Emma said, her feet moving restlessly. "Can't we *do* something?"

Emma knew there had been a problem at court on Thursday which delayed opening statements to Monday; but she had no idea what had really happened. Kathryn had always tried to shield Emma from anything that might cause her to fear for her mother's life, these days more than ever. Emma had worked through a very difficult period following the shooting that claimed her father's life. Kathryn would never take chances with so delicate a matter.

"Aw, Mom, c'mon, I'm *bored,*" Emma said impatiently.

Kathryn smiled. Emma's appetite for Sunday trips with frozen yogurt at the end of them was insatiable. And although it was definitely not Kathryn's favorite, when it came to Mexican food, insatiable didn't begin to cover it.

"I really ought to stay home and finish my opening."

"I know," Dave said. "Look, we won't be late. Maybe if you come at it fresh later, it'll come easier. You can sit in the backseat and think all the way down there and all the way back. Emma and I will keep nice and quiet."

"Mom?" Emma pleaded.

23

"We can stop off and show Emma the new research center at Elkhorn Slough on the way, make it educational," said Dave.

"Elkhorn Slough, isn't that where they do the kayak tours?" Kathryn asked.

"What are kayaks?" her daughter asked.

"Kind of a one-man canoe, Em," Dave said. "Some people race them on rivers."

"One-person, not one-man," Emma corrected, "you chauvinist."

Kathryn grinned. Her daughter was a quick learner.

"Right. Sorry." Dave was a quick learner, too. "They use them on the Slough to take tours into the tidelands and view wildlife and native plants that can't be seen any other way. There's a walking trail around the tidal pools, but you can't see nearly as much as by kayak. Did you know they're talking about allowing people to mine for minerals in the Slough? Jade, I think."

"That's disgusting," Emma said. Her schoolwork was making her very conscious of environmental matters. "We going there?"

"Maybe we'll swing by," Dave said. "On the way."

They piled into Dave's red Jeep Cherokee and headed for Laguna del Mar via Shelter Beach Drive, northeast on Liberty Boulevard, and then west again.

"Pinos Altos?" Kathryn said as the sign slipped by. "I thought you said we were going to Mooney's Landing."

"Just a little detour," Dave said. Kathryn shook her head.

"What are you up to, Granz?" she said, feigning sternness.

24

"Yeah, what, Granz?" Emma said, aping Kathryn's mock pugnacity.

"Brunch," Dave said.

"We just had breakfast," Emma said.

"You call that breakfast?" was the cheerful response. "One lousy muffin and coffee? Okay, lunch, then."

Kathryn turned her head and gave her daughter one of those what-can-you-do-with-a-man? looks. Emma nodded agreement: clearly a hopeless case.

They rounded a bend and saw a sign: "Pinos Altos Sausage Company." A long, low redwood building resembling a hunting lodge stretched along the road for at least half a block. Cars lined the road and overflowed onto a side street across from the store.

"Sausages?" Kathryn said as Dave slid the Jeep into a parking space beneath a ten-foot-high menu.

"Sixty-one different kinds," Dave said. "Best sandwiches in California."

"That's quite a claim," Kathryn said.

Dave grinned. "I'll just get one," he said. "So you can taste. Anything on the list you'd particularly like to try?"

"What's venison, Mom?" Emma asked.

"Deer meat," Kathryn told her.

"Yuck," Emma said, grimacing with genuine horror. "People eat deer?"

"Sure," Dave said. "You want some?"

Emma shook her head. "No way! I think I'm becoming a vegetarian."

They both looked at her in surprise. "When did you decide that?" Dave wanted to know.

"Oh, lots of the kids in my school are vegetarians,"

Emma said loftily. "Valerie Beshore and Brittany James are vegans."

"This place does vegetarian sausages," Dave offered.

"No, just a Coke," Emma said.

"Me, too, except make mine diet," Kathryn told him.

Dave made an exasperated face. "Wimps! I bring you guys to the best sausage sandwich place on the West Coast, and all you want is a Coke?"

"Go get your sandwich," Kathryn told him. "Nobody said you can't have one."

"If you're trying to make me feel guilty," Dave said, "it's not working."

"Just don't get venison." Kathryn smiled.

She watched him fondly as he went inside. There were times when he acted more like a naughty little boy than the tough cop she knew him to be. Part of his appeal. It would have been nice to have him working on the Hudson case with her, but they both knew their personal relationship had grown to a point that precluded the normal prosecutor-investigator working partnership.

*Quit thinking about work, damnit,* she told herself. *Have fun. Be like other people.* She smiled at her own thoughts. She, more than anyone, knew she wasn't like other people and, truth be known, did not want to be. She looked up as Dave came back.

"That's a sandwich?" she said. "It looks more like a blimp."

"Good, though," Dave mumbled with his mouth full.

"What's in it?" Emma asked.

"Don't ask," Dave said. "A vegetarian's nightmare, utterly unspeakable."

Emma giggled. Dave loved that giggle and spent a lot of their time together provoking it. When they had finished their snack, they drove from Pinos Altos down to Liberty Boulevard and then headed south through Catalina to pick up Elkhorn Road.

"How were you and Jim Field getting along?" Dave asked. Field was only in his second year as a DA's Inspector, and the Hudson case had been his first high-profile assignment.

"I like him," Kathryn said. "He's bright. Reliable. Thorough. Right now, though, all I'm concerned about is how he's going to pull through this."

Dave nodded as though what she had said confirmed his own thoughts.

"You really want to go to Elkhorn Slough, Em?" he said over his shoulder. "Or would you rather go straight on down to Mooney's Landing?"

"Where's the frozen yogurt place?"

"Mooney's Landing."

"Okay, let's go there."

Kathryn stared at him, and he put on a mock-wounded look.

"Just trying to save time," he said. "You said you want to get back early."

"And you said the trip would be educational."

"Give me time," he said. "You know the story of Pinos Altos, Em?"

"What story?"

"They teach you anything about the Spanish missions in your school?"

"Li'l bit," Emma said.

"You know the Spaniards came here first."

"Yeah, and founded the missions."

"The leader of the first Spanish expedition was called Don Gaspar de Portola. He came here from San Diego in 1769. It took him three months. His men were the first white men to see this area."

"Was that his name, Don?"

"No, honey. In Spanish, to call someone 'Don' is a mark of high respect. Like we might call a judge 'Your Honor.' "

"What did he come here for?"

"To claim all the land around here for Spain. He made his camp right here in Pinos Altos. They called it Bolsa de Pájaro because they found a stuffed bird left here by the Indians. The next day they marched north to where Santa Rita is now. It was Portola who gave the place its name."

"What was here then?"

"Nothing," Dave said. "About seventy years after Portola passed through, there was a big ranch here, what the Mexicans called an *estancia*. They had redwoods growing all the way down here. It was good lumber country. About 1853, two Americans built a sawmill. Pretty soon they had a couple of stores, a blacksmith shop, a schoolhouse, and a church."

"But there's nothing here anymore. What happened?"

"They cut down most of the good trees, and the lumber business moved on. So did most of the other businesses. People moved away, over to Catalina, or north to Santa Rita. After World War Two, it opened up again, but it was mostly a tourist and summer residential area."

"And a sausage factory," Emma said.

"That's right," Dave agreed. "And a sausage factory."

"Mom, did you hear what Dave was telling me?"

Emma liked to share newfound knowledge with her mother. Kathryn looked up, startled. She had been staring out the window, deep in thought, or reflection. "What, honey?"

"Mom, you were working, weren't you? We're supposed to be having fun."

"I know. Yes, I was. I couldn't help it. I'm sorry."

Emma gave Kathryn her most mature smile. "It's okay, Mom. We understand."

She rolled her eyes at Dave in a conspiratorial grimace, which he returned with a wink. Kathryn shook her head in fond tolerance. Emma had always been close to Dave, even when he was no more than just her mother's friend and colleague. Although she had never referred openly to the growing intimacy of their relationship over the last year or so, it was clear it had her approval. Well, they said a child's instincts were usually right.

"Mooney's Landing," Dave announced, as if he'd built the place himself.

Below them, they could see the little fishing village, comprising a small residential area, a shopping district where old stores had made way for antique shops and boutiques, a couple of run-down but fully functional fish processing plants, and a well-developed harbor where commercial fishing vessels shared their moorings with an occasional sailboat or powercraft. The road went down the steep hill in tight curves. Boats bobbed on the glimmering water, and a squadron of pelicans banked to starboard overhead.

Signs directed them along Hill Street to the parking

area. Granz slid the car into the parking lot straddling a white painted stripe, occupying two parking places. Emma grabbed the meter-money purse and jumped out. She loved feeding meters.

"Hey, hey, take it easy!" Dave remonstrated as Emma industriously fed the machine. "We're not staying all week. And be sure to put money in both meters."

"I know you're going to say this is a dumb question," Kathryn said, letting her puzzlement show, "but why are you taking up two parking places?"

"Typical woman." He smiled. "This is a brand-new car, yes? So I plan to keep it free from parking lot dings as long as possible, even if it means paying for two parking spaces. *Capisce?*"

"Isn't that illegal?"

"Beats me. Probably. Tell you what, you can file charges Monday before you start trial. I'll confess and throw myself on the mercy of the court. Besides"—he waved his arms in an arc to indicate the half-empty parking lot—"it looks to me like Mooney's Landing can use the revenue."

This time, it was Kathryn and Emma's turn to exchange conspiratorial grins. Men!

"Is it time for frozen yogurt, Mom?" Emma said.

"Let's walk a little first, sweetheart," Kathryn said. "You'll get your yogurt, don't worry."

Emma made an impatient face, and Kathryn smiled. Everything was now-now-now when you were nine years old.

They walked down Water Street, which sloped steeply to the harbor, where abandoned marine railway tracks bisected a wide paved area that stretched about half a mile around the tight little bay around which the town nestled. An old crane bent over the empty docks like a rusty scarecrow. Along the old-fashioned pier, anglers were hunched over their rods. Kids trundled along on tricycles, and teenagers on rollerblades swooped past, threading their way through the sightseers. Dave bought Emma her frozen yogurt, and then they strolled along the old waterfront toward the steep hill at the south end of the bay, where a walkway led up to the lighthouse that dominated the point.

"I used to come down here weekends with my dad when I was a kid," Dave said. "My uncle was harbor master. We used to fish off the pier. Hardly ever caught anything, but I didn't care. Probably weren't more than a hundred and fifty people living here then."

"It's still pretty," Kathryn said. "What's up this street?"

"It leads to the square," Dave said, turning into a narrow, curving street that led them up into a small, old-fashioned plaza with a little bandstand. Around the square were little boutiques and specialty shops, one selling paintings and prints, a secondhand bookshop, another that sold tea and coffee. Shaded by pollarded trees, elderly couples sat on the benches feeding the birds.

Emma was fascinated by the antique shops with their little treasures laid out on tables, exclaiming with delight over a pretty set of beads, a tiny gold locket on a fine gold chain, a silver-backed child's hairbrush and mirror.

At one counter, Kathryn stopped to look at a

beautiful old half-hunter cased Waltham pocket watch with a gold chain. It would make a wonderful present for Dave's birthday, just a couple of weeks away, but it was very expensive. And if she bought it now, she thought, would Emma be able to keep the secret until the big day?

"Beautiful watch," the owner of the stall remarked. He was a short man with a round, jolly face and shrewd eyes. He wore a linen jacket with a vest that looked like it had been made from an old tapestry.

"How old is it?" Kathryn asked.

"Turn of the century, maybe a little earlier," the man said. "Original case and movement. You don't see too many in that kind of condition anymore."

"I don't know," Kathryn said. "Four hundred dollars is a bit rich for my blood. How about three-fifty?"

The man drew in his breath sharply, then shook his head slowly from side to side as if saddened by her lack of knowledge.

"That's a twenty-two-karat gold case," he said. "Hallmarked. I couldn't . . . tell you what, three-eighty."

"Three seventy-five," Kathryn said.

"What are you, a lawyer?" the man said. "A lawyer, right?"

"Does it show?" Kathryn smiled. "Is Amex okay, or do you prefer a check?"

"Nothing personal," the man said. "But I'll take Amex."

Emma watched wide-eyed as the man wrapped the watch in three layers of tissue paper and then put it into a flat box which he sealed with Scotch tape.

"Mom," she whispered, wide-eyed, as the man

filled in the sales ticket. "Three hundred and seventy-five *dollars?* For an old *watch?*"

"It's a very special watch, Em," Kathryn said. "And it's for someone very special."

"Dave?" Emma whispered back. "Is it for Dave? For his birthday?"

"Yes, it is," Kathryn said. "But you've got to promise not to tell. It's our secret, you understand? Yours and mine. Promise?"

"Sure," Emma said. "Gosh, Mom, you'd think I was just a little kid or something."

Kathryn signed the sales slip, and they went out into the square.

"We better go find Dave," she said. "He'll think we got lost."

Dave had left them to look around the antique shops at their leisure while he browsed in the book-store. They walked across the square and found him in a back room, looking through a drawer of old postcards.

"Find anything?" Kathryn said.

Born and raised around Santa Rita, Dave was always on the lookout for old pictures of locations in and around the county. He knew more about the early history of the county and its surroundings than anyone Kathryn had ever met. He turned one postcard over.

"Look," he said. "The old covered bridge across the Alameda Valley. About 1894."

"Can I see, Dave?" Emma asked. He smiled and showed her the old sepia picture.

"My dad used to cross that bridge every night on his way home from work," he said.

"What happened to it?"

"Highway One," Dave said, and put the postcard back into the box. "You guys hungry yet?"

Kathryn looked at her watch and was surprised to find it was already after five.

"What did you have in mind?"

"We could eat here, drive back early. That would give you plenty of time to finish your opening statement."

"Sold," she said. "Where do we eat?"

"We had Mexican food last time, right? There's a fish place on the pier," he said. "It's called Mike's. They do a great cioppino."

"What's cioppino?" Emma asked.

"It's a spicy fish stew," Dave said. "They usually serve it with sourdough bread."

"Fish stew?" Emma said, making a dubious face.

"It's great, Em. They cook it with onions, garlic, peppers, tomatoes, basil, oregano, parsley, lemon . . . yum."

Emma's expression suggested she wasn't altogether sold. Kathryn smiled and took her daughter's hand.

"Let's go take a look," she said. "It'll make a change from watching you two eating Mexican."

They walked the length of the pier until a sign appeared: "Mike's Fish Market and Eatery." Behind the windows on beds of ice lay lobster and crab, abalone, black-shelled mussels, oysters, clams, sea bass, tuna, snapper, shark, Monterey Bay salmon, squid, scallops, sand dabs, and tiger shrimp.

"Dave," Emma said, pointing. "What are these fish called?"

Dave frowned as if concentrating seriously. "Let me get this right," he said. "I don't want to make a mistake here." Then he nodded sagely. "That one there is called Tom," he said, pointing. "The one next to him is Dick. And the one on the right is Harry."

"Oh, Dave!" Emma giggled. "Be serious."

He grinned unrepentantly. "Never on a Sunday, Princess," he said. "Never, never on a Sunday."

# 3

Mornings were always a circus. Usually, before she ever got to the DA's office, Kathryn was exhausted, as if she'd already done a full day's work. And often she had. Make breakfast, pack Emma's lunch, do a load of laundry, iron the clothes she and Emma would wear that day, empty the dishwasher, put food and water out for the dog. Then, after sweeping yesterday's cookie crumbs out of the front seat, hop into the car for the short sprint to Lighthouse Drive to catch the school bus. She nearly always managed to get there in time for Emma's bus, although on rare occasions they were a bit late and she had to drive all the way over to the school.

This morning, Kathryn awoke at five-thirty. She had slept little, and fitfully. Nightmare visions of Jim Field's mangled hand, or the smoke-filled courtroom, or the distinctive muffled blast and orange flames jolted her awake each time her weary mind slipped into sleep. She was glad to get up and face the situation, tired but alert. She went into the kitchen, started water heating in a black and chrome whistling teakettle, ground a scoop of fresh coffee beans, dumped them into a Melitta filter cone, and went outside to pick up the newspaper. Big headlines led on a front-page in-depth investigative piece, delving into the Santa Rita bombing and tying it to a larger national phenomenon. Coverage in last weekend's papers had been sketchy; now she saw why. An involuntary shudder ran through her entire body as she read the account. She folded the paper quickly and secreted it under the clothing in her bottom dresser drawer to prevent Emma's reading it. As she did so, she mentally noted the date on the front page. The nineteenth of the month.

"BSE," she reminded herself. During her last checkup, almost a year ago, her doctor had recommended she carry out a monthly breast self-examination.

"BSE isn't just to detect breast cancer," Dr. Ota had explained. "It's also part of the larger process of becoming acquainted with your own body. The sage said: 'Know thyself.' It's good medical advice, too. But for it to be effective, you must do it religiously at the same time each month."

Like most women her age, Kathryn knew BSE was an element of self-health care that no woman could afford to ignore or forget. She had begun by doing BSE every day for the first month so that she really got to know the contours and feel of her breasts. Familiarity made it easier to notice any changes. She would be looking for anything unusual, Dr. Ota told her. A lump, obviously, but also dimpling or puckering of the skin, or a discharge from the nipple.

Now Kathryn stood naked in front of the full-length mirror in the bathroom and looked at her reflection. She saw a petite woman in her early forties, with long, dark hair and wide-set brown eyes. The body reflected in the mirror was a good one, strong and healthy. She prided herself—privately, since she was far too modest to say as much to another person—on the fact that she stayed in better shape than many women ten or fifteen years her junior. Of course, that was not by accident; she routinely read legal briefs, studied court decisions, prepared for trial, and even read personal letters while working out on the Stairmaster set up in the spare bedroom.

She clasped her hands behind her head and pressed forward, feeling her chest muscles tighten. No change. Good. Now hands on hips, leaning slightly forward. Okay, good.

It was much easier to do the next part of the exam in the shower, because the soap lubricated the skin, making it slippery and easier to feel the underlying tissue. She started the water and allowed it to run until it was very hot, despite admonitions of local water officials concerning water conservation, a superfluous carryover from the drought years. Hot showers are one of life's nicest indulgences. She stepped into the steamy shower stall and grabbed the soap, an expensive clear amber glycerine soap, another of her little extravagances. Her mind turned to the Hudson trial, reviewing the reasons she would advance in her motion to continue the trial that she would make in court this morning.

In criminal cases, the defendant has a statutory right to a speedy trial, and continuances are granted only for good cause. The big question was, would

Field's unavailability constitute that good cause? Probably not. Field was her investigating officer and not a material witness. In addition, Public Defender Marty Belker would oppose the continuance for no better reason than the fact that anything that disadvantaged her automatically benefited him.

She shrugged. Perhaps her argument would not prevail, but she intended to try. Belker was an old adversary. She had prosecuted the first murder case he ever defended, and she had won, making him another of the many defense attorneys who had made the mistake of underestimating her. The difference was he had never forgotten or forgiven. She didn't like Belker, and he made no effort to conceal his distaste for her.

As she soaped herself vigorously, the cascading water enveloped her in a warm cocoon. Putting her left hand behind her head, she lifted her left arm, gently but firmly pressing with the pads of her fingers, moving in small circles toward the nipple to explore her breast carefully and thoroughly, paying special attention to the area between the breast and the underarm as the literature instructed. And there was a lump. Small but unmistakable.

*No. It can't be.*

Carefully, she tested the spot a second time. It wasn't her imagination. There was a lump. Small, hard, undeniable.

She stood stock still, hardly able to breathe. Everything else in the world was exactly the same as it had been ten seconds earlier—the smell of coffee coming from the kitchen, the sounds of Emma readying herself for school. Only now she had a lump in her breast.

*It's a mistake,* she told herself. *It's got to be.*

For the third time, she moved her fingers carefully, her body cold even in the warm torrent. No mistake. There was definitely a lump under the skin, between her left breast and underarm. She turned off the water and dried herself. Sure, this was cause for concern but nothing to panic over. Little lumps usually indicated something benign—an infected lymph node, most likely. Glands and lobules in the breast could feel like lumps. Maybe it was something like that. Sure, that was what it was. No need for concern, but she would talk with Dr. Ota, just to make sure.

But . . . what if . . . ?

No.

*I won't allow myself to think about what if,* she thought angrily.

But she knew she would.

# 4

*COUNTY BUILDING, SANTA RITA.*
*MONDAY, JUNE 19, 11:55 A.M.*

The County Building would never win any prizes in an architectural beauty contest. Built in 1966 at the height of the Cold War, its uncompromising gray concrete structure suggested its main purpose had been to withstand a nuclear attack, and it probably had been. Five stories high, squat and square, it accommodated the offices of the Sheriff, the District Attorney, Environmental Health, the Planning Department, and the County Clerk. With its wide stone-floored corridors, the flat white fluorescent light, its public hallways featuring ever-changing art exhibits by talented local artists that few people took the time to look at, it was a place to work, functional and unloved.

Fending off reporters and TV crews hoping for sound bites, Kathryn hurried across the partly open-air atrium that linked the County Building to the Courts Building, and up to her office on the second floor. Once inside, she closed and locked the door and

41

walked directly to her desk. Pausing only slightly, she drew a deep breath, picked up the telephone, and dialed a number she had memorized.

"Women's Medical Clinic."

"Good morning," Kathryn began. "I'm a patient of Dr. Ota's, and I need to speak with her before she leaves for lunch. It's extremely important."

"I'm sorry. Dr. Ota is with a patient and isn't available," the receptionist said in a regretless singsong. "May I ask what it is you need to see the doctor about? I'd be happy to make an appointment for you."

"No, I need to talk with her immediately," Kathryn insisted. "This is Kathryn Mackay, and Dr. Ota is a close personal friend. She won't mind being interrupted if you tell her who it is. Why don't you check with her while I wait?"

Without another word, the receptionist clicked her onto hold. Kathryn waited no more than a minute or two before JoAnn Ota answered the phone.

"Kathryn, this is a nice surprise," she said. "What can I do for you?"

"I'd like to come and see you, JoAnn," Kathryn said, wondering if her voice sounded as tense as it felt. "It's rather urgent. I found . . . I think I have a lump in my breast."

"I see." Dr. Ota's voice was suddenly brisk and formal. "We'd better get you in to see me right away. I'm just checking my schedule. How would eleven-thirty tomorrow work for you?"

"I'm in trial, JoAnn. Could you make it late this afternoon sometime?"

"Four-forty-five? I'll wait if you're a little late."

"Thank you. I'll be there."

42

She gently cradled the handset in the phone base and stared at it. JoAnn Ota was her friend as well as her doctor. Just telling her had eased the pressure, but the black thing lurking at the back of her mind remained there, and she knew it would not go away. Well, she would know soon enough, one way or the other. One of Kathryn's strengths was her willingness always to confront an enemy head-on; she would play this the way she played everything else.

Her phone rang almost as soon as she put it down. It was Dave Granz.

"I just got off the phone with Dr. Death—oops, sorry," he said. "Didn't mean to say that."

Although the Sheriff, Jake Gylam, was *ex-officio* coroner, in Santa Rita, as in most counties in California, the actual work was contracted out. Dr. Morgan Nelson, the forensic pathologist employed by the county as its coroner, was a close friend. Dave had never been able to completely shake the habit of using the nickname one of the tabloids had given Nelson years earlier when they discovered he had carried out more than nine thousand autopsies. Kathryn sometimes wondered if Dave used it because he knew how fond she was of the man. She let it go.

"Yes, and?"

"He ran preliminary tests on fragments the bomb squad dropped off," Dave went on. "Located traces of sulfuric acid, nitric acid, and methyl alcohol—classic kitchen bomb ingredients. Looks like a fairly crude homemade device to him. Maybe you should call him."

"Okay," she said.

"You all right, Kathryn?" he asked.

"Sure, fine."

43

"You sure?"

"Dave, I'm perfectly all right," she said, a shade more forcefully and formally than she meant to.

"It was just you sounded . . . worried," he said, and she heard the concern in his voice.

"I'm sorry, Dave," she said. "Just keyed up like always when I'm going to trial. Everything's fine."

No sense in him worrying over nothing, she reasoned, and smiled ruefully. Who was she trying to convince—Dave? Or herself?

# 5

Kathryn sighed as the phone rang yet again. No rest for the weary, she thought. This time it was her boss, District Attorney Hal Benton.

"Got a minute?"

"For you, always," she said. "I'll be right in."

When she walked into Benton's office, he was on the phone. The District Attorney was never informal; today he was wearing an impeccably conservative gray single-breasted suit with a white cotton dress shirt and a red and dark gray striped tie. He put his hand over the mouthpiece.

"Be right with you," he said, and waved her to a chair. "Yes, fine, fax the details to me and I'll get back to you," he said into the phone, and put it down. Although he had lived in California most of his adult life, his voice still retained a trace of its Southern drawl.

"I've been trying to reach you for half an hour," he said.

45

"It's been one of those days," Kathryn said, and it was true. She felt as if she hadn't touched the ground since she arrived at the office.

"So what's the situation on the Hudson case?"

Hal always hoped for the best but expected the worst, she thought. She shook her head.

"Motion denied," she said tersely. "No continuance. We resume tomorrow morning."

Benton made a face. "Are you ready?" he asked.

"I'll be ready," Kathryn promised. "But you're going to have to help."

"What do you need?"

"First and foremost, an inspector to replace Jim. Dave Granz is helping out on a temporary basis, but I want him assigned permanently."

Benton leaned back in his chair, regarding her levelly. Fifty-five years of age, he was a good-looking man, with blue-gray eyes and dark blond hair. A graduate of Stanford Law School, his first job had been as an ADA in the Santa Rita District Attorney's Office, back then a small office with only five prosecutors. He had run for DA the first time in 1978 and served in that capacity ever since.

"A year ago, I would have agreed. But your relationship with Dave has changed things."

"Ordinarily I'd agree with you, Hal, but we both know Dave is the best inspector in the office. And right now I need the best."

"No danger we're going to lose this one, is there?" he asked, a trifle edgily. "This is a high-visibility case, Kathryn. Lots of political fallout. The media are all over us. I don't want Hudson walking free. That's why I made sure you were on it from the start. If anybody can convict him, it's you."

Benton took it for granted that when he assigned a case to her, she would win it. The pressure his expectations might have generated in most prosecutors did not affect her; it was no less than what she imposed on herself. She went into every trial expecting to win and settled for nothing less. The personal cost of doing so, great as it was to her, was immeasurably less than the cost of mediocrity. And there was another, even more important consideration. She never forgot she was the sole voice for the victim. It was what gave Kathryn her passion, her complete involvement in every case she prosecuted.

"He won't walk," Kathryn said. "Not if you give me Granz."

Benton thought about it for a moment, then nodded in reluctant agreement. He knew Mackay and Granz were the best prosecutor-investigator team in his office. And if Kathryn said her relationship with Granz wasn't going to be a problem, then it wasn't.

"Okay, I'll talk to Norm about cutting Granz loose from his other cases. What's the news on Jim Field?"

"They amputated," Kathryn said, hoping she wasn't revealing how hard the news had hit her. "No choice. Morgan Nelson knows the surgeon, and he said there was practically nothing left of the hand anyway."

"How is he taking it?"

"How do you think?"

"Goddamn lunatics," Benton exclaimed angrily. Kathryn's eyebrows arched. Harold Benton was an old-fashioned gentleman, and such language was untypical, a sign of extreme emotion. He stood up and walked to the window, staring at the parking lot below. "It's like there're more lunatics out there than sane people. And you can't tell who they are by looking."

"It feels like that sometimes," Kathryn agreed. "Has anyone claimed responsibility?"

Benton shook his head. "That's what's odd," he said. "Someone plants a bomb in a courtroom, there has to be a reason."

"The thing is, it might not be what you and I or any other normal person would recognize as a reason, Hal," Kathryn said. "People like that don't think the same way we do. You should know that better than anyone."

"Nothing from DOJ?" Benton switched to his professional persona. DOJ was the Department of Justice crime lab. Though the bomb that had destroyed Field's hand had itself been destroyed, tiny grains of the explosive mixture hadn't burned and were being analyzed by DOJ criminalists. They would no doubt confirm and expand on Dr. Nelson's preliminary analysis.

"It'll be a while before we hear from them. Doc Nelson seems to think it was a homemade device. Kitchen-table job, no finesse. And probably no signature."

"I hope that's not supposed to make me feel better," Benton said sourly. "A homemade bomb with no signature is virtually impossible to trace."

"We'll just have to hope DOJ comes up with something, Hal. We're all in the dark otherwise."

Benton sighed and went back to his seat behind the desk. "I guess," he said. "Anything else happening I need to know about?"

Kathryn shook her head. "Not as of ten minutes ago, but give it timc. Look, I better get back to my office. If I'm going to be ready tomorrow, I've got a lot of work to do."

She was at the door when Benton said her name. She stopped and turned.

"One other thing," Benton said. "The sheriff's office is setting up a task force to investigate the bombing. As of now, you're assigned to it. Granz, too."

"Hal!" Kathryn protested. "We've got a major trial starting tomorrow, Dave isn't even up to speed yet, and you want to assign us to a task force?"

"It's just a preliminary meeting," Benton said. "Walt Earheart, George Purington from the bomb squad. But I want you in there."

"Okay, Hal," she said. Benton was effectively doubling her workload. He knew it, she knew it, and he knew she knew it, but there was no way of ducking. "If that's how it is, that's how it is. When do we start?"

"S.O. conference room at five-thirty."

"Then I'd better get moving."

"Good luck," Benton said as she closed the door.

*I could use some,* Kathryn thought.

# 6

Kathryn checked her watch as she slid her car into a parking space. Twenty minutes late for her appointment with JoAnn. She sat silently for a moment, preparing herself for what lay ahead. It was not fear—a dread of knowing the worst, maybe. Until you know for sure, you can deny. Scenarios flickered through her mind, nagging thoughts that just would not go away. A lump could mean cancer. Cancer meant surgery and radiation. A lot of women died from breast cancer.

Emma. Who would look after Emma?

The obvious answer was Dave. He loved Emma, Emma loved him, it was that simple. He was the best thing in the world for her—as long as Kathryn was there as well. Her mind took her back to a night about a year ago, in the dark weeks after Jack, her ex-husband, had been shot. Dave had come over unexpectedly, and they sat and talked for a while. Then, almost without preamble, he had asked her to marry

50

him. "Right now you need someone," he had told her "So does Emma."

She remembered how she had felt, off-balance, uncertain how to reply.

"Dave, Emma isn't your responsibility, she's mine," she'd said.

Emma was only a part of it, he'd said. "This is about you and me. I'm ready to make the commitment. The question is, are you?"

Part of her had wanted to say yes. But another, pragmatic part of her knew it would be the wrong way to go. The very nature of what they both did for a living made independence an asset rather than a liability. And deep down she knew, they both knew, they didn't need marriage to affirm the deep affection and respect they had for each other, or his love for Emma.

If she had made the commitment then, would it have been different now? She shook her head. Dave was a darling man, but there was no way he could juggle the work he did and the life he lived to include being both father and surrogate mother. But if not Dave, then who? The interior of the car felt suddenly cold, and she shivered. She could not recall ever having felt more alone.

She got out of her Audi and locked it. Dr. Ota's office was one of two in a modern single-story building next to the post office on Salmon River Drive. From its large parking lot, wheelchair ramps and stone steps led to the main doors. On the righthand side of the doorway was a large brass plate on which were engraved the names of Dr. Ota and her partner, Dr. Carolyn Jensen.

"Hi, Ms. Mackay," the receptionist said. In her early twenties, Amy Martinez had a mane of curly black hair and a smile that could light up a room. "You're right on time." Kathryn looked at her quizzically. "Dr. Ota said to expect you around five o'clock. How's Emma?"

"She's fine, thank you," Kathryn said, taking a seat at the far end of the waiting room. Amy was a pleasant young woman, but Kathryn didn't feel much like making conversation.

"Kathryn, come in."

She looked up to see Dr. Ota standing in the hallway. So petite she made Kathryn feel tall, JoAnn Ota wore a spotless white coat with a stethoscope around her neck, white trousers, and white hospital shoes. Her hair was jet black, parted in the middle so it fell in long wings beside her high-cheekboned face. When she smiled, she was beautiful.

"How are you?" she said, motioning Kathryn to one of the examination rooms. Her green eyes were sympathetic as she asked the question.

"A little shaky," Kathryn confessed.

Dr. Ota nodded, as if she'd heard the same thing many times.

"Slip off everything from the waist up, put on this paper gown, and I'll be back in a few minutes."

By the time Dr. Ota returned a few moments later, Kathryn had undressed and put on the gown. She looked up expectantly as the doctor sat down facing her.

"I'm going to do a manual examination now," she said. "It's called palpation. Just relax."

Her fingers were cool and firm as she applied light

pressure to Kathryn's armpits and the area just above her collarbone.

"That's not where—" Kathryn began.

"I know, Kathryn," the doctor told her with a smile. "I'm just checking your lymph glands. That's fine. Now, lie down on the table for me, will you?"

Kathryn stared at the ceiling, feeling strangely detached as JoAnn made a careful, inch-by-inch examination first of her left breast and then of the right.

"You were right," Dr. Ota said. "There does seem to be something there. Very small, but something."

Kathryn sat up. "And?"

"Get dressed first," Dr. Ota said. "Then we'll talk in my office."

Kathryn slipped on her bra and blouse, fastening the buttons with fingers that trembled slightly. She followed Dr. Ota into her brightly lit office and sat down on the couch.

"What do you think it is?" she asked.

"We won't know until we do a mammogram."

"How soon can I have that done?"

"Let's see, today is Monday, I can probably get you an appointment with the radiologist for Friday. How does that sound?"

"The sooner the better," Kathryn said.

"Let's do it now," JoAnn said, and punched a button on the desk console. Kathryn could hear the "Close Encounters" music clearly as the machine dialed the preprogrammed number.

"Santa Rita Breast Center," a disembodied voice said, and she realized JoAnn had left the phone speaker on so she could hear what was being said.

"This is Dr. Ota," JoAnn said. "I'd like to make an

appointment for one of my patients. Mammogram and ultrasound scan."

"Oh, hi, Dr. Ota," the voice said. "Sure thing. Name of the patient?"

"Mackay, that's M-a-c-k-a-y. First name Kathryn, K-a-t-h-r-y-n. She'd like to come in as soon as possible. How about Friday . . . " She looked at Kathryn with raised eyebrows. " . . . morning?"

Kathryn nodded.

"Morning," Dr. Ota confirmed. "Do you have an opening?"

"How about ten-thirty A.M., would that be acceptable?"

Kathryn nodded again.

"Ten-thirty will be fine," Dr. Ota said. "Thank you, Karen."

"You're welcome," the woman said automatically as she hung up.

"All set, Kathryn," JoAnn Ota said. "Is there anything you want to ask me?"

"Yes, what do you suggest I do between now and Friday?" asked Kathryn.

"First, take a deep breath," said Dr. Ota. "Use the time to educate yourself. Information is often the most powerful tool we have."

"Any suggestions?" asked Kathryn.

"Start with *Dr. Susan Love's Breast Book.*"

Kathryn made a mental note of the title as she gathered up her suit jacket and purse.

"Call me Friday," JoAnn said as she gave Kathryn a quick hug, "when you get through at the center. Meantime, don't brood. Try and put this out of your mind."

"I'll try," Kathryn said, holding everything in tight. "Thank you, JoAnn."

She managed to hold back the tears until she got out the door and into her car. Then, after a few moments, mustering the inner strength that always sustained her when the going got tough, she started her Audi and headed back to town.

**7**

Fluorescent lights in ceiling panels, brown shell chairs, two scarred metal tables set up to make a T, and a wood-framed map of the county on the wall did nothing to give the cramped conference room inside the Sheriff's office a personality.

Lieutenant Walt Earheart sat at the end of the T with Commander Purington of the bomb squad to his right. Kathryn and Dave took seats on opposite sides.

"Purington has been in contact with BDC," Earheart said, for Kathryn and Dave's information. "They're prepared to assist if we need them."

BDC, the FBI's Bomb Data Center, was responsible for the technical training of public safety bomb disposal technicians, preparation and dissemination of explosive-related publications and bombing incident summaries, sharing of technical information and bombing incident statistics, and providing technical support in crisis management situations.

"Probably won't be necessary," George Purington

interjected. "I'm trained to conduct bomb crime scene investigations."

"That being the case, maybe George ought to head up this task force," Earheart said. "Everyone agree?"

All heads around the table nodded in agreement. Purington's credentials were beyond reproach. He had received his training at the FBI Hazardous Devices School at the Redstone Arsenal in Huntsville, Alabama. HDS is the only school in the United States that trains and certifies local public safety officials as bomb technicians.

"Okay, here's our situation as of now," Purington said. "We don't know who we are dealing with or who the target was."

"Wait a minute," Earheart said. "I thought the package was addressed to Marty Belker."

"It would have to have been addressed to an attorney, Walt," Kathryn pointed out. "We have papers and packages coming into court all the time. No one takes any notice of them. Otherwise it would have been checked by security."

"So our bomber knows that much about courtroom procedure," Dave said thoughtfully.

"Or he just got lucky," Purington added. "Bombers will lift a name from a newspaper, a TV news report, anything to get the device into the intended area. Look, the name on the bomb doesn't mean that's who the target was. It could just as easily have been you, Kathryn."

"Kathryn? Why?" Dave's voice betrayed his concern.

"Why not?" Purington snapped back. "A lot of these guys are nuts, pure and simple. Maybe the bomber doesn't like women lawyers. Maybe he doesn't like you prosecuting a guy with AIDS. Or maybe it's someone who has a grudge against you."

"Same could apply to Jim Field," Kathryn cautioned. "Or the judge, for that matter."

"Which means we've got a helluva wide-ranging investigation on our hands," Walt Earheart said heavily.

"Let's start with Belker, anyway," said Purington. "Does the fact the device was addressed to him suggest anything, anybody? Is he a man with a lot of enemies?"

"He's represented his share of psychos over the years," Kathryn offered.

"Okay," said Purington. "We'll need to look at all the defendants he's represented this past year. Anyone recently paroled who might hold a grudge against him."

"I'll have one of my detectives take care of that," Earheart said. "You know, I'm surprised he hasn't screamed for protection knowing that bomb was addressed to him."

"Not Marty," Kathryn said. "He might be scared to death, but no way would he let anyone see it—especially anyone in law enforcement."

Earheart shrugged. "One less bell to answer," he said unsympathetically.

"What about Jim Field, George?" asked Kathryn.

"Him, too. Have someone pull all the cases he's investigated since he's been with your office. While you're at it, better have all the cases you've prosecuted in the past couple of years pulled as well," Purington suggested.

As Kathryn nodded her agreement, Dave asked a question.

"Judge Woods? Yeah, he's a possible, too," Purington said. "We better get a list of every case he presided over for the past year or so."

"What if this bombing isn't an isolated event?" asked Kathryn.

"We're ready for that," Purington said reassuringly. "If we get a bomb threat, we have a total containment vessel with a bomb containment sphere that can withstand the pressure, heat, and fragmentation of most high-powered explosive devices. The bomb truck has a bomb disposal robot, protective suits, screening and disruption equipment. Not to mention some of the best bomb disposal specialists in the country."

"Works for me," Earheart said.

"Only if the bomber delivers a threat ahead of time," Kathryn argued. "What if he doesn't?"

A silence descended on the room. Nobody had any answers for that question, because nobody knew what the bomber would do next.

Except the bomber.

# 8

Getting away from the mundane routines of the job was always strangely exciting, a feeling remembered from childhood of anticipation, of something wonderful about to happen. The twenty-minute drive to Mission Hills allowed plenty of time to go over every detail of the plan. Even dream a little, seeing it through Angel's eyes. How it would be. What would be said. All of it.

Angel had played her part perfectly in disposing of Lawrence Sutterfield. But she could not do what she did so well alone. That was why they were the perfect team. One to design the instrument, the other to unleash its awesome power.

Bombs came in two varieties. Explosives or incendiaries: bangers or burners. All you needed for a perfectly effective banger was a plastic explosive made from potassium chlorate, Vaseline, and a blasting cap. Or a moist explosive mixture made from aluminum bronzing powder bought in a paint shop and carbon tetra-

*chloride, extracted from a fire extinguisher or obtained from a dry cleaner's.*

*Or add weed killer—ninety percent of the people who used it in their gardens didn't know it was simple sodium chlorate—to copper sulfate from your friendly local hardware store, some pure alcohol, ammonia hydroxide from a bottle of smelling salts, and you had a primary explosive, tetrammine copper chlorate— TACC for short.*

*There were plenty of others, the ingredients set out like recipes in the two slim black paperbacks on the bookshelf behind the table, available by mail order or at any public library to anyone with a library card. All of them reliable. All of them deadly. And all of them absolutely untraceable.*

*Only damned fools bought traceable quantities of chemicals, thousands of pounds of ammonium nitrate like those lunatics in Oklahoma. Using the equivalent of fifteen hundred pounds of dynamite to achieve one's ends was crude, unnecessary, and stupid, like using a .357 Magnum to shoot a worm.*

*Buy small, buy often, that was the secret. Never use the same store twice in succession. Wear different clothes every time you shop. Avoid chatting with whoever waited on you. Leave nothing for anyone to remember.*

*And so to work.*

*Neatness was important.*

*A place for everything, and everything in its place. Stainless steel mixing bowls on the table to the left; glass retorts on the right; tool kit open in the middle. Ingredients laid out in a neat row, waiting. Perfection in preparation leads to a perfect result.*

*Today it was another burner. Simple ingredients*

*again. Thermite scraped out of a highway flare. Magnesium. Iron filings. A length of bicycle inner tube. Stuff you could buy at any hardware store without leaving any record or drawing attention to yourself. Put 'em together and what have you got? A small, totally deadly device about the size of a sausage that fit in your pocket easily, absolutely untraceable to its creator. Add a fuse made from a couple of inches of drapery cord soaked in potassium nitrate—saltpeter mixed with sugar if you wanted it to burn slowly—and you had an incendiary bomb that would burn a hole through sheet steel.*

*As the deft fingers meticulously fashioned the deadly device, music blared from the forty-watt speakers. 'Eighties sounds like Duran Duran, Spandau Ballet, the Police. Right now, Elton John was singing a favorite, "Candle in the Wind."*

*Smiling, every step carried out with scrupulous care, without haste. When the burner was completed, it was laid to one side. Next came the delay switch. Like everything else, the secret of the thing was to keep it simple, to use untraceable everyday materials: a cigarette, a paper match, and a shoelace. Use the shoelace to bind the cigarette to the fuse of the burner with the paper match sandwiched between them, its head on the actual fuse. Simple as that.*

*Then, when the time came, light the cigarette and walk away. In still air, a common dry cigarette burns about an inch every seven or eight minutes. So if the match head is placed one inch from the burning end of the cigarette, it will ignite the fuse six or seven minutes after being lit.*

*Six or seven minutes, plus two more for the fuse to*

reach the bomb. For the intended victim, an eternity of horrified, helpless terror.

The CD machine clicked and hissed, and Sting's sinuous voice filled the room. *"Ev'ry move you make, ev'ry step you take, I'll be watching you."*

# 9

Kathryn Mackay half-turned in her chair at counsel table to survey the courtroom. Behind the waist-high oak barrier, the rows of bench seats reserved for the public were crammed shoulder to shoulder with reporters, photographers, camera crews, and spectators. Kathryn recognized two or three faces as regular visitors to the courts—court groupies, they were sometimes called. Outside the double doors, a sheriff's deputy barred entry to jostling latecomers who protested their exclusion vociferously but were denied nonetheless.

There was a mounting urgency in the courtroom during the moments before a trial began, as all involved in it readied themselves for what was to come. Kathryn watched as court reporter Kathleen Havill inserted a fresh roll of paper in her machine with deft, precise movements. When she was satisfied, she stood, put her hands to the nape of her neck, and tossed her gray-streaked blond hair, eyes sweeping the courtroom. Then she sat down again, gazing blankly ahead. Court reporters were an incredible group, Kathryn thought. To anyone watching them during the trial, they appeared detached, almost nonchalant, but their casual demeanor concealed an uncanny ability to transcribe with absolute perfection every word uttered "on the record," irrespective of the speakers' accents, poor diction, or inadequate projection.

Now a rising buzz of interest emanated from the audience as the bailiff escorted the defendant, Richard Hudson, into the courtroom. Hudson wore a plaid shirt with the collar outside the neck of his cotton sweater, and dark brown Dockers. He looked like a yuppie. Martin Belker had obviously gone for the casual look for his client, Kathryn thought. A formal suit and tie would have inspired a different reaction. The jury would perceive him as they would any other young, affluent Santa Rita resident. It was all a necessary part of the elaborate game of justice.

By virtue of being charged by the State with the commission of a serious crime, and by being referred to continually as "the defendant," a powerful and pervasive presumption of guilt attaches to an accused person. The judicial system attempts, not altogether successfully, to mitigate that presumption on the part of the jury by permitting jurors to see the defendant only at his or her contrived best.

Kathryn had often wondered whether jurors had any idea of the lengths to which the State went to enhance a defendant's appearance of normality, if not outright innocence, prior to a court appearance. Take Richard Hudson. About half an hour before his scheduled court time, two sheriff's deputies would have arrived at his county jail cell, conducted a strip-search, then placed him in manacles, leg-irons, and a restraining chain that connected to the handcuffs, passing through a waistband and in turn locked onto the leg-irons. Clad in standard jail-issue bright orange overalls, escorted by the heavily armed deputies, he would be signed out through security and led shuffling across the street to the bowels of the court building.

There, in an area referred to by law enforcement and prisoners alike as "the Tombs," he would be placed in a holding cell, unshackled, stripped of his orange jumpsuit, and dressed in whatever civilian clothing his lawyer had delivered to the jail that morning. If the prisoner was considered a flight risk, as Richard Hudson was, a metal leg brace would be placed under his pants to restrict mobility.

After he was thus clothed and secured, he was again placed in handcuffs and leg-irons, escorted through interior passages, and brought to the inside door of the courtroom, where all visible restraining devices would then be removed.

Not until the judge was satisfied that the prisoner's appearance was as normal as possible under the circumstances (there was an old prosecutor's joke to the effect that the defendant frequently looked more normal than the defense attorney) would the jury be allowed to file into the jury box. This routine would be repeated each and every day the defendant was seen by the jury, no matter how long the trial lasted.

If they only knew, Kathryn thought as Hudson crossed to the defense table on the righthand side of the well in front of the bench, his arms swinging loosely, eyes dead, face completely expressionless. He sat down with a heavy sigh and stared straight ahead.

*Why am I being put through all this?* His expression said. Belker had coached his client well.

She watched Bailiff Chris Taylor, who had brought in the defendant, retrace his steps across the courtroom and take his position behind and to the left of the bench near the door. She recalled hearing someplace that Taylor was studying for the sergeants' exam. Like all SO deputies, he was doing a stint in Court Security on a rotational basis. He looked alert and confident, not like the shaky kid she had interviewed on a night long ago when he responded to a 911 call placed by a rape victim named Karen Esterhaus. Only recently assigned to the Patrol Division, he had never been called out on a rape before, and he was still in shock when she talked to him. She saw Taylor draw himself up and knew the judge was coming in.

"Ready, Dave?" Kathryn asked. Benton had lost no time in arranging Dave's full-time assignment to the case. She was glad to have his reassuring presence at her side.

"You bet," he whispered. Anyplace else, he might have reached over and squeezed her hand. Not here. It wasn't just a matter of how it looked; in court, Kathryn was all business. It was one of the things he liked best about her—the ability to be strong, decisive, and totally in charge in the courtroom, while maintaining her own special and undeniable femininity outside it.

"All rise!" Bailiff Taylor intoned loudly. "Department Eight of the Santa Rita Superior Court, State of California, is now in session, the Honorable Jesse Augustus Woods presiding!"

As he spoke, the door on the righthand side of the

wall in back of the bench swung open, and Judge Woods swept in past the jury box in flowing black robe to seat himself in the leather chair behind the bench overlooking the courtroom. He was a big man with broad shoulders and large hands. Dark hair crowned his leonine head, and his dark, deep-set eyes missed nothing that transpired in his court.

"Be seated."

As the jurors and audience resumed their seats, the judge slid his half-frame reading glasses over his nose and nodded to the court clerk, Cathy Radina, who stood up.

"In the Superior Court of the State of California, in and for the County of Santa Rita, the People of the State of California, Plaintiff, versus Richard John Hudson, case number CR1432," she began, her clear, well-modulated voice carrying to every corner of the courtroom. "The People of the State of California hereby accuse Richard John Hudson of the crimes of attempted murder, to wit: violation of Section 664/187 of the Penal Code, in that said Richard John Hudson did willfully, unlawfully, and feloniously commit an attempted murder against the persons of Victoria Mitten, Jane Sorensen, and Marian Browning. Signed Harold Benton, District Attorney, to which information the Defendant entered pleas of not guilty as charged."

As the court clerk sat down, Judge Woods looked up, his glance shifting from the jury to the defense table on his left and then on to the matching table on his right where Kathryn sat with Dave Granz.

"For the record," he said, "the court will grant the prosecution's motion to exclude witnesses. Inspector

Granz will be designated the prosecution's investigating officer and will be permitted to remain."

By court order, witnesses remained outside the courtroom until their testimony was required. It was a common pretrial motion brought by either the defense or the prosecution—often both—to avoid witnesses' memories being influenced, or contaminated, by the testimony of other witnesses.

"All right, Ms. Mackay," Judge Woods said. "Are you prepared to make your opening statement?"

"Yes, Your Honor."

"Proceed."

Kathryn put down the glass from which she had taken a quick sip of water while the judge was speaking and rose to face the jury. This was her battlefield. In this battle, as in all her battles, Kathryn intended to be the victor. A prosecutor's case begins as a jumble of unintelligible facts, bits and pieces of information, some relevant and some not. Her job was to mold that mass of information into a coherent presentation of the truth that the jury would clearly understand. This was their first exposure to the facts. She must tell them a story with a beginning, a middle, and an end. She must do it all in an hour or less. And do it better than anyone else.

She looked around. Except for one or two muted whispers among the reporters and the soft sigh of the air conditioning, there was hardly a sound in the courtroom.

"Good morning, ladies and gentlemen," she said to the twelve men and women sitting in the jury box and the three alternate jurors seated in chairs in front of them. They looked at her expectantly.

"I want to talk to you about AIDS," she said, and paused for effect. "Acquired immune deficiency syndrome. It is a disease caused by a virus—the HIV virus—which cripples the body's immune system, depriving it of its defenses against common ailments that unaffected people would easily survive. Once the HIV virus infects the body, the progression of the disease toward its terminal stage is irreversible, remorseless, and inevitable. There is no vaccine. There is no cure. There is no hope. For the victim, the prognosis and the future are always the same: death."

The courtroom was perfectly still. The emotive words Kathryn had just spoken seemed to hover in the air.

"A year ago, the defendant, Richard Hudson, was diagnosed with AIDS. He, of course, knew—because his doctors told him—that the disease from which he was suffering was sexually transmitted, contagious, and deadly."

Kathryn spoke slowly and clearly, looking from one face to another, careful to make eye contact with each individual and hold contact just long enough that the juror felt he or she was being addressed directly, but not so long as to cause discomfort.

"In spite of what he knew, shortly after he was told he had AIDS, he began placing what are called 'romance connection ads'—ads for people searching for new companions in hopes of entering into long-term relationships—in a local tabloid, the *Coastal Times.*"

Another pause. This time, Kathryn consciously reminded herself, as she always did, to convey a real story, so the jury understood that the people involved were people like them, that the people who had been hurt were people like them, and that it was because of that fact that people like them must render judgment.

"The defendant met Victoria Mitten through one of the ads he had placed in the *Coastal Times*. They rendezvoused at a downtown coffee house and several times after work for drinks. He invited her to dinner at his home. Over drinks, he told her it had been years since he had had a relationship with a woman, assured her she had nothing to fear because he had recently tested negative for HIV in connection with outpatient surgery. They had unprotected sexual intercourse on a number of occasions. Then, one day, the defendant called her, and told her he had AIDS. She was shocked, astonished that he could have deliberately lied to her about such a thing. He told her it wasn't his fault she was stupid. She asked him for help. He told her she'd find it in the Yellow Pages and hung up on her. Within weeks, Victoria Mitten tested positive for HIV."

Kathryn glanced at the clock. *Don't rush it. Plenty of time.* Every eye in the courtroom was fixed on her.

"Jane Sorensen responded to a similar but differently worded ad. She agreed to meet the defendant for coffee, at the same coffee shop he and Victoria Mitten had frequented. Ms. Sorensen was cautious: they met exclusively at the coffee house, for more than a month, before she agreed to join him for dinner at his home. Up to this time, she still had not revealed to him where she herself lived. He told her, as he had told Victoria Mitten before her, that he had not been intimate with a woman for several years, and that in connection with a minor outpatient surgical procedure, he had recently tested negative for HIV.

"Hudson had Jane Sorensen perform unprotected

oral sex on him a number of times. Oral copulation was the only sexual activity they engaged in. Soon after, as he had done with Victoria Mitten, Hudson unceremoniously terminated the relationship, this time by letter informing Jane Sorensen he had AIDS. Four weeks later, and again four weeks after that, Jane Sorensen had herself tested for the HIV virus. Those tests were negative; she is not yet HIV-positive. Not *yet*."

Just a brief pause. She did not need to overdo it; she could see the jury was hanging on every word.

"Like the others, Marian Browning replied to an ad in the *Coastal Times*. As with Victoria Mitten and Jane Sorensen, the defendant met her at the Santa Rita Coffee Roasting Company on Mercado Street. After they had dated a few times, going to the downtown movie theater, he invited her to his home for dinner. Not surprisingly, he told Marian Browning the same kind of lies he had previously told to Jane and Victoria. He lied about his relationships, or lack of relationships, with other women, and he lied about having tested negative for HIV.

"Repeating the pattern he had established with Victoria and Jane, he had unprotected sexual intercourse with the unsuspecting Marian. He terminated his brief relationship with her exactly as he had with Victoria and Jane, coldly, unfeelingly, and without the slightest trace of sympathy. Terrified, she had herself tested for HIV, and—" a tiny pause "—the results of that test were positive: Marian Browning has been infected with the HIV virus."

As she stopped speaking, every eye in the jury turned toward the defendant. He stared blankly ahead, swinging slightly on his chair, as if what was being said had no relevance or connection to him.

"Attempted murder of the second degree, ladies and gentlemen, is the attempted unlawful killing of a human being as the proximate result of an act involving a high degree of probability that it will result in death, an act committed for a base, antisocial purpose, with wanton disregard for human life."

Kathryn turned slightly so that she brought Richard Hudson into her sightline. She wanted the jury to be under no misapprehensions about whom she was referring to.

"The defendant had unprotected sexual relations with Victoria Mitten, Jane Sorensen, and Marian Browning fully aware of the fact that he had AIDS. The sexual acts in which Richard Hudson engaged each of these three women involved a high degree of probability that they would result in their deaths, and he committed those acts for a base, antisocial purpose and with wanton disregard for the lives of Victoria Mitten, Jane Sorensen, and Marian Browning."

Kathryn drew in a long, deep breath, her throat dry with tension. She walked away from the podium, over to the jury box, and stood before the jury.

"This is the last time I will speak directly to you until the conclusion of this trial. During the trial, I will confine my communications to witnesses, who will relate to you facts that will prove those matters I have spoken to you about this morning. At the conclusion of the trial, I will ask you to find the defendant guilty of three counts of attempted murder. Thank you."

As she turned and walked back to her chair, she

glanced surreptitiously at her watch: Fifty-eight minutes.

"Thank you, Ms. Mackay," Judge Woods said. "Does the defense wish to make an opening statement at this time?"

Martin Belker rose. "May we approach, Your Honor?"

The judge signaled his assent, and Kathryn and Belker approached the Bench.

"Before I answer, I need to consult with my client, Your Honor," Belker said. "I suggest I use the noon hour to meet with him and advise the Court of our decision at the start of the afternoon session."

Judge Woods's annoyance showed, but he controlled it. "All right, Counsel," he snapped, waving Kathryn and Belker back to their tables. "But be ready after noon recess. Step back."

"We'll take our noon recess at this time," he announced, "and resume at one-thirty. I'll ask the jury to return at two o'clock in order that we can handle a few housekeeping matters outside their presence."

He swiveled around to face the jury and regarded them gravely for a moment.

"Ladies and gentlemen, please be mindful of the fact that at all times, whether you are in the courtroom or out of it, it is your duty not to discuss this case among yourselves, nor may you permit anyone to speak to you about the case. Further, I enjoin you at all times until the matter is finally submitted to you by me, and you go into the jury room, that you keep an open mind on all the issues of the case. Thank you."

He rose and swept out in a flurry of black, and the bailiff led the jury out of the courtroom. Kathryn glanced at the clock: it was exactly eleven-thirty.

"Good opening, Kathryn," Dave said as she sat down. "Strong."

"Good to know," Kathryn said. She felt limp, the way she always did in the aftermath of an hour of such high tension.

"You want to get a bite to eat?"

"Thanks, Dave, not today," she replied. "I need to go over some files, and I've got a stack of phone messages to return. I'll grab a Yoplait in the cafeteria and eat in my office. See you later."

Something in his eyes told her Dave had detected a strange tone in her voice; all she could do was hope he'd write it off as trial stress. He nodded in agreement as they gathered up their files and headed out of the courtroom into the waiting rabble of media people jostling to get to phones or set up here-and-now news items and sound bites.

As she emerged from the courtroom, one or two of the reporters shouted her name, but Kathryn shook her head and kept walking. On October 1, 1995, as a result of the sensationalism surrounding the O. J. Simpson trial, the California Supreme Court had issued the "trial publicity rule." The spectacle of attorneys having daily press conferences on the courtroom steps was now a thing of the past. She had already made her position clear to the media before the trial began: she would state whatever was on the record, comment on the scheduling of the trial, but otherwise no comment. Quite apart from the fact that any attorney who violated the rule would be subject to disciplinary action, trying her case in front of the TV cameras was not her style, and the reporters knew it. And since there were no witnesses for them to pursue today, they were just going to have to manage the best they could with what they had.

She shrugged. Things were tough all over.

# 10

Kathryn had barely enough time to gulp down her tea, finish her yogurt, and repair her makeup before dashing back through the atrium to Superior Court Eight. Judge Jesse Woods made almost a fetish out of being punctual and demanded the same standards from everyone appearing in his court.

The Courts Building was a single-story hollow rectangle, the courtrooms and other offices forming a box within a box skirted by long, wide corridors whose walls were lined with the same unfinished cedar paneling as the courtrooms themselves. Severe, uncushioned oak benches flanked the entrances to each court, with more beneath the floor-to-ceiling exterior windows. Here attorneys and clients met, families sat worrying, witnesses bit their nails, spectators checked the notice boards, jurors awaited their summons.

"Hi, Kathryn."

"Hello again, Jack," Kathryn said, plopping her

77

bulky briefcase and box full of files on the table in front of him. The smiling deputy's name was actually Peter Kennedy, but everyone in law enforcement called him Jack. Seeing him triggered a flashback in her mind to a chilly night on Shelter Island and the mutilated body of a young woman lying dead in the dunes at the edge of the ocean. Jack had been on duty at the crime scene that night. It seemed like a century ago.

"Hey, sorry to hear what happened to Jim Field," he said. "That courtroom. Jeez, what a mess."

She nodded quickly, not wanting to relive it, and slid through the Magnascanner arch. Alice Hernandez, the deputy manning it, smiled hello but said nothing.

"Same bailiffs this afternoon as this morning, Alice?" Kathryn asked her.

"Yeah. Chris Taylor on the jury, Kennedy on the defendant, I'm on the doors."

Superior Court Department Eight was a new, specially built courtroom in which high-security cases were heard. It was similar to yet different from other courtrooms in the annex. Its heavy double doors were steel lined. Spectators, press, and attorneys alike checked in through the Magnascanner, a metal detector exactly like those at airport security stations. Briefcases, camera bags, and other items were hand-inspected by an armed deputy. On a chair to one side was a metal-detector wand ready to run over anyone who tripped the Magnascanner. Occasionally, a lawyer complained about violation of privacy, but prosecutors, especially Kathryn, felt the courtroom security was long overdue.

Inside, the differences between Superior Eight and other courtrooms were striking. The basics were the same: variegated wood strip paneling, twin light oak counsel tables and swivel chairs, lectern facing the jury, state and national flags behind the judge's wooden bench, carved wooden Great Seal, the judge's high-backed leather chair, a Santa Rita Land Title Company calendar on the wall. A sectional bookcase was on the right wall, the jury box on the left.

Protecting the judge's bench from a frontal attack loomed a five-foot-high bulletproof plexiglass shield. Similar armored shields protected the windows, the jury box, and the witness stand.

Although Kathryn realized the shields were necessary and that they would eventually—inevitably—become standard in courtrooms everywhere, she could not help but feel such protective measures made a mockery of everything the law stood for. They conjured up memories of the day last year when her ex-husband, Emma's father, had been killed by a criminal defendant in an L.A. County courtroom shooting. Judges and lawyers practiced an increasingly dangerous profession; courtrooms could become battlefields as some disgruntled litigant or desperate criminal vented his impotence on the system with a weapon.

Or a bomb.

Martin Belker was already seated at the table to her right as she entered the courtroom, his notes piled in front of him, the defendant sitting unshackled beside him. The jurors were not yet seated, nor was the judge in the courtroom. As soon as the lawyers had been admitted, bailiffs allowed spectators and press into the seating area. As Kathryn put her files on the table, Dave Granz entered the courtroom and joined her at the prosecution table.

"Did you get something to eat?" she asked with concern. Dave often got so engrossed in what he was doing that he forgot meals completely.

"No time," he said. "I've been reviewing reports, trying to get up to speed on this."

"It's complex," Kathryn said. "The facts and the law. There aren't any precedents."

"I'll get there," Dave said grimly. "But it isn't gonna be easy. Especially now we're assigned to the task force as well."

"That's life in the DA's office." Kathryn grinned. "Just one long round of pleasure."

She opened her briefcase and placed a yellow legal pad in front of her, ready to take notes. She knew Marty Belker would make an opening statement for the defense; the business he had given the judge about consultation with his client was just a ruse. He had not wanted his opening to follow immediately after her own, while her words were still fresh in the jury's minds.

She looked up as Belker sauntered across toward her, a slight smile hovering around his thin lips.

"I figure my opening will take about two hours," he said. "Do you plan to start with a witness this afternoon?"

"I doubt it, Marty," Kathryn said. "If it's going to take you until three-thirty or later for your opening, my guess is Woods won't want to start hearing testimony until tomorrow. But if he changes his mind and wants to go late today, I'm ready. My first witness is in the Victim/Witness office."

Belker's lips moved into something between a smile and a sneer. "Surprise, surprise," he said sourly. "When was the last time you *weren't* ready?"

He turned and ambled back to counsel table, where Richard Hudson sat wearing his usual vacant stare. Belker leaned over and said something to him. Hudson nodded and looked at Kathryn as if she were a hunk of meat on a butcher's tray. Now, for the first time, she wondered how any of his victims had found him attractive.

"All rise!"

Judge Woods took his place on the bench and directed bailiff Chris Taylor to provide each of the jurors with paper and pencil. It was an unnecessary directive; Taylor was an experienced peace officer and was perfectly able to take care of his duties without direction, but he never presumed. There was gentleness in his acquiescence, Kathryn thought, but then learning forbearance was what bailiff duty was all about.

If the judge needed more water in his decanter, he asked the bailiff. If the jury wanted coffee during their deliberations, they asked the bailiff. Bailiffs were charged with the security of the defendant. They called the next witness into the courtroom, watched over courtroom security scanners, directed people to the rest rooms, patroled hallways, and sat stone-faced in courtrooms. Whether it was a senior citizen asking nervously if the rays of the Magnascanner were radioactive or an attorney challenging their right to search his briefcase, the bailiffs had to deal with it, calmly, tactfully, and with dispatch.

After the paper and pencils were distributed, Judge Woods addressed Belker.

"Counsel, are you prepared to give an opening statement, or do you wish to waive?"

Belker stood. "No, Your Honor. The defense wishes to address the jury."

"Very well. Can you advise the court as to the length of your opening statement?"

"No more than two hours, Your Honor." Belker glanced at the clock; it was almost one forty-five. "I should be finished no later than four o'clock."

The judge nodded. "Proceed, please, Mr. Belker."

To a prosecutor as experienced as Kathryn, the line Belker took in his opening statement was as predictable as summer fog on the central California coast. She had shown his client to be cruel, vindictive, uncaring. His job was to establish the opposite, laying a foundation for the line he was going to use in Hudson's defense. He began by painting a picture of Hudson as a victim from an early age—an only child whose parents had been religious zealots who forbade him to have friends of his own age and systematically abused him physically and sexually. Placed in a series of foster homes by Child Protective Services, he had never had the benefits of a normal home life.

"Yet in spite of these experiences, Richard Hudson determined to better himself," Belker told the jury. "He studied hard and graduated near the top of his high school class, put the past behind him, and moved to California. He worked by day in a travel agency and attended college at night to learn computer science. He was diligent and hardworking and moved up the ladder to the position he holds now with one of the best-known computer assembly firms in Silicon Valley. He has never been in trouble of any kind, not so much as a speeding violation. In spite of the traumas he suffered in his childhood, he became a hardworking, decent citizen, popular with his colleagues, many of whom are convinced, as I am convinced, that he is a blameless man wrongly and falsely accused by overzealous prosecutors."

There was a lot more in the same vein. Emotional and outraged, he scorned the State's case, which, he promised he would show them, was comprised of nothing but unreasonable circumstantial evidence. He indicted the prosecution as shameless puppets pandering to hysterical, "politically correct" extremists who were looking not so much for justice as for a dumping ground for society's guilt about a disease it neither understood nor tolerated.

The fact of the matter, he told the jury, was that Richard Hudson was not a criminal, and the State should be ashamed for victimizing rather than helping him. If the State were to spend half as much of its time and money developing a cure for AIDS as it did persecuting AIDS victims like his client, they could all go home.

"Thank you for your careful attention, ladies and gentlemen," Belker concluded. "I say again, Richard Hudson is not the criminal here, he is a victim, as much a victim as the unfortunate women the District Attorney will parade before you in a feeble attempt to subvert your rightful sympathy for them into misguided antipathy toward him. Richard Hudson is the victim of an uncaring state with distorted financial priorities; the victim of an insensitive but politically correct District Attorney; the victim of the most insidious and terrifying disease ever to afflict mankind. Do not make him a victim of the judicial system as well. You must find my client not guilty at the end of this trial."

He sat down next to his client with a that-showed-them expression on his face. Not bad as defense openings go, Kathryn thought to herself. Belker had been emotional and moving, but, like most defense attorneys, he had steered clear of the facts. Kathryn banked on there being little fire behind the smoke screen. She shivered slightly at the thought of fire and smoke and wondered how Jim Field was getting along. Maybe she would be able to get up to the hospital to see him tonight.

It was exactly four o'clock. As she had expected, Judge Woods adjourned court immediately, following the usual admonishments to the jury not to discuss the case with anyone. Presentation of evidence would commence tomorrow morning with testimony from the first prosecution witness, he told them.

Kathryn quickly scooped up her files, her mind already going into Mom Mode, as Dave called it. Between now and the time she picked Emma up from school and dropped her at her violin class, she would consciously shed the formal identity of Kathryn Mackay, prosecutor, and adjust to being the mother of a freckle-faced hoyden who asked far too many questions.

*Oh, Em,* she thought, *I love you.*

# 11

Kathryn stood at the stove using a wooden paddle to stir white cornmeal in an unlined copper pot. Emma sat at the kitchen counter immersed in the homework spread out before her. They had only been home a few minutes. In spite of her best intentions, Kathryn had been late arriving and paid a penalty for picking up Emma late from day care—again. To say Emma had been unhappy was putting it mildly.

The phone rang, dispersing the slightly tense silence. Kathryn let the answering machine pick up the call, monitoring it without revealing her own presence. A glance showed Emma's face already wore a resigned expression. She knew only too well what evening phone calls meant.

"County Communications, Ms. Mackay," a terse female voice said. "We have a possible homicide at 380 Cabrillo Avenue, Alameda Heights. An explosion and fire."

"Damn," she said, and quickly picked up the

85

phone. Emma rolled her eyes heavenward. "This is Kathryn Mackay, I'm here."

"SO requests you get to the scene as soon as possible. Do you know how long you'll be, so I can advise them?"

Kathryn was on permanent call for homicide investigations. Though they "belonged" to the police until charges were filed, she was present and involved at their invitation to assist and advise on legal and investigatory matters that might affect potential prosecution.

"Tell them I'm on my way now," Kathryn said. "It should be no more than fifteen minutes. Would you notify Inspector Granz and ask him to meet me there?"

She hardly heard the dispatcher's automatic "ten-four." Her mind had already moved into overdrive. Possible homicide, explosion and fire. Explosion? Bomb? She picked up the phone again and called her friend Ruth Draper, who lived on the floor below, to come up and stay with Emma.

"Has something bad happened again, Mom?" Emma asked, a thread of fear in her voice. She knew the answer before she asked.

Kathryn nodded. "Someone is dead, Em. I have to go out for a while. Ruth will be here in a couple of minutes. She'll finish cooking the polenta for you."

"But we just got home!" Emma protested. "You said if I promised to try for all A's, you'd help me with my homework. It isn't fair. Can't someone else go?"

"I have to go, Em, you know that. I'm sorry, sweetheart, but it's my job, and I can't help it. But I'll get home as soon as I can. If it's too late to help with your homework, we'll do it tomorrow morning, I promise. Be sure to take a shower and wash that beautiful face—only, listen, don't scrub off any of those freckles or I won't recognize you."

The little joke evoked a grudging smile which Kathryn decided to read as Emma's acceptance, and she headed for the bedroom to change out of her sweats. But her daughter wasn't too disappointed to miss an opportunity like this.

"Mom," she called, "if I eat all my dinner and take my shower and do my homework, can I have a Snickers ice cream bar for dessert?"

Kathryn shook her head ruefully. Caught again, she thought.

"Okay, but only one," she agreed as she hastily put on a pair of jeans and a shirt. "Then, if you have time, you can watch TV with Ruth for a little while before bed. Brush your teeth after you eat, too, and don't forget to give Sam some fresh water. G'bye."

"Take care, Mom," Emma said, and blew her a kiss as she went out the door on the run. She'd told the dispatcher she'd be at Cabrillo Avenue in fifteen minutes.

She made it in twelve.

# 12

The crime scene was easy to find. The strobe lights of the police cars and fire engines lit up the sky as soon as she turned onto the avenue. Even though each was different in its own way, at first sight every crime scene appeared the same—the yellow taped cordon, the carelessly parked patrol cars, the background squawking of police radios, the weary cop telling curious neighbors to keep moving, the crime scene van outside the house. Here, however, fire hoses snaked across the street, and firefighters in yellow slickers stood by.

A skinny deputy held up a hand to stop her as she approached. The nameplate above his pocket said CAREY. He bent down to peer into the car as Kathryn wound down the window. When he saw Kathryn, he touched the brim of his hat. "Hi, Kathryn."

"Hi, Jeff," Kathryn said. "Okay to park here?"

"Pull over to the right some," Carey said. "Ought to be okay there."

Kathryn parked her Audi behind one of the green and white patrol cars and got out. The deputy lifted the yellow tape so she could duck under it. As she headed up the path, she saw Dave's Jeep pull to a stop behind her Audi. He hurried over to join her.

At first glance, the house looked unremarkable, a Victorian-style home on a large lot. But as they drew closer, they spotted a huge gaping hole, part blasted, part burned through the roof, and black scorch marks on the exterior siding. Brittle shards of shattered window glass glinted in the damp lawn. Anybody in front of the window when that bomb went off would have been skewered like shrimp on a barbecue. The smell of scorched brick and dark, wet smoke hung heavy in the air.

They followed the corridor of tape to the front door of the house. The curious faces of neighbors resembled ghosts with sunken eyes and black lips in the flickering neon lights of the police and fire apparatus. At the door, another deputy logged them in. His nameplate said PETERSEN.

"Hi, Carl," she said. "Bad in there?"

Petersen made a face. "I've seen some bad ones," he said grimly. "But this . . ." He shook his head sadly. "Top of the stairs."

The acrid stink of still-warm soot, burned wood, and something else, richer and sweeter, pervaded the house. As she led the way up the stairs, Kathryn realized what it was. Suddenly, vividly, she recalled the smell of roast pork and Sunday dinners when she was growing up in Kansas City.

Detective Henry Chu came out of the bedroom as they reached the landing. Short, solidly built, conservatively dressed, Henry was a fastidious man, choosy about his clothes; he looked more like a CPA than an investigator. Soot flecks dotted his dark gray suit and marred the otherwise spotless white shirt. He didn't look so good.

"What have we got, Henry?" Dave asked.

"A mess," Chu said disgustedly. "Take a look for yourself."

A criminalist who was carefully examining what was left of the bedding looked up as they came in, then returned to his painstaking work. The routine rarely varied. The crime scene was photographed, measured, and diagrammed. Investigators dusted for latent and patent impressions; others collected trace evidence. Hairs, semen stains, blood. Nobody hurried, nobody took shortcuts. There were no second chances at a crime scene.

The interior of the bedroom was a blackened ruin, every surface covered with greasy soot. The smell of cooking was a stink now. On what was left of a collapsed king-size bed lay the charred, spread-eagled figure of a naked man. His arms and legs were extended in an exaggerated X, feet and hands tied to the bedposts. Below the navel was a huge volcano of charred tissue, a hole about eight inches across burned right through the body, completely destroying the genitals. The dead man's face was frozen in a rictus of agony, eyes protruding visibly. A froth of bloody foam surrounded the gaping mouth.

"Jesus," Dave said involuntarily. "What the hell happened here?"

"Looks like somebody tied the poor bastard up, put some kind of incendiary device on his belly, lit the fuse, and then walked away," Chu said, a thin trace of anger in his voice. "I don't know what the hell he used, but whatever it was, as it burned down through the body it ignited the body fat—that's why we got so much soot—and then set the bed on fire. Flames touched off the ceiling, then the roof—fat burns really hot. Luckily, a neighbor smelled smoke and called 911."

"Luckily," Granz said bleakly.

"He's right," Kathryn said. "If the house had burned down, all we'd have would be a pile of carbon. Have you made an ID?"

"The neighbor lady says a middle-aged guy named Patrick Hanlon lived here by himself," Chu replied. "Odds are that's who it is, but we'll need dental records or X-rays to confirm."

"Has Doc Nelson examined the body?" Dave asked.

"Been here and left for the Hellhole," Chu said.

A long time ago, Morgan had unwarily referred to the high-tech morgue complex that occupied the basement of County Hospital as the Hellhole. The label had stuck; now there wasn't a cop in Santa Rita who ever called it anything else.

"We'll catch up with him there," Dave said. "You want a ride, Henry?"

The detective shook his head. "I got to stick around until the meat wagon gets here."

In a broken mirror that lay askew against one wall, Kathryn caught sight of herself looking down at the ghastly thing on the bed and wondered how many victims like this one she had seen—shot, strangled, stabbed, burned, beaten to death. She tried always to maintain an air of professional dispassion at murder scenes, but she had never attended one yet that did not move her to pity and anger. You could let the pity out; it helped mask the horror. The anger she banked. One day, someone would stand trial before her for this atrocity. And she would recall that anger and then and draw strength and conviction from it. She touched Dave's shoulder.

"Nothing we can do here now," she said. "Let's go."

# 13

After stopping off for a welcome cup of coffee, and to give the coroner's deputies time to transport the body to County, Kathryn and Dave headed for the morgue. Morgan Nelson was waiting for them in the VIP room when they arrived.

"Hello, Katie," he said. "Dave."

Morgan Nelson was the only person Kathryn knew who called her Katie. In his late fifties, tall, slightly stooped, with cropped gingery hair and wire-rimmed granny glasses, he looked tired and irritable. Hardly surprising, Kathryn thought. It was a rare day he didn't work fifteen hours, and often—like tonight—it was more like eighteen. The dead are not helpful; moving their inert, leaden bodies was hard, punishing work.

"We got a confirmed ID on him yet, Doc?" Dave said, gesturing toward what remained of Patrick Hanlon on the steel operating table.

"His X-rays and medical records were on file here

93

at County. Patrick James Hanlon, forty-six, unmarried. Industrial designer, office in Espanola. Family in the Westwood area of L.A. Henry Chu is trying to locate them."

"Chu told us they found signs of forced entry at the house," Kathryn said. "Did you find any contusions or bruising consistent with a robbery?"

"I already told Henry, nothing overt," Nelson said. "Of course, I won't be able to tell you for sure until I open him up."

"It doesn't make any sort of sense to me," Granz said flatly. "Robbers don't use bombs."

"You have any idea what the thing might have been made of, Doc?" Kathryn asked.

Nelson shrugged. "I could make a guess. Anything that generated such intense heat would probably have been thermite-based. We'll probably never know what the carrier was, the fire destroyed everything. But I'd bet on it having been a fairly basic device, a simple ignition fuse, and—zap."

"Big, bulky?" Kathryn asked.

"On the contrary," Morgan replied. "Something you could carry comfortably in your jacket pocket."

"What's troubling is the way he was tied up," Kathryn said. "It's not consistent with a home robbery or an interrupted burglary."

Nelson smiled appreciatively. "I thought I was the only one who'd noticed that," he said. "Go on, Katie."

"The whole scenario suggests bondage to me rather than restraint," Kathryn said.

"Are you saying a sex partner tied him up? And then offed him with a bomb?" Dave asked.

"Short of duress, suggest some other way you could

persuade a man to allow himself to be tied to a bed naked like that," Nelson said.

"But why use a bomb?" Kathryn argued. "Why kill him at all, come to that?"

"There's a reason," Morgan said. "We just don't know what it is yet. Maybe whoever killed him was someone he knew."

Dave looked up sharply. "Because?"

"Depending on how far the parties involved go, S&M can be dangerous," Morgan explained. "So your partner has to be someone you trust implicitly, someone you can rely on to stop the moment it becomes unbearable."

"Hanlon's neighbors said he lived alone. S&M takes two: one to give pain, the other to receive it," Kathryn observed. "Which, if Morgan is right, means his visitor was someone he knew. Dave, would you have CSI search for and seize any address books, check his desktop for e-mail, any forums he might have been using on the Net? I'll get a warrant for his phone and fax, credit card, and bank records. If any safe deposit boxes turn up, we'll search them."

Dave nodded, scribbling rapidly in his notebook.

"You said you already have his medical records, right, Doc?" he said. "Okay, I'll run his rap and DMV and have CSI seize and search any vehicles the printout turns up. Maybe we'll get lucky."

Kathryn felt a wave of tiredness sweep over her. As if he could read her mind, Dave looked at her and lifted his chin. *Let's go.* She nodded.

"When are you planning to do the autopsy on Hanlon, Doc?" Dave asked.

Nelson shrugged. "All being well, Thursday. If not, Friday. You want to sit in?"

"No," Kathryn said. "But I think we'd better."

Dave walked Kathryn to her car, where he kissed her good night.

"Give Em a kiss for me when you get home," he instructed her.

"She'll be sound asleep by then," Kathryn lamented.

"That's okay. Kiss her anyway."

He watched until her taillights disappeared down the curving driveway, then turned and walked back into the hospital. To his surprise, the first person he saw in the reception area was Jim Field's wife, Rochelle. A slim, athletic woman with a cloud of dark brown hair framing a heart-shaped face, she was wearing a single-breasted cotton blazer with wide-leg trousers. Dark shadows beneath her eyes hinted at sleepless nights.

"Hey, 'Chelle, I'm glad I bumped into you," he said, giving her a hug. "I've been meaning to call."

They had known each other a long time. He'd been an usher when she married Jim Field. It was 1986, he recalled, the year Tyson became heavyweight champion and *Challenger* blew up in that cerulean Florida sky. Where did the time go?

"I was just leaving," she said. "I'll be back in the morning with the kids."

"How is he tonight?" he asked.

Rochelle drew in a deep breath, held it, then exhaled. "We were planning a trip to Cleveland, it's Jim's hometown, did you know? We were going to stay with his sister and her family, take the kids to see the Rock and Roll Hall of Fame. Now . . ." She shrugged.

"You can still go. He'll be out of here in a few days."

"I guess," she said, looking away, her wide brown eyes suddenly tearful. "He keeps saying he's finished, can't even zip up his own pants."

Dave nodded. He'd seen a few maimed cops, men who lost the use of an arm or a leg, and knew from personal experience something about what was going on in Jim's head. The first reaction was always a sort of panic. Everything was a mountain. Simple functions you had never even given a thought to—tying a shoelace, buttoning a shirt, opening a beer—suddenly became major tasks requiring total concentration or, worse, asking for help. Other skills had to be relearned completely, like driving or writing a letter. Field was a good tennis player, a member of the Sheriff's Office Police Olympics Shooting Team. One of his stress releasers was lifting weights at the spa. All that would have to go on hold until he was fitted with a prosthetic hand and learned how to use it. And even then . . .

"He's a cop, Dave. He doesn't know how to be anything else."

"He's still a cop, always will be," Dave assured her. "Look, I'll talk to him, okay?"

"I wish you would," she said fervently. "I don't seem to be able to give him the reassurance he needs right now. I think it's something only another man can talk to him about—another cop."

"You mind if I ask you a question, 'Chelle? Did Jim . . . did he have any enemies? Anybody he ever mentioned to you?"

Rochelle looked bewildered. "Enemies?"

"He hasn't been threatened? No hate mail, crank phone calls?"

She shook her head. "Nothing like that." Her eyes widened. "You don't think the bomb was *intended* for Jim, do you?"

"I don't think anything, 'Chelle. I'm just running through the possibilities, that's all."

"What are you saying, Dave, it might have been someone he put away in the past?"

"That's possible, too. We're checking through his old cases right now. Defendants, inmates, parolees, even suspects in ongoing investigations."

"I know some of them were . . . bad people. The ones he put in prison. I still find it hard to believe any of them might have . . . done this."

"Someone did."

Rochelle Field shivered, as if a cold wind had touched her.

"You okay, 'Chelle?" Granz asked. "Have you talked to anyone?"

Rochelle shook her head. "I'm not one of those people who think you can talk this kind of hurt away as if it were a headache, Dave. But I'm working my way through. I'll be all right."

"Never doubted that."

"I heard on TV there was another bombing," Rochelle said. "Any connection?" She tilted her head in the direction of her husband's room.

"No reason to think so," Dave said. "It was a different kind of thing. An incendiary device."

"What makes someone do such a terrible thing?" she said fiercely. "Such a terrible, *wasteful* thing?"

"I wish I could tell you," Dave said. "The fact is, there's no simple reason. This one is paying off a grudge, that one is making a protest, or else it's some weirdo group that thinks it's the only way to get the world to pay attention to their grievances."

"Why don't they bomb bad people, Dave?" Rochelle said fiercely. "Why is it always innocent people who get killed or maimed? Damnit, why couldn't he have been an accountant or something? Anything but a cop."

There was no answer to that.

"How are the kids handling it?" Dave asked.

"Tracy's fine. A thing like this has no real significance to a four-year-old. It's just Daddy had an accident. But Clark—"

Clark was six, nearly seven. His dad was his idol. Dave remembered visiting the Fields one time and saying something about his air conditioner having broken down. Little Clark, a fine-looking kid with marmalade hair and bright brown eyes, tugged at his sleeve.

"My dad will show you how to fix it, Dave," he said, adding proudly, "My dad can fix *anything.*"

"If you think it would help, I could maybe drop in Sunday. You know, talk to him."

"He'd like that. You're one of his heroes. And he knows you and Jim are buddies."

"'Chelle, I have an early morning," Dave said. "I better go in and see Jim."

Rochelle nodded her understanding. "Thank you, Dave," she said, her face serious. "I appreciate you doing all this."

"See you Sunday," he said.

Jim Field's room was like hospital rooms everywhere, with the usual sterile steel and Naugahyde furniture, the same tautly made bed, the electronic monitors, the saline drip suspended on its F-shaped stand. Field lifted his head as Dave came in. His face was blank, unreadable. There was no welcome in his eyes.

"How are you, Jim?" Granz said.

Field made an impatient sound. "Me? Never felt better. Losing a hand has put a whole new gloss on my life."

"Jim, this isn't the end of the world. They have prostheses today that look like the real—"

"Cut the bullshit, Dave," Field rasped. "It's bad enough having to lie here thinking about all the things I won't be able to do anymore without you coming on like some fucking Little Mary Sunshine."

"Look, you got a tough break," Dave said. "But tough breaks go with the territory. Nobody knows that better than me."

He gestured toward the scars that ran down the left side of his face. Field's face was immediately contrite.

"Aw, shit, I'm sorry, Dave. It's just . . . I keep thinking, is this what I worked my butt off for all those years, to end up in a back room filing reports? I don't even know if I can do that. What if they retire me on a disability? I don't know how to do anything but be a cop."

"They're not waiting to get rid of you. They want to know when you're getting off your butt and coming back to work."

"Yeah, tell me about it. And while you're at it, tell me how I'll be able to play catch with my son. Jesus, Dave, I don't know what the hell I'm gonna do or how I'm gonna do it. I just keep thinking, why me? Why the fuck did it have to be me?"

"Think of it another way," Granz told him quietly. "You could be dead."

"Lemme tell you, I wanted to be," Field said bitterly. "At first, I just wanted to die, to not have to face it or think about it. I just lay here with the same question going through my mind, over and over and over: Why me? Why the hell did I have to pick up that stupid fucking package?"

"Kathryn said it was addressed to Belker."

"Right," Field said. "Just his name. 'Personal attention Mr. Martin Belker.'"

"How was it sealed, do you remember?"

"I already told the bomb team all this. Brown paper, Scotch tape."

"Light, heavy?"

"Like a videotape. That would be, what, half a pound?"

"And you've got no idea how long it had been there."

Field shrugged. "It was there when we came in, but, you know, the courtroom had probably been unlocked for almost an hour. Anybody could've walked in there and left it. My best guess would be someone who knew the courtroom was unlocked about nine, waited till the bailiff went for coffee or to the john. Wouldn't have taken more than a few seconds."

"When are they letting you out of here?"

"Couple of days, they said. What's happening on the Hudson case?"

"I've been assigned to take your place. As of this morning, we're back in trial. In fact, I oughta be reviewing reports right now. Gonna be a long night."

Field nodded. "Go ahead, g'wan, get outta here. I'm okay."

As Dave turned to go, Field abruptly asked, "Why do we do it, Dave? Why do cops like us go out there every day of the week and put their lives on the line? And keep on doing it?"

"You mean you don't know, or you want to hear what I think?"

"You . . . you nearly got killed. Yet you're back on the street."

"It's what I do," Dave said. "It's what I'm good at."

"Is that enough?"

"Maybe there's more to it. Maybe it's because we can feel good about ourselves out there. It's simple. We know who the good guys are, we know who the bad guys are, and we're doing what we can to balance the books."

"I wish I could be so . . . certain."

"The only thing I'm certain about is that I'm not certain about anything," Dave said. "Look, Jim, I gotta go. Anything you need?"

"Keep an eye on 'Chelle for me, will you, Dave? And the kids? Make sure they're okay. Especially Clark."

"Sure," Granz said. "And listen, I'll be back. I need to pick your brains so I can get up to speed on Hudson by the time Kathryn needs it."

"Anytime," Field said.

His manner had all at once become lethargic, and Dave remembered his own hospitalization, the conflicting emotions, the abysses of depression, the way you looked forward to your visitors arriving and ended up being glad to see them go.

"Hang in there," he said. If Field noticed him leaving, he gave no sign of it.

# 14

After requesting a brief sidebar before testimony commenced, Kathryn asked Judge Woods to order the media not to film, photograph, or identify on TV or in print the victims about to testify before the jury.

"Your Honor!" Marty Belker protested. "This is grossly unfair. The media have already filmed my client and identified him by name. These women—"

Judge Woods held up a silencing hand. "Are victims and deserve this court's protection, Mr. Belker," he said. "Ms. Mackay has a valid argument. Justice will be in no way better served by their being submitted to that kind of an ordeal. I'm going to rule in Ms. Mackay's favor and issue an order prohibiting such coverage."

Belker scowled and slouched back to his seat. It wasn't that he had lost anything, Kathryn thought. He just hated her winning. She returned to her table as Chris Taylor brought in her first witness, Victoria

CHRISTINE MCGUIRE

Mitten, only half listening as court clerk Cathy
Radina swore in the witness.

". . . swear to tell the truth, the whole truth, and
nothing but the truth, so help you God?" the clerk
droned.

"I do," Victoria Mitten said. About medium
height, she wore a simple black jacket over a light
yellow blouse, and a long black skirt. Her very white
skin, long straight black hair, dark eyes, and full lips
made her otherwise plain face oddly exotic. She sat in
the witness chair as directed by the court clerk and
fidgeted nervously.

"State your name and spell your last name, please."

"Victoria Mitten, M-i-t-t-e-n."

As Judge Woods looked expectantly toward the
prosecution table, Kathryn rose and strode purposefully to the far end of the jury box. It was crucial that
the jury hear what the victim said, and that she
appear to speak directly to them. The goal of good
direct examination was to explain the facts to the jury
clearly and simply, telling a story from beginning to
end. During a trial, Kathryn became a storyteller, her
witnesses the pages and chapters of her book.

"Are you married, Victoria?"

The young woman shook her head. "I live alone. It
used to be my mother's house."

"How old are you?" Kathryn asked.

"Twenty-eight."

"Would it be correct to say that you have never had
a long-term romantic relationship?"

Victoria Mitten nodded. "I . . . my mother was
disabled. I took care of her. It didn't leave much time
for . . . other things."

"Your mother died recently?"

104

"In January of this year."

"And would I be right in saying that it was after your mother died," Kathryn said, "that you started reading romance connection ads?"

"I was so lonely with Mother gone. I had very few real friends. And it seemed . . . safe enough."

"Is this the advertisement you replied to, Victoria?" Kathryn said, handing her a newspaper identified as People's Exhibit 5. "The one with the red ring around it?"

Victoria Mitten reached into her purse and brought out a pair of reading glasses. She put them on, looked at the newspaper, and nodded. "That's it."

"Victoria, would you read the ad out loud for the jury, please."

During direct examination, the witness became the central character in the story that was being told. The accomplished prosecutor orchestrated, emphasized, and punctuated, but remained always in the background.

"'Are you twenty-five to thirty, looking for romance, kindness, fun, adventure?'" Victoria Mitten read in a clear voice. "'Sweet nothings at unexpected times, and support when you need it? Reply with photograph to Box PZ2245.'"

"Was this the first ad you had ever replied to?"

"Yes."

"What was there about this particular ad that attracted you?"

"I thought . . . it was the last part. Support when you need it? It sounded so sincere. Like whoever placed it would be a real caring person."

"So you replied to the ad. How, exactly?"

"I wrote a note to the box number and included my

first name and telephone number. I didn't put my last name in the note, and I have an unlisted number. I figured that was a safe thing to do."

"I see. Then what happened?"

"I got a telephone call a couple of days later." Victoria Mitten kept her eyes fixed on Kathryn. She had not looked at the defendant since seating herself in the witness chair. "From him. From Richard Hudson."

"Victoria, would you please identify Richard Hudson for the jury."

Almost painfully, Victoria Mitten looked directly at Hudson for the first time and pointed to him. "Him. There."

"Let the record indicate that the witness has identified the defendant, Richard Hudson," Kathryn requested. From now on, Kathryn would never refer to Richard Hudson by name, but only as "the defendant."

"So ordered," replied Judge Woods.

Kathryn returned her attention to the witness. "So the defendant called you. Then what happened, Victoria?"

"He—Richard Hudson—suggested we meet at the Santa Rita Coffee Roasting Company on Mercado one evening."

"And you agreed."

"That's right." The look on her face left no doubt she wished she had never done so.

"And after you met him there, what happened?"

"I thought he was very nice. Polite, pleasant. I thought he . . . he was a gentleman." She blushed. "We talked about all sorts of things. TV shows we liked. Books, movies. He drove me home. We decided to meet again a few nights later. We went to a place in Espanola for pizza and beer."

"What did the defendant tell you about himself, Ms. Mitten?"

"He said he worked as a systems analyst at a computer assembly firm over the Hill," she replied.

"By 'over the Hill,' you mean Silicon Valley?"

"Yes. I'm sorry. Outside San Jose."

"That's okay, no need to apologize. You're doing fine. Did he tell you anything else about himself?"

"He told me he had been married but was now divorced and there were no children. He said the reason he placed the ad was he was tired of being alone but the idea of going to singles bars was repulsive to him. He seemed shy, so it made sense to me. He wanted to meet a nice woman and, you know, have a more stable relationship."

"And you agreed to see him again?"

She nodded. "I met him again a couple of times, weekdays after I got off work. I thought he was . . . you know, attractive. Intelligent. He said he really liked being with me. He said I was fun."

"Did your relationship with the defendant undergo a change at some point?" Kathryn asked.

"Yes."

"In what way?"

"He invited me to dinner at his home."

"Did you accept?"

"Yes, I wanted to go. I wanted to see where he lived. And . . . I really liked him."

"At that time, did you believe you had fallen in love with the defendant?" Kathryn kept her voice gentle but insistent.

Victoria Mitten looked up at the ceiling, blinking

away tears. She swallowed and then nodded her head, taking off her glasses and fumbling them back into her purse.

"Yes," she replied almost inaudibly.

"Victoria, I know this is difficult for you, but can you speak a little louder, please, so the jury can hear you?" Kathryn urged the witness.

Louder, "Yes."

"Tell us what happened the first night you went to the defendant's home for dinner."

"I went to his condominium, up in Mission Heights. It was nicely furnished, books, music on the CD. It was very clean and neat. I didn't know men kept their homes so clean." The remark brought an audible chuckle from everyone in the courtroom. "We drank champagne. We had a lovely meal—crab, brie, and French bread. He said it was his favorite for special occasions."

"Did the defendant suggest making love?"

"After dinner, we sat on the sofa. We were kissing and, you know. He said I was very sexy, he wanted to touch me all over with no clothes on. I . . . wanted to. I had no real . . . experience with men. But I knew . . . I told him he had to use a condom."

"You suggested he use a condom?"

"Yes. I knew it was dangerous not to." Her voice caught as she spoke.

"Victoria, this is very important," Kathryn said gently. "You asked him to use a condom, but he refused?"

Victoria Mitten shook her head. "No, it wasn't . . . he didn't refuse, exactly. He said it wasn't an issue. He was very intense, very sincere. He told me I was the first woman he had been serious about for years. "I've lived like a monk," he said. I remember we laughed. And then he said, 'Victoria, if you're worried about AIDS, don't be. Trust me, there's nothing to be afraid of. I had minor surgery a couple of months ago, and I tested negative.'"

"And what happened then?"

"We drank more wine, and talked some more. And then we . . . we . . . made love."

"Where, exactly, did you make love?"

Victoria Mitten's face flushed. "Right there on his sofa in the living room."

"I see. And, once more—did the defendant use a condom?"

"No, he did not."

"Was that the only occasion on which you had sexual intercourse with the defendant?"

"No. We were seeing each other twice a week. He always wanted to . . . to do it."

"How long did this go on?"

"Three weeks."

"And then what happened?"

"I came home from work one day, and . . . I was making some tea. The phone rang. It was him, Richard."

She looked up at the ceiling again, her throat working.

"Take your time, Victoria," Kathryn said softly. "I know this must be very distressing for you."

Victoria Mitten took a little handkerchief out of her purse and blew her nose.

"I'm sorry," she said.

"There's no need for *you* to be sorry about anything, Victoria," Kathryn said firmly, putting emphasis on the personal pronoun. "What did the defendant say when he called you that evening?"

The jurors looked expectantly toward the witness, who cleared her throat before speaking.

"He just said, 'I'm calling to tell you I've got AIDS. You'd better get yourself a blood test.'"

Kathryn heard one or two of the jurors gasp and saw them cast surreptitious glances at the defendant, who stared impassively at Victoria Mitten. She turned back to the young woman on the stand.

"And what did you say, Victoria?"

"I didn't know what to say. I was stunned. I couldn't believe what he was saying. But . . . I said, 'You must have known. How could you lie to me about something like that?'"

"And he said?"

"He said, 'It's not my fault you're stupid.'"

"He said it wasn't his fault you were stupid?" Kathryn repeated, looking at the jury. "And what did you say?"

"I said, 'I have to see you, I have to talk to you.' He said he didn't want to see me again, ever. I said, 'I need you to help me.'"

"You asked the defendant to help you. What was his reply?"

"He told me to try the Yellow Pages and hung up."

Once again, Kathryn heard the jury's hushed gasp of shock.

"Did you try to contact the defendant again?" she asked.

"I tried to call him a dozen times, but I always got his answering machine. I went to his condo. I don't know if he was home or not, but he never answered the door."

"And what was your state of mind after you received that call and were unable to contact the defendant?"

"I was afraid, I was frantic, I didn't know what to do, who to turn to. I felt so . . . hopeless. I cried for a week. I couldn't believe what he had told me was true."

"And then what did you do?"

"I called my doctor. He said there was a new test called OraSure that can determine if the antibodies to the HIV virus are in your saliva. He said it wasn't as accurate as a blood test, but it would tell me whether or not I needed one."

"And did you submit to an OraSure test?"

Victoria Mitten nodded meekly. "Yes."

"And what was the result?" Kathryn knew the answer to this question, and so did the jury, but they must hear it from Victoria Mitten herself.

"It was positive."

"By positive, do you mean the test indicated the presence of HIV virus in your saliva?"

"Yes."

There was a profound silence in the courtroom now. No one moved.

"Then what happened?"

Victoria Mitten's eyes were teary. "My doctor arranged for me to have a blood test. I got the results a few days later. I am HIV-positive."

Kathryn allowed Victoria Mitten's words to hang in the silent air for a long, long moment. Behind her, someone in the jury box sighed audibly.

"Thank you, Victoria," she said. She looked up at the judge. "I have no more questions for this witness at this time, Your Honor."

"Mr. Belker?" Woods said.

"Thank you, Your Honor," Belker said. He remained seated for a long, considered moment. Then he stood, putting his hands on both sides of his face and looking thoughtfully at the floor as he walked across toward the witness stand. Kathryn, who had seen it many times, knew it was a rehearsed pose. But, of course, the jury did not. To them, Belker appeared to be a man concentrating deeply on what he was about to say. Which was precisely the impression he wished to give them.

"Ms. Mitten," he said, "I have only a few questions, but they're important ones. Please let me know if you don't understand my questions and I'll repeat them for you. All right?"

"Yes, sir," Victoria Mitten said. She shifted perceptibly in her seat.

"Now, Ms. Mitten, you said you have never had a long-term romantic relationship with a member of the opposite sex, is that correct?"

"Yes, sir."

"Never?"

"No, sir, never. My mother—"

"Ms. Mitten, you don't need to explain your answers. If you can answer my questions with a simple yes or no, please do so. If I need an explanation, I'll ask. Now, have you ever had sexual intercourse with a man besides Mr. Hudson?"

"Objection, Your Honor! Irrelevant!" Kathryn was on her feet instantly.

Woods frowned, looking from her to Belker and then back again. "Approach," he commanded. Kathryn and Belker approached the judge's bench.

"Where is this going, Mr. Belker?" he asked in a hushed voice so the jury could not hear.

"Your Honor, the State alleges my client deliberately infected the witness with the AIDS virus. Surely we are entitled to establish whether she has had sex—perhaps unprotected sex—with other men?"

Kathryn demurred. "Your Honor, the People have charged the defendant with *attempted* murder. Defense counsel knows full well that whether or not his client actually infected her isn't relevant. The prosecution doesn't have to prove successful completion of the offense in an *attempted* murder. It is sufficient we prove he *knowingly tried* to infect her."

Woods's frown deepened. "Thank you for that lesson on criminal law, Ms. Mackay, but I'm going to allow it. Step back," he ordered, waving them away.

"Objection overruled," he announced. "Go ahead, Mr. Belker."

Belker nodded and turned to face the witness again. "Would you like me to repeat the question, Ms. Mitten?" he said.

"I can't . . . " The young woman's hands fluttered in front of her. She cast an agonized look at Kathryn.

"Answer the question, Ms. Mitten," the judge ordered, not unkindly.

"I'll ask you again," Belker said, clearly unabashed. "Is Richard Hudson the only man with whom you ever had sexual intercourse?"

"No."

"There were others?"

"Yes."

"How many others?"

"A boy in high school. And one other."

"When was this . . . other relationship?"

"Two . . . no, three years ago."

"Three years ago, you had sexual intercourse with a man, Ms. Mitten?"

"I . . . yes. Yes."

"When you engaged in sexual intercourse with Mr. Hudson, you said you asked him to use a condom, is that correct?"

Kathryn shook her head, letting her vexation show. Changing topics abruptly was a shopworn defense tactic, intended to confuse the witness. The trouble was, it often proved effective.

"Yes, sir."

"And what, exactly, did he say when you asked him to put on a condom before you had sex? Did he say no?"

"I . . . I don't remember exactly what he said . . . his exact words. But he told me it wasn't necessary, that he wasn't HIV-positive."

The witness was clearly uncomfortable with this subject, and Belker saw it.

"And you believed him?" Belker let his disbelief show. "Did you *insist* that he wear a condom? Did you ask him more than once?"

Kathryn stood. "Objection, Your Honor. Counsel has asked the witness several questions. Which one does he want her to answer?"

"I'll rephrase my question, Your Honor," Belker interjected smoothly before the judge could sustain the objection. His point was already made. "Now, Ms. Mitten, were you aware at the time you had sex with Mr. Hudson that HIV—AIDS—can be spread by unprotected sex?"

The witness stammered. "Yes, but . . ."

"Please, just answer the questions yes or no, if possible." Kathryn could see Belker felt he was making considerable headway with this line of questioning, and enjoying his success. "So, although you were aware of the risk of contracting HIV—AIDS—from unprotected sex at the time you engaged in intercourse with Mr. Hudson, you still chose to engage in sexual relations with him not once but several times without using a condom, is that correct?"

"You don't understand. He was very insistent, very domineering, and I—"

"Thank you," he interrupted, cutting her off. "Did you ever ask him again to put on a condom before having sex?"

"No. I could see it made him angry. We never discussed it again."

"Did you ever discuss condom use with your other sexual partners, what was it you said, in high school and two or three years ago?" Belker queried, switching subjects again.

"No, we never . . . I never . . ."

"Okay. So, on numerous other occasions you assumed the risk of contracting HIV by engaging in unprotected sex, just as you did with my client. Is that correct?"

"Objection!" Kathryn jumped to her feet. "If defense counsel is going to ask *and* answer the questions, he doesn't need a witness."

"Sorry, Your Honor."

There was no contrition in his words; Belker was not sorry, and his suppressed smile of triumph showed it. He turned ceremoniously and walked back to counsel table, picked up his notes, and perused them, brow furrowed, flipping pages for a full minute. Kathryn knew this was an elaborate show for the jury's sake. Belker knew exactly where he was heading. He walked back and stood directly in front of the witness.

"Only a few more questions, Ms. Mitten. Now, think carefully before you answer, please. Are you absolutely certain that it was *you* who brought up the subject of condom use before you engaged in sexual intercourse with Mr. Hudson? Given your prior sexual escapades . . ."

"Your Honor!" Kathryn was on her feet again.

"Sorry, Your Honor." Again, Belker was clearly not sorry. "Given that you never even discussed the use of condoms in your previous sexual relationships, much less insisted on them, isn't it possible that it was Mr. Hudson who suggested that he use a condom, and you who were too eager for sex to wait?"

Astonished by the question, Victoria Mitten stared at Belker, unable to reply. Kathryn rose to object, but Judge Woods raised his hand as if fending her off.

"Overruled," he said before she could speak. "Answer the question, Ms. Mitten."

"It's possible. I don't remember for sure." Victoria Mitten's voice was scarcely more than a whisper.

Martin Belker spoke more kindly this time. "Ms. Mitten, you need to speak up so everyone can hear. I ask you again, isn't it possible it was Richard Hudson who suggested using a condom on that first occasion when you had sex, and you who were so eager to have sex that you chose not to use one?"

There was absolute silence. Every eye in the courtroom was fixed on Victoria Mitten, every ear awaiting her reply.

"It's possible, but I don't think so," she replied, this time loud enough for everyone to hear.

"Nothing further, Your Honor." Belker turned and walked slowly back to his table, shaking his head in sad disbelief as a buzz of whispered speculation mounted in the courtroom. Kathryn was already on her feet. What was needed now was some damage control.

"Redirect, Ms. Mackay?" Judge Woods smiled, since the answer was obvious.

"Victoria, you told the jury you had a relationship with another man two or three years ago," Kathryn said. "Do you believe it could have been he who infected you with HIV?"

"No, it couldn't have been him," she replied, grateful for the chance to explain.

"Please tell the court why."

"Objection, calls for a conclusion," Belker said.

"I'll rephrase it," Kathryn said. "How long did that relationship last, Victoria?"

"It was . . . it happened just the one time. In the summer of '93."

"Can you tell us who the man was, Victoria?"

"He was a friend of my mother's." Embarrassment reduced her voice to a near whisper, but it was audible to everyone.

"How old was he?"

"Do I have to say?" she asked. The judge assured her she did. "He was fifty-nine. His wife and my mother were friends."

"Did he ever tell you how long he'd been married?"

"Yes. He said thirty-five years."

"And in the summer of '93, what happened?"

"His wife died. He came to see my mother and me, to tell us. My mother was ill herself. He was so sad." She shook her head slightly. "So very sad."

"Your Honor," Belker protested. "May we ask where all this is going?"

"Ms. Mackay?" Judge Woods said. "I take it you are going to make a point here?"

"Just a couple more questions, Your Honor," Kathryn said. "Now, Victoria, do you remember a specific occasion when this man came to your house?"

"Yes. He was very upset, and I felt sorry for him. He was crying. About Alice. About his wife. I didn't think, just put my arms around him, rocked him like a baby. Then it . . . started to become something else. And I thought, it doesn't matter. I let it happen. It was just . . . consolation, really."

"Did it ever happen again?"

"No."

"So your only other sexual experience in the last ten years—apart from your relationship with the defendant—was the one you have just told us about, with a man who had been happily married to one woman for more than thirty years."

"Yes."

"Thank you, Victoria. No further questions."

"Mr. Belker?" the judge said.

Belker shook his head. "No questions," he said.

"The witness is excused," Judge Woods said. "You may step down, Ms. Mitten."

As Victoria left the stand, he looked up at the clock and nodded.

"It's eleven forty-four," he said. "I think we'll adjourn for lunch. Ladies and gentlemen of the jury, remember my admonition not to discuss this case with anyone or with each other. Court will reconvene at two."

"All rise!" the bailiff shouted.

As Judge Woods retired to chambers, the corps of reporters in the courtroom erupted in a scrimmage of noise and movement, crowding the doorway and shoving each other in their haste to get outside to their microphones and cameras, to transmit their sound bites and updates to a waiting world. Kathryn ignored the ruckus and went across to where Victoria Mitten sat on the witness stand, staring dully at the floor. She looked up as Kathryn approached, tears in her eyes.

"Victoria, I'm sorry," Kathryn said, taking her hand. "I know that was difficult for you."

"It's not your fault. You prepared me for him," Victoria said, shaking her head. "It's just . . . I didn't expect it . . . him to be so . . . horrible."

"Would you like some tea?" Kathryn said. "We could go down to the—"

Victoria shook her head vehemently. "I just want to go," she said. "I just want to get a long way away from here."

"There's a car waiting to take you home," Kathryn told her. "Inspector Granz will go with you, get you past the reporters. You'll be fine."

*I hope,* she thought as Dave led the young woman out of the courtroom. She looked across the room at Marty Belker. He felt her glance and grinned maliciously, light blanking the glass of his spectacles. A few minutes later, Dave Granz came back in.

"You want to grab a sandwich?" he said. "Hey, you look angry."

"It's nothing," Kathryn told him, shrugging off her irritation. "Yes, a sandwich sounds good. Your treat, right?"

Dave grinned and shook his head admiringly. "You never quit, do you?" he said.

"No," Kathryn replied. "Never."

She was looking at Marty Belker as she said it.

# 15

The light fixture over the table had three adjustable sockets, allowing the triple hundred-watt bulbs to rotate and point in any direction. They were presently adjusted to illuminate all parts of the room in a hard, brilliant white light. The harsh glare of the spot lamps picked out highlights on the bottles lying on the table. Raw materials for the delay fuse were already laid out neatly. A few preparatory tasks needed to be completed first.

"You're so clever," Angel said.

"No," he replied. "It's simple."

And it was, bomb making was so simple. It didn't require a degree in chemistry to construct one; a child of ten could do it. Well, maybe not a child of ten, but it was no problem if you were careful and reasonably intelligent. The care and intelligence were in the execution. Angel smiled at the double entendre.

"Will he suffer?"

"Oh, yes," he replied. "I can guarantee that."

121

*People might see what was happening to these victims only as a particularly bizarre revenge, but it was much more than that. They had all betrayed the gifts of beauty and gratification Angel had brought them. They had sullied something beautiful, something irreplaceable, and they must pay. That was the real reason for the bombs. It was a cleansing, a fire to consume and cauterize.*

This one was for Peter, whose imagination the Marquis de Sade would have admired. Peter with his clamps and hot needles, gagged and bound, body wet with sweat, arching with welcomed pain, gasping with explosive relief at the end. The adjective triggered another small smile. Angel had a wicked sense of humor.

"You have to be quiet now," he told Angel. "I have to concentrate." He hated to be harsh, but it was getting more and more difficult to make Angel leave him alone. He waited until his mind was clear, until he could no longer hear Angel's voice. Then he began.

First, sulfuric acid. The only ingredient necessary was car battery acid, concentrated by boiling it in a glass oven bowl—Pyrex mixing bowls were perfect. Then you set it aside to cool, taking care not to slop any on your skin or to inhale the deadly fumes. The lights were hot. Careful not to sweat into the mixture; sweat is salty, and salt water would create deadly chlorine gas.

Next, use potassium chloride and ordinary granulated sugar to make sugar chlorate. All you needed to do it was some boiling water.

"You're brilliant," Angel told him. "Brilliant."

"It's easy," he said. "Now hush. You have to be quiet."

*Next, roll a tube from a square of cardboard, just large enough to fit around a small glass jar with a lid. Tape the sides and one end closed, pour the sugar chlorate crystals into the tube, then set it to one side to dry.*

*Now, drill a hole through the lid of the jar. Cut a rubber disc from an old bicycle inner tube that will fit snugly inside the lid. Check that the seal is reliable, put in the sulfuric acid, cap tightly, then carefully wash the outside of the jar to ensure there is no acid residue that might injure your hands.*

*Voilà, the delay fuse.*

"Tell me what you're going to do," *Angel begged.* "Tell me what will happen."

*When the time comes, place the tube containing the sugar chlorate crystals over the incendiary device itself. Start the delay fuse by turning the jar of acid upside down and sliding it into the tube. After a time—if the inner tube was thick enough, it would take ten, maybe fifteen minutes—the acid would eat through the rubber disc and ignite the sugar chlorate, which would in turn ignite the incendiary device beneath it.*

*Ten, fifteen minutes, endless eons of unbearable fear. And then . . .*

"Adios, mi amor," *Angel whispered.*

# 16

"How strong is Sorensen?" Dave asked.

He sat to Kathryn Mackay's right at the prosecution table in Superior Court Department Eight. Kathryn's files and trial notes were on the table in front of her. As before, Martin Belker and the defendant, Richard Hudson, were seated at the defense table to their right, to the judge's left as he presided from his elevated position in front of the courtroom.

Today, Hudson's clothes were again informally casual. As usual, Belker was dressed conservatively, except for the Bruno Magli loafers. Shoes were his big indulgence. He had once told Kathryn he had more than a hundred pairs, and she'd sensed he was miffed when she wasn't impressed.

"She's pretty solid," Kathryn replied. "I've worked with her like I did with Victoria, prepped her for direct and cross. We've gone over the areas of her testimony where she's most apt to get upset or angry. I can only hope she doesn't let Belker get to her."

"It's always a crap shoot," said Dave.

Kathryn nodded in agreement.

She glanced up at the clock. Court was about to convene. Taylor led the jurors in and waited while they took their places before coming to his desk behind the jury box. As he passed counsel table, Kathryn noted there were dark shadows beneath his eyes as if he hadn't slept well. The sergeant's exam was just days away, Kathryn thought to herself, or maybe it was a new girlfriend. She vaguely recalled that Taylor was still single and lived with an aunt someplace.

With the jurors settled into their seats, the door behind and to the left of the bench opened as Bailiff Chris Taylor shouted, "All rise!" Judge Woods swept in. Their flowing robes and grave demeanor always gave judges the appearance of making a spectacular entrance, as in the theater; they never simply came in. All part of the pomp and circumstance. Kathryn loved it.

"Ready or not," Kathryn whispered, as much to herself as to Dave. "Here we go."

"Good morning, ladies and gentlemen," the judge said briskly to the jurors.

He looked next to the defendant, then at Martin Belker, then finally at Kathryn.

"The record should reflect the defendant, Richard Hudson, is present with his attorney, as is the district attorney." A nod to Kathryn, which brought her to her feet. "Your next witness, Ms. Mackay?"

"The People call Jane Sorensen, Your Honor," said Kathryn. Heads turned as Dave Granz escorted the witness into the courtroom from the outside corridor and directed her to the witness stand.

Jane Sorensen was blond, petite, and pretty, with blue eyes and a deep tan. She wore a dark blue trouser suit and cameo earrings, a necklace pendant, and two very thin gold bangles on her right arm. In repose, her face appeared composed and confident. She swore her oath, stated and spelled her name, then glanced a trifle apprehensively at the jury.

"Good morning, Ms. Sorensen," Kathryn said as she moved toward the rear of the jury box. "May I call you Jane?"

"Yes, thank you, I prefer that."

One of the surest ways to put a witness at ease was to use her first name. By dealing with it up front, she could further alleviate the nervousness.

"Okay, Jane. You look a little nervous. Are you?"

"A little," the young woman said, her mouth turning up at the sides when she smiled.

"There's nothing to be nervous about," Kathryn said. "Just answer my questions and tell the truth. Now, where do you live, Jane?"

"I have an apartment in Mountain View."

"And what do you do for a living?"

"I'm an editor with a publishing house in San Jose. We publish self-help books, cookbooks, travel guides."

"Are you married?"

"My husband and I were divorced in April last year."

"Do you mind telling us why?"

"He . . . it was another woman."

"How long had you been married?"

"Eight years."

"Children?"

"No."

"Have you been seeing anyone since your divorce?"

Jane Sorensen shook her head. "No. After my husband walked out on me, I was pretty low. I needed to . . . work on my self-esteem. That was why I thought . . . why I began reading the romance connection ads. I couldn't bear the thought of singles bars or blind dates."

"Was that how you met Richard Hudson?"

"Yes."

"Which paper did the ad appear in, Jane?" Kathryn asked.

"The *Coastal Times*. I don't usually read it, but that's where those ads are."

She was obviously embarrassed. To put it mildly, the *Coastal Times* was a rag. Kathryn handed her a folded copy of the paper, premarked as a people's exhibit.

"Is this the ad, Jane?"

Jane Sorensen glanced at the ad, which was highlighted in yellow, and nodded. "It is."

"Read it aloud to the jury, please."

" 'Honest above all, and looking for a kindred soul, I am easy-going and intelligent. If you share these attributes and are between twenty-five and thirty-five, please respond with photograph.' "

"And did you respond?"

"Yes," Jane replied. "I wrote to the box number in the paper, enclosing my phone number and first name as the ad stipulated."

"Then what happened?"

"He—Richard Hudson—telephoned me, and we arranged to meet."

"Please identify Richard Hudson to the jury," Kathryn directed her.

"He's seated over there." Jane pointed toward the defense table.

"Your Honor," said Kathryn, "may the record reflect that Ms. Sorensen has identified the defendant?"

"It will so reflect," said Woods.

"So, you arranged to meet. When was that?" asked Kathryn.

"It was on Wednesday, September fourth of last year," Jane Sorensen said. "We met at seven-thirty P.M. at the Santa Rita Coffee Roasting Company on Mercado Street."

"And then?"

"When I sat down, the first thing he said was, 'I am now going to utter the most boring sentence in the world. My name is Richard Hudson, and I work in computers.' It was pretty corny, but it broke the ice."

"Go on."

"He seemed likable, well adjusted, a good personality. It turned out we were the same age, thirty-three, and both from Texas. I told him about my divorce, and he said he knew how I felt, his wife had cheated on him. Like me, he had no children. We both agreed the singles scene was a pretty gruesome way to meet people. I liked his sense of humor. We talked all evening. It was amusing, it was friendly, it was relaxed."

"Did you decide to see each other again?"

"Yes, we had a date about a week later. Afterwards, he told me it was the best evening he'd had in a long time, he really enjoyed being with me. It made me feel . . . special. I guess I was pretty silly."

"Did you see him again after that?"

Jane Sorensen's chin lifted slightly. "Yes. I wasn't

desperate, you understand. But he kept calling, and I thought, why not? So he would come by and meet me after work. We'd go to a movie or a concert. Something simple."

"How long did this go on?"

"Four or five weeks."

"And then what happened?"

"He asked me if I would like to see where he lived. Maybe have dinner at his place. I said yes. I wanted to know more about him."

"Were you attracted to the defendant at that time?"

"Yes, very." Jane Sorensen looked across at Richard Hudson. "He was—he's a good-looking man. Intelligent. We seemed to have so much in common."

"Did you eventually go to his home?"

"Yes, I did."

"And where did he live, Jane?"

"In Mission Heights on Lassaigne Drive. His condo was on the second floor. It had a beautiful view. He had champagne on ice and soft classical music on the stereo. He asked me if I liked seafood; he'd cooked scallops. It was wonderful; he's a good cook."

"Then what happened?" Kathryn prompted.

She knew the next part was going to be tough on both of them. Tough for her to get the answers she wanted, even tougher on Jane Sorensen to give them.

"We talked and laughed a lot, and I helped him with the dishes. His place was so clean. He said he hated clutter, like it was a big thing. Before I realized it, it was ten o'clock. It was a weeknight, and I knew I should go home, but he persuaded me to sit down on the sofa for a few minutes to talk. Then we, you know, we started kissing, and . . ."

"I know this is embarrassing, Jane," Kathryn said

as the witness hesitated. She kept her voice sympathetic but encouraging. "And I wouldn't ask you if it weren't important. But we need to know exactly what happened. It went a lot further than kissing, didn't it?"

Two high spots of color became visible on Jane Sorensen's cheeks as she replied. "It just went on and on, and then we both had most of our clothes off, and he said why not spend the night with him," she said. "He said we were both adults, and anyway I shouldn't drive after drinking so much wine. He was . . . not demanding, exactly, but forceful. Like only someone stupid would say no to a simple thing like that."

"So did you spend the night with him?"

"No. I told him I couldn't stay. I didn't want to, Ms. Mackay. I hadn't slept with a man since my husband."

Jane Sorensen appealed to Kathryn with her eyes, pleading not to be asked the next question. But Kathryn knew there was no way to spare her.

"You didn't stay the night. But did you have sex with the defendant that evening?"

Jane Sorensen locked her fingers together and looked down at them as she spoke. "Yes. Well, not . . . exactly. He wanted to, but I . . . he was so insistent, almost angry about it, as if I was being childish. That was the first time I saw the other side to his character. I sensed a rage burning deep down inside him, and it frightened me a little, so I agreed, provided he used a condom. He told me he didn't have one. I said in that case I wouldn't . . . I wouldn't do it without a condom, and he pushed . . . I'm sorry, I—I can't, I'm sorry."

Kathryn's heart went out to the young woman in

front of her, but she could not let her avoid the issue: it was imperative the jury hear the entire story from the witness herself.

"Jane? Jane, it's all right," she said encouragingly. "We're almost finished. Just tell us exactly what happened."

Jane waited a few moments, then took a deep breath and squared her shoulders.

"He said, 'Come on, damnit,' something like that, and then he just sort of . . . pushed my head into his lap with his hand on my neck, and I couldn't get . . . I was just . . . I did it, oral sex. When he . . . when we finished, he just stared at the ceiling as if I wasn't even there anymore. So I went into the bathroom and got dressed."

"I know this sounds like a ridiculous question, but I have to ask you—did the defendant wear a condom when he had you perform oral sex on him?"

There were one or two snickers from spectators in the well of the courtroom. She ignored them.

Jane Sorensen shook her head. "No, of course not."

"What happened when you came out of the bathroom?"

"He hadn't moved. I was embarrassed. I didn't know what to say. Then he said, 'You going now?' I said something about it being late and I had to go. I got my purse, and then he came to the door with me. He took me in his arms. Suddenly he was so—caring. He said, 'Listen, in case you're worrying, don't, that was safe sex.' I asked him what he meant. He said, 'I had a small cyst removed three months ago, and took a blood test. I was negative for HIV.' He showed me the scar on his shoulder. Then we kissed good night, and I drove home."

"Did you see the defendant again?"

"Just twice more, that weekend. Both times at his place."

"And did you have sex on both those occasions?"

"The same as the first time."

"The defendant had you perform oral sex on him?"

"I was . . . I sensed an anger in him. I thought at the time it was because I'd refused to sleep with him. But now I realize it was deeper than that, a kind of resentment. As if he had a right to use my body any way he wanted to."

"You mean you were afraid?"

"Not afraid. It's hard to explain. He had a way of making me feel guilty for not gratifying him somehow."

"I see. Did the defendant have you perform unprotected oral sex on him both times?" Kathryn asked.

"Yes." Jane nodded.

"Now, Jane, I'm sorry if this embarrasses you, but I must know if the defendant ejaculated in your mouth. Did he?"

Jane waited a long moment before answering the question. She drew in a deep breath and exhaled. "Yes, he did."

"You're absolutely certain?"

Jane Sorensen looked surprised, then realized what Kathryn was asking her. "Of course I'm certain. My husband and I . . . yes."

Kathryn paused for a moment to let the witness compose herself, then asked another question. "Why did you stop seeing the defendant, Jane?"

"On the Tuesday following that last weekend, I got a letter from Richard Hudson. He sent it to my P.O. box. I hadn't told him where I lived."

"Is this the letter?" Kathryn handed a folded sheet to Jane Sorensen marked as a people's exhibit. She glanced at it and nodded.

"Yes, that's the letter."

"Would you read it to the jury, please?"

" 'Dear Jane,' " the witness read. " 'I have decided not to see you anymore. Please don't write or call.' " She looked up. "It's signed, 'Richard.' And there's a P.S.: 'I think you should know I have AIDS.' "

"Thank you, Jane," Kathryn said, taking the letter from her. "How did you feel when you received this?"

"I was devastated," Jane Sorensen said. "I felt as if I'd been opened up and everything inside me had been ripped out. I tried to call him, but all I got was an answering machine that said he was out of town. I went to his condo a few times, but he was never home. Eventually, I gave up trying to get in touch with him."

"Then what did you do?"

"I called the AIDS 800 help line number, and they referred me to a clinic where I could have a blood test."

"Did you take a blood test?" asked Kathryn.

"Not right away. I picked up a brochure from the lobby and took it home. But when I read that the HIV virus can be transmitted even by oral copulation, I got scared and went back for a test."

"What were the results?"

"Negative. I didn't have the HIV virus. But they told me more than ninety percent of people who are infected with the AIDS virus won't test positive for at least three months after exposure. So I waited another three months and had my blood tested again at the same clinic. I'm still negative."

"And how did you feel about what the defendant did to you?"

"I'm still afraid, and I'm angry he put me at such risk!" Jane Sorensen said fiercely, glaring at the defendant as she said it.

"Thank you, Jane," Kathryn said. "No further questions."

As she returned to her seat, Judge Woods nodded at Martin Belker. He rose and walked empty-handed to the witness chair, a scowl on his face that announced he did not intend to treat Jane Sorensen as considerately as he had treated the previous witness.

"Ms. Sorensen," he began, his voice sharp, "you said you refused to engage in sexual intercourse with the defendant unless he wore a condom, is that correct?"

"That's right."

"Is that what you said to him? Did you say, 'If you don't wear a condom, I won't have sex with you'? Did you call it a condom, or did you refer to it as a 'rubber'?"

"What difference does it make?" Jane Sorensen was clearly not intimidated by Belker's hostile manner. "I told him he had to wear one, but he said he didn't even own any."

"I'll ask the questions, Ms. Sorensen," Belker snapped maliciously. "Again, did you refer to it as a 'condom' or a 'rubber'?

"I don't remember."

"I see.

"Ms. Sorensen, it's common knowledge that there is a risk of contracting HIV from unprotected oral sex, isn't that true?" asked Belker.

Kathryn leaped to her feet.

"Sidebar, Your Honor!"

She was headed for the bench before the judge could respond. Belker had no choice but to join her there.

"Your Honor, the witness isn't an expert on HIV," Kathryn protested *sotto voce*. "She isn't qualified to answer the question."

"She doesn't have to be an expert to testify on matters of common knowledge," Belker argued.

"I'm inclined to agree, Ms. Mackay," Woods said. "But be very careful, Mr. Belker. Step back, please."

As both lawyers returned to their tables, Judge Woods turned to the witness.

"Did you understand the question, Ms. Sorensen?"

"Could I have it read back, Your Honor?"

Kathryn concealed a smile; she had prepared her witness well.

"Withdrawn. I'll ask the witness another question," Belker said smoothly, anxious to regain control of his cross. "You were aware there was some risk involved with oral sex, right, Ms. Sorensen?"

Jane Sorensen took a moment to think about her answer.

"I knew there might be a small risk, I suppose. I'm not sure."

"You knew there was a risk even before you picked up those brochures at the clinic, didn't you?"

"I suppose so."

"How? How did you know this before you read those pamphlets, Ms. Sorensen?"

She shrugged, reluctant to answer. "I just knew. I guess everyone knows, don't they?"

"And yet in spite of knowing it's possible to contract HIV through oral copulation, you performed oral sex on Mr. Hudson not once but on three separate occasions." Belker pounced. "Three times, isn't that correct?"

If looks could have killed, Kathryn thought, watching her witness's face, Martin Belker would already be owl bait.

"Yes," Jane snapped. "I told you he was . . . very insistent."

"Really, Ms. Sorensen, you're not trying to tell us you did this under duress, are you?"

"Not exactly," Jane said. "But—"

"No more questions for *this* witness, Your Honor," Belker snapped, cutting off whatever she might have been going to say. He smiled triumphantly at the jury, wheeled around, and headed back to the defense table. Judge Woods looked over at Kathryn and then ostentatiously at the clock.

"Ms. Mackay, anything more?"

"No, thank you, Your Honor," Kathryn said. "No further questions."

"The witness is excused," Judge Woods said. "You may step down, Ms. Sorensen. And we'll recess at this point. Court will reconvene tomorrow morning at ten o'clock. The jury is again reminded of its obligations not to discuss the case among themselves or with anyone else."

"Not so good," Kathryn observed, rising to her feet as the judge left for his chambers.

Dave touched Kathryn's arm gently. "Like I said, a crap shoot."

He stood up.

"As soon as I get your witness into a car, I'm going to go upstairs to the SO, see if anything's breaking on the bomb investigation," he said. "Can you go with me?"

Kathryn shook her head. "I'm leaving now to pick up Emma. I promised her I'd pick her up early for a change."

Dave nodded. "Okay. See you later in the Hellhole, right?"

"Be still, my heart," Kathryn said.

# 17

At ten at night, the reception area of County Hospital was empty. Apart from a couple of drunks who'd gotten into a fight and were being patched up under the eyes of a bored cop in the emergency room, nothing was happening, and, barring an outbreak of small-hours violence, it would probably remain that way for the rest of the night.

"You okay, Kathryn?" Dave asked as the elevator lumbered down toward the basement complex Morgan Nelson had dubbed the Hellhole. It was an apt if irreverent moniker: over the years, thousands of poor souls had been dispatched to the big sleep from here, many of them probably headed for the destination for which the complex was nicknamed. "You didn't say a word all the way up here."

"I guess I'm just not in the mood for this tonight," she said, wrinkling her nose. The elevator doors rolled back, and the chilled air and familiar all-pervasive antiseptic death odors of the morgue assailed her

138

nostrils. No matter how many times she came here, Kathryn never quite escaped her sense of being an intruder in an alien environment. The place had a familiar but not quite identifiable ambience, redolent of the red-tiled corridors of the city swimming pool she remembered from her Kansas City childhood, an odor somewhere between chlorinated water and Lysol, the air flat and inert, the neutral-colored walls slightly slick, as if coated with a film of moisture or something even more unpleasant.

"Aw, come on, Kathryn," Dave chided her with a grin. "What are you trying to do, spoil my fun?"

"I'd have liked to get home before Emma goes to bed for a change, that's all," Kathryn said, realizing it probably sounded like a whine but unable not to say it.

The largest of the three autopsy suites was to their right as they exited the elevator. In addition to the usual scales, steel lockers, sinks, sluices, and sound-proofed booths for dictating notes, it contained three fully equipped stainless steel operating tables. Further down the corridor on the right was what Morgan called the VIP room, used for cases requiring special or extended study. Directly across the hall from the VIP room was the isolation suite, which was used for the examination of advanced decomposition cases or those where infectious diseases were present. Fitted with high-powered extraction fans to siphon out harmful gases and direct them to an incinerator, it always conjured up gruesome associations that put a chill into Kathryn's blood.

At the end of the corridor, next to the huge cold storage room where bodies were kept after autopsy, was the staging room where, after being prepped and photographed, bodies were put on gurneys and taken to the designated autopsy suite. Inside, air conditioning maintained the temperature at a level that had earned the suite the name "Siberia." Walking into it was not unlike walking into a deep freeze, except that spending a few hours in a deep freeze was a lot more fun.

"At least we're not in court tomorrow," Dave said. "Did I hear you say something to Hal about coming in late?"

"I have to stop off in town," Kathryn said, without elaborating. Tomorrow morning she was scheduled for her mammogram and ultrasound. *And maybe that's really what's bothering me,* she thought. With the thought of all that awaiting her, watching Morgan Nelson dissect an incinerated cadaver wouldn't have been her first choice of things to do tonight.

Morgan's cramped office was empty; one of the deputy coroners, Les Dougherty, told them Nelson was waiting for them in the VIP room. They hurried down the corridor past the staff meeting room and a larger room that contained the X-ray and photo processing facility, record storage shelves, and rows of jars containing specimens of vital organs from each autopsied body.

Morgan lifted a hand in salute as they came into the VIP room. He was wearing a green surgical robe and a face mask, and his lab pants were tucked into pale green rubber boots. The legend "Santa Rita Co. Coroner" in untidy capitals was printed in laundry-proof pen on the left breast pocket. His eyes glinted mischievously behind the gold-framed granny glasses. He seemed to be in a good mood.

"I was just about to start without you," he said cheerfully. "You're late."

"We got hung up downtown, Doc." Dave grunted, hitching one hip on a tall stool in the corner of the room. "And I didn't think the guest of honor would mind waiting."

Nelson grinned. "He's got all the time in the world," he said. "I'm the one in a hurry."

He adjusted the rake of the shining table so the cockroach-shiny body of the bomb victim lay tilted feet-down toward the sinks and constantly flowing water. On a bench to one side lay one large knife and the series of smaller ones that would be used for various procedures during the autopsy. Morgan picked up one of the knives and started to whet it on sharpening paper. Kathryn had seen him do it a hundred times or more, but somehow tonight the sibilant sound raised goose bumps on her skin.

"Anything new on the courtroom bomb?" Morgan asked.

"That's what held us up," Kathryn said. "We met with Purington. He says DOJ identified the components."

"And?" Nelson said.

"Pretty much what you predicted," Dave said. "A kitchen-table job. How they can figure it out from what CSI scraped up in that courtroom beats the hell out of me."

"They put all the fragments gathered at the scene— everything, no matter how microscopic—through a gas chromatograph spectrograph," Morgan explained. "It separates each element of the mixture into its individual components. Those components are then

141

identified by comparison of their mass spectra with known explosives. What they're looking for are taggants."

"Taggants?"

"A taggant is a microscopic chip, color-coded with eight or nine pigmented layers. Basically an identifier designed to survive the explosion. It's a government requirement that all commercial explosives manufacturers not only include them during manufacture but report the code used and the purchasers of each batch to the National Explosives Tracing Center. Your average half-pound of dynamite will contain around two thousand taggants. If an investigator can come up with enough taggants at the crime scene, he can contact the NETC and identify the plant, the date of manufacture, and who it was purchased by."

"But in this case . . . ?"

"With a kitchen-table job as opposed to a commercial explosive, there wouldn't be any taggants," Morgan said. "Kitchen-table devices are usually made from ordinary, everyday ingredients, not commercial explosives."

"Purington says it was probably some kind of homemade plastic explosive in a pressure-tight container, maybe a length of copper tubing sealed at both ends to maximize decomposition," said Kathryn. "They're trying to ID the type of pipe used. He says they can sometimes even determine its manufacturer from the fragments."

"Sometimes," Morgan said. "But not by any means always. How was it detonated?"

"A simple clothespin device," Kathryn said. "You open up a clothespin, wind copper wire around each of the jaws, put a piece of wood or polystyrene between the jaws to hold them open. One wire to your battery, the other to the initiator. Link the battery and the initiator. When the package is opened or jarred in movement, the wood falls out of the peg, the jaws snap shut, and—boom."

"Everything homemade," Dave said. "Even the box it came in. Purington says whoever put that thing together was either lucky as hell or sure knew how to cover his tracks. And George doesn't believe much in luck."

"Do they have any leads on who the bomb was intended for?"

"Right now they're concentrating on Belker's clients," Kathryn said. "He's won and lost his share of cases. Considering the caliber of his clientele, there are probably plenty of defendants *and* victims out there with a grudge against him."

"Checking lists," Dave growled impatiently. "You want the truth, we're chasing shadows, Doc. We don't have a lead worth a damn."

Morgan shrugged. "Goes like that sometimes," he said. "You know my motto: 'Attempt the end and never stand to doubt, nothing's so hard but search will find it out.' Robert Herrick, 1591 to 1674."

"I'll pass that along to George Purington." Dave grinned.

"What about this guy, Doc?" Kathryn asked, with a gesture toward the body on the table. "Any similarities between the courtroom bomb and the one that killed Hanlon?"

Morgan looked up sharply. "Why? Do you have some reason for thinking there might be a connection between the two cases?"

"Two bombings within days of each other sounds

like more than a coincidence. And you know me, I'm a skeptic."

"Well, that might change things. Let's make sure we're all on the same page," Nelson said. "The device that blew Jim Field's hand off was a bomb. Primitive, maybe, but still a bomb. And as far as we know, Field wasn't the intended victim. Our friend Hanlon here, on the other hand, was quite deliberately killed by someone who tied him to a bed and ignited an incendiary device on his body. To my un-detective-like eye, the modus operandi is completely different."

"What kind of incendiary device?" asked Dave.

"From chemical traces I found on the body, it looks as if it was a length of bicycle inner tube filled with a mixture of thermite, magnesium, and iron."

"I've seen fire victims before, but I never saw anything do that much damage to a body," Dave observed. "It must have burned hotter than hell."

"Hell probably isn't as hot," Morgan said grimly. "Thermite—it's a mixture of powdered aluminum and iron oxide—generates enough heat to melt most metals. You've heard of them using thermic lances to cut open safes." He gestured at the body of Patrick Hanlon on the table. "You can see what it does to the human body."

He tossed each of them a lab coat and a paper envelope containing a face mask, which they put on. Besides the mess made by bodily fluids that would soon be released from their corporeal wrappings, there was always the risk of infection from TB, hepatitis, or HIV. Kathryn positioned herself on a stool next to Dave and tried to watch dispassionately as Morgan unhurriedly began his examination.

"What do you two know about burn degrees?"

"You mean like first degree, second degree, third degree?" Kathryn said.

"The scale was first formalized by a Frenchman called Guillaume Dupuytren, chief surgeon of the Hotel Dieu in Paris. He recognized six degrees of burns. Later his six groups were merged into three by an Austrian dermatologist named Ferdinand Ritter von Hebra, whose classification was adopted. Burns like these, with gross distruction of subcutaneous tissue and muscle, even bone, third degree on the Hebra scale, would have been sixth on the Dupuytren. I expect to find the air passages acutely engorged and significant amounts of mucus and soot in the trachea, respiratory tract, and lungs."

"Meaning what?" Kathryn asked.

Nelson didn't look up from his work. "Meaning he was alive and breathing while the incendiary device was consuming his body. He could hear it, feel it, and smell it. Until he lost consciousness, at least."

"Jesus," Dave breathed.

"What are those cuts on his legs and torso, Morgan?" Kathryn asked. "They look like they could be wounds."

"No, they're heat ruptures, Katie," Nelson explained. "Produced by a splitting of the soft parts— as in cooking. Which is pretty much what happened to this poor guy. He cooked in his own fat."

"Morgan, let me just back up a minute," Kathryn said thoughtfully. "The incendiary mixture you just mentioned that was used—thermite, magnesium, iron filings. It's not something just anyone would know, is it? Wouldn't whoever did this need some kind of special knowledge?"

Morgan shook his head. "Afraid not, Katie. Any

third-year high school chemistry student could probably come up with the formula. No special knowledge required. Okay, let's get started . . ."

Grunting with effort, Nelson carved a giant Y onto the trunk of the body on the table, beginning at each shoulder and meeting at the gaping hole in the belly. The crisp burned flesh crackled as he sliced through it, charred pieces breaking away to fall onto the table. Next he peeled away the V of chest flesh from the upper incisions and folded it back across the dead man's face. A small rivulet of black blood wormed down the dead man's cheekbone and formed a pool in his left ear.

Grabbing each of the two flaps left by the long belly incision, pulling and cutting simultaneously, Morgan separated the flesh from the ribcage and peeled it back.

"You might want to step back a bit while I do this," he muttered as he switched on the miniature buzz saw he used to separate the sternum and for the two side cuts needed to remove the ribs. Flakes of incinerated flesh rose in the still air and fell back onto the body like strange black snow. As he stepped back, the glistening, closely packed interior organs were fully revealed.

"Okay, now we can see exactly what happened here," Morgan said. "See how the center of the abdominal injury is roughly equidistant between the shaft of the penis and the umbilicus? The question I kept asking myself was, if he knew what it was, why didn't this guy do something? He could lift his backside, twist from side to side. Why didn't he try to shake the damned thing off?"

"Okay, why not?" Kathryn said.

"Because he knew it wouldn't make any difference."

"How do you know?"

"I ran some tests," Morgan said. "Found microscopic traces of cyanoacrylate in the cavity. Superglue to you."

"You mean the device was glued to his body? He couldn't shake it off?"

"Exactly."

"Jesus H. Christ, Doc, are you saying he just had to lie there and watch the damn fuse burning down?" Dave exclaimed. "What kind of animal does that to another human being?"

"Someone who hated him very much indeed," Morgan said quietly. "Someone who wanted him to suffer very badly. Not just while he was lying there waiting for the thing to ignite, but also after it did. It would have taken several minutes to burn through the epidermis and subcutaneous fat and then down through to the abdominal aorta and the iliac arteries to kill him."

"Damn," Dave breathed. "So he wasn't just alive— he was awake and watching when his own body caught fire?"

Nelson nodded. "You saw the bloody froth around the mouth. That suggests to me we'll find that his larynx is ruptured. From screaming."

There was a little silence. The grisly blackened thing on the table had once been a living man. It needed little imagination to picture what its last few minutes on earth must have been like.

"Morgan, is there any question at all in your mind that this man died from any cause other than the bomb—the incendiary device?" Kathryn asked.

"None whatsoever," Nelson said. "Look at him. Unless there's a bullet in his brain or a pint of prussic acid in what's left of his kidneys, a ten-year-old kid could tell you what killed him. Even his innards are cooked."

"Then if it's all the same to you, I'm going to call it a night," Kathryn said. "Dave, why don't you stay and keep Morgan company?"

"Hell, no need for that," Morgan said. "Autopsying a body burned as badly as this one is a long job. You have to dissect right down to the bones. It'll be three or four A.M. before I get through."

"You going to sleep here?" Although she knew Morgan frequently crashed out on a cot in his office, Kathryn had never really gotten used to the idea.

"Sure." Morgan grinned. "That time of night, I'm a lot safer in here with the corpses than I would be out on the street."

"You may be right at that." Dave grinned. "Okay, I'll pick up your protocol sometime tomorrow afternoon if that's okay with you."

"I'll put a priority sticker on it," Morgan promised. "Drive safely."

The air outside felt warm and friendly after the chill of the autopsy suite. There was practically no traffic, and the freeway heading south was almost empty. A thin mist rolled in off the ocean, drifting across the highway like wraiths, and the road signs loomed up and then disappeared into it like ghostly galleons on some still sea. It was a while before Dave broke the silence.

"What's wrong, Kathryn?" he asked her.

"Wrong?" she said, and heard her own voice. *Too bright, damnit,* she thought.

"I never saw you quit on an autopsy before," Dave said. "Ever."

"It wasn't the autopsy, Dave," she said.

"What, then?"

She shook her head. "Not now," she said. "Just . . . let it rest, okay?"

She wanted to tell him, but somewhere in her heart she knew this was not the right moment. She reached out and touched his arm with her right hand.

"Bear with me, Dave, please. I've got a lot on my mind."

"You mean the trial?"

She shook her head again and did not reply. Dave shrugged and looked out the window.

"You know," he said quietly, "this is the first time you ever held out on me, Kathryn."

Again she made no answer. They drove in silence, the mist-shrouded trees lining the road spectral in the pale moonlight.

# 18

Housed in a drab single-story masonry structure two blocks from County Hospital, the Santa Rita Breast Center was the first free-standing facility in the region for comprehensive breast diagnostic services. It offered comfort, convenience, and privacy to the women it served, as well as state-of-the-art mammography. An added distinction was the fact that all its doctors and technicians were women.

The receptionist was a motherly-looking woman in her middle forties who directed Kathryn to the waiting room off the hallway that ran the length of the center of the building. National Institute of Health posters hung on the plain cream walls, one showing how to do BSE, another explaining mammography.

"Would you like anything?" the receptionist asked. The badge on her neat gray hospital coat said her name was Leonora Kinney. "Some coffee or tea?"

"Thank you, no," Kathryn said, although her mouth was already a little dry. She settled into a leather chair in the corner of the waiting room and pulled a "daily" out of her leather tote bag, reading through the transcript without really absorbing a word. The electric clock on the wall gave a small tock each time a minute elapsed.

"Kathryn Mackay? I'm Pat Miller."

The slender woman standing in the doorway was about the same height as Kathryn, but heels made her slightly taller. She was in her mid-forties, and her blond hair was streaked with silver strands. She had the bluest eyes Kathryn had ever seen.

"You're here for a mammogram, yes?"

"That's right," Kathryn replied.

"Shall we go in?"

Kathryn nodded and followed the technologist out of the room and down the corridor, then through a door marked "Mammography." In it stood a machine that looked like a giant photographic enlarger with various sizes of adjustment wheels and controls. The overhead lights were hard and unfriendly.

"Slip off your blouse and bra," said Pat Miller, handing Kathryn a hospital gown. "Then we'll get started."

"What do you want me to do?"

"Just stand in front of the flatbed, here," Pat Miller told her. "I'm going to take two X-rays of each breast, one from the top and one from the side."

"What about radiation exposure?"

"The risk is quite minimal," the technician answered. "About what you'd get walking nude on the beach for ten minutes. You ready? Okay, just lift your breast and lay it on the flatbed. Let me help you, that's it. Good, good, now hold your breath, these things are cold."

She moved down a pair of metal plates, each about the size of a large book, and placed one vertically on each side of Kathryn's breast, squeezing it between them. The metal felt alien and hostile, and Kathryn shivered.

"Not hurting?" Miller asked.

"It's fine."

"Good. The flatter we can get your breast, the better the picture will be. Okay, ready, here we go."

The big machine buzzed, and light passed through a lens somewhere inside it. Next, Miller moved the plates so they were horizontal, placing one beneath Kathryn's breast and the other on top. Once again, she pressed the exposure button, and the machine emitted another heavy hum. Then they repeated the procedure with the other breast, and it was all over.

"That's it?" Kathryn said.

"It'll take a little while to develop your X-rays," Pat Miller told her. "As soon as they are developed, Dr. Snyder will review them and meet with you. Would you like some tea or coffee while you wait?"

"Tea would be wonderful," Kathryn said, realizing as she spoke that her throat had become parched.

She was shown to a private cubicle, where she sat waiting until the receptionist brought in a steaming cup of tea. Kathryn sipped gratefully, realizing as she felt the warmth of the drink spreading through her body that she had been cold. She sat waiting, resolutely not thinking. Somewhere a phone rang.

Dr. Marie Snyder was a small, dark, intense-looking woman with a slight accent that hinted at European origins.

"I've reviewed your X-rays," she said. "And they

do show an abnormal area of density. A lump, if you like. Now we need to know what kind of lump it is."

"I'm sorry, I don't understand," Kathryn said.

"It's fairly simple. When we're young, in our twenties, our breasts are made up mostly of breast tissue and are very dense. As we get older, the tissue ages, much as the skin does, and by the time one is in her forties, it's about half tissue and half fat. The thinner you are, the more tissue there'll be. You, for instance, still have quite dense breast tissue, and that's the problem. Cancer and benign lumps are the same density as breast tissue. So if there's this little white cancer right in the middle of an area of dense tissue, it won't show up. There's something there; it may be a cyst, it could as easily be a fibroadenoma. The ultrasound scan will enable us to locate it precisely."

She left the room, and a few moments later, Pat Miller came back in.

"Hello again," she said. "You finished your tea?"

"Finished."

"This won't take long," Miller said. "I'll just put some jelly on your breast to make it slippery. Then I'll slide a small instrument called a transducer along your skin, sending sound waves through your breast. If something gets in the way, the waves bounce back. If nothing does, they pass right through."

"What will the ultrasound tell you?"

"Primarily it helps us determine whether a lump is solid or fluid-filled. If it's solid, like a fibroadenoma or a cancerous lump, we get bounce-back. If it's some kind of cyst, the sound waves go right through."

The ultrasound scan was over in less than ten minutes.

"Why don't you put your clothes on?" Miller said

as she picked up the printout from the machine. "I'll run this over to Dr. Snyder for analysis. Come on in when you're dressed."

Kathryn nodded and dressed slowly, suddenly aware of the beat of her heart, the soft pulses of life in her body. *I can't have it,* she thought fiercely. *I won't have it.* She crossed the corridor, pulled in a deep breath, and knocked on Dr. Snyder's door.

"Well, it's not a cyst," Dr. Snyder said briskly as Kathryn sat down in a chair facing her. Kathryn's heart sank. She could feel a sort of tingling sensation all the way up from her toes to her face. And she recognized it: fear.

"What happens now?" she said. It seemed to her as if her voice sounded like a croak, but if it did, Dr. Snyder appeared not to notice.

"I'll send my report to your doctor. She'll discuss the various options with you. You're a prosecutor, aren't you? I saw your photograph in the paper. The AIDS case."

"You've been following it?"

"It's very interesting," Dr. Snyder said. "It's not often you read about a trial where there are moral as well as legal issues to be considered. Have you found it difficult with . . . this hanging over you?"

"The hardest part is the not knowing," Kathryn admitted.

"I hear that a lot," Dr. Snyder said. "Have you talked about it to anyone?"

"No," Kathryn said. "I've wanted to, but somehow there never seemed to be a right moment. I guess what it is, you just want a chance to say you're scared."

"I've heard that before, too." Marie Snyder smiled. "You're worrying the whole time, have I got cancer, will I lose my breast, will this thing kill me? Let me tell you something. Every year, 182,000 American women are told they have breast cancer. What you have to hang on to is that fewer than a quarter of them die of it. And most of all, don't brood."

"I'm not the brooding type," Kathryn said, getting up to leave. "Thank you, Dr. Snyder."

"No thanks necessary," Dr. Snyder said. "And Ms. Mackay? Do you have someone you can talk to about this? A significant other?"

"Yes, I do."

"Talk to him," Dr. Snyder said.

## 19

*Men only wanted the body, few of them ever caring, ever wanting to know what was behind the face, under the skin. But Angel believed—knew—the mind was much more important than mere physical beauty. The intellect was what separated the dross from the gold.*

*That was why, from the outside looking in, joining one of the organizations for intelligent people— MENSA, for instance—had seemed like a logical step to take. MENSAns needed an IQ of 132 even to qualify for membership, the top two percentile of the population—121 was gifted; 143 was considered to be genius level. Perhaps there one might find that special other person, that longed-for meeting of minds that happened so rarely in the workaday world.*

*But the MENSA meetings had lost their appeal very quickly, forty or so very ordinary people packed into the small living room and dining area of someone's home for a morning of breakfast and conversation, carrying plates of waffles and fruit or glasses of juice, sitting on hard chairs talking about Bosnia. They seemed just a shade too self-satisfied, even the ones who weren't obviously on ego trips. Being bright on cue was boring, boring, boring. There had to be more to intellect than IQ tests.*

*Then there was Intertel, whose members were required to score about the ninety-ninth percentile to qualify. There was Prometheus, where the requirement was a score at the 99.997 percentile. And above them all, the Mega Society, where only one person in a million could meet the 99.999 qualification for membership. The Mega Society's entrance exam was the most difficult in the world; being one of its twenty-six members was confirmation of special, unique qualities.*

*Of course, genius-level IQ was a curse as well as a blessing. It made so many of the people one encountered in daily life appear lead-footed and slow-witted, their world narrowed down to what they had seen on TV the preceding night, their opinions formed by whatever some bearded jerk wrote in a newspaper. Art was a framed print, music was a rock station, literature was a book of poems by a geriatric movie star.*

*True intelligence was about being apart from and above such crass common denominators. It was about learning how to be what Nietzsche had called Übermensch, a superior being, a person of extraordinary power or achievements, beyond mere good or evil, someone who had the pride and strength to make rules or break them, to cast aside petty moral strictures, to act and exist on a level to which the dull masses could never even aspire.*

*"Do you understand, Peter? Do you understand what I'm talking about?"*

*The darkened room was heavy with incenselike*

*perfume. The window overlooking the small boat harbor of Laguna del Mar below was covered by heavy drapes that shut out the late-evening light. Muted traffic sounds from East Laguna Drive over-laid the Vivaldi concerto playing softly on the stereo system.*

"*Let's stop talking now, Angel,*" *Peter Valenzuela said hoarsely.* "*Let's begin the game.*"

"*You're wicked. When I want to talk.*"

"*Afterwards. After.*"

"*Mmmm,*" *Angel said, pushing back long blond hair.* "*And which game do you want to play tonight?*"

"*You know. You know what I like. The moon, Angel.*"

"*So that's what you want. Have you been a bad boy?*"

"*Yes. I didn't mean to be . . . but yes, I did the bad thing again.*"

"*You promised me you wouldn't do it anymore.*"

"*I know. But I couldn't help it.*"

"*Very well. Then you must be punished.*"

"*Yes,*" *Valenzuela breathed.* "*That's what I want, Angel. Punish me. I've been so bad.*"

"*Bring me a glass of champagne first,*" *Angel said sternly.* "*Then we'll see.*"

*Valenzuela poured the champagne, his hand trembling so badly that the neck of the bottle rattled on the rim of the glass. He handed it to Angel, then sank to his knees, kissing the painted toenails.*

"*Angel, please,*" *he said.* "*Angel, please, now.*"

"*You want me to begin?*"

"*Yes, yes.*"

"*You want the moon?*"

*Peter Valenzuela looked up, smiling dreamily. It was their code for his erotic fantasy: Fly me to the moon. "Yes, the moon. The moon, Angel."*

*"Shhh," Angel said, stroking his hair. "There's no hurry. We have the whole night."*

# 20

Ed Hatch no longer paid much attention to women.
He was not a misogynist, but as far as he was
concerned, the Bible was quite clear on the subject:
"Abstain from fleshly lusts, which war against the
soul." Anyway, he wasn't interested. At sixty-eight
years of age, he was happy to forgo the pleasure of
admiring women's bodies as they walked by. Had she
not so obviously tried to conceal her face as she
hurried out into the street, he would hardly have
noticed the slim blond woman he passed in the lobby
of his apartment block on Palmetto Drive.

Funny, he thought as she pushed the door open and
hurried off down the hill toward Altamira Boulevard.
Why would she want to hide her face like that? Then
he shrugged. These days, a woman could have plenty
of reasons for not wanting to be recognized, if that
was what she had been doing. She might have been a
married woman, visiting someone who was not her
husband. She might have been a call girl. Or a drug

160

runner. Best to keep your nose out of it, whatever *it* was.

He pushed the button for the third floor, and the elevator doors sighed shut. The elevator crawled upward at no great speed. Ed Hatch had lost count of the number of times he had complained to the manager about it. Nobody did his job properly anymore. Hell, nobody gave a damn about anything anymore. The world was going to hell in a handbasket.

The tinny Muzak was playing a jaunty version of "Once in a While." Even though his hearing wasn't as good as it might have been, it sounded odd, as if the tape was wowing. Overlaying the tinkly tune, Hatch could vaguely hear what sounded like long, high-pitched notes in the background. Or . . . was it someone shouting?

The elevator doors opened on the third floor, and he stepped out. Almost immediately, the acrid tang of smoke touched his nostrils, and at the same time he heard, louder than before, the sound he had detected over the Muzak in the elevator. There was no question about it: what he could hear was the sound of a man screaming. He stopped dead in his tracks, frozen with fear and indecision. *Lord God Almighty,* he thought, *someone is being murdered. What are you supposed to do if someone is being murdered?*

Heart pounding with terror, he scuttled along the hall toward the door of 3C, his apartment. His mind momentarily blanked out the stink of smoke. All he could think was *police, police, call the police.* As he reached his door, the screaming stopped abruptly. Now from apartment 3B, opposite his own, he saw tendrils of smoke swirl out under the door, thickening even as he watched to become a black, oily sheet that climbed up the door, coating it with soot.

Other than the fact that the name of the man who lived in 3B was Peter Valenzuela, Hatch knew nothing about him. He looked around wildly as a door opened further down the hall. A horsey face framed in a halo of unkempt hair poked out. It was Henry Thorn, the insurance salesman who lived in 3D.

"What's that screechin'?" he shouted. "Ya hear it?"

"Call 911!" Hatch screamed. "There's a fire, the place is on fire!"

Thorn's jaw dropped open. He disappeared back into his apartment. Hatch ran for the fire alarm, tearing off his shoe to shatter the glass. The strident bell deafening him, he grabbed an extinguisher, wrenching it from its bracket. Outside the door of apartment 3B, flickering tongues of flame were beginning to lick their way up the wood. He leveled the nozzle and hit the trigger. The chemicals whooshed out with a frightening noise, blanketing the blackened door with foam.

For a moment, Hatch thought he had controlled the fire, but then suddenly the door ignited with a sharp crack like a rifle shot. As it collapsed into the hallway, a ball of flame leaped outward, causing Hatch to skitter backward in involuntary panic, dropping the fire extinguisher and almost losing his balance.

Inside the apartment, he could see nothing but a sheet of fire. He looked down. Before his horrified eyes, evil little ripples of flame spread from the fallen, burning door and along the carpeted hallway. He picked up the fire extinguisher again and doused them, coughing and choking as smoke billowed from the open doorway. He could hear people shouting, a woman screaming. His throat felt as if it was on fire, and he could hardly bear to keep his streaming eyes open.

Out of the roiling smoke, a tall man with a towel wrapped around his face appeared beside him with another fire extinguisher, shouting, gesturing. Confused and dazed by the noise and heat, Hatch did not understand a word. The man grabbed his arm and pulled him away from the fire.

"Leave it!" he heard the man scream. "Get the hell out of here!"

At that moment, the sound of a dull explosion ripped through the burning apartment. It sounded like a gas boiler igniting, then, as if from the mouth of a giant unslain dragon, a huge yellow and red breath of flame roared out the gutted doorway, scorching the wallpaper and the picture rails on the opposite wall. Throwing up his hands to shield his face, totally disoriented and close to asphyxiation, Hatch stumbled and fell, vaguely aware of the sound of sirens, of breaking glass, of men shouting. By the time the firefighters dragged him clear and stretchered him to an ambulance, he was unconscious, one of three casualties on that floor.

Four, if you counted Peter Valenzuela, whom they found on the bed in the apartment. Or what remained of him.

Kathryn and Dave were drinking coffee in her living room when, shortly after noon, County Communications paged Kathryn to the crime scene.

"We'll take my car," she said. "Okay?"

"No sweat," Dave agreed. He knew Kathryn usually insisted on driving alone to any crime scene. For one thing, it afforded her maximum flexibility, and for another, more personal reason, she preferred being totally self-sufficient.

Palmetto Drive sounded a lot classier than it actually was, except to those who knew that what they called a palmetto bug in Florida was in fact a giant cockroach. It was a short curving street that ran down the hill from the center of Laguna del Mar, crossing Altamira Boulevard before passing under the Alvarado Freeway where it became First Street in Marina Village.

The apartment house was just below the Southern Pacific railroad tracks, sandwiched between a recreation area with basketball hoops surrounded by ten-foot-high wire fencing and a peeling stucco-faced block on the corner of Altamira Boulevard that housed a dry cleaner, a print shop, and a hairdressing salon called American Hairlines.

As they rounded the bend, they observed the familiar crime scene—flashing strobes, the scattered array of police vehicles, fire engines, a Channel Eight satellite truck, and the white CSI van parked at an angle in front of the building. Firefighters in yellow slickers and helmets were rolling up their hoses on the wet pavement. Curious locals clustered in groups outside the yellow perimeter tapes, watching enthralled as the police went about their business oblivious to the audience scrutinizing their every move. Kathryn braked the Audi hard to slow the car on the slope. A deputy waved them to a parking spot.

As they stepped out of the car, Kathryn spotted Walt Earheart lumbering toward them. His loose-fitting tan sportcoat flapped as he hurried up the slight incline, a sheen of perspiration on his forehead.

Late June is usually the warmest time of year along the central California coast.

"Thought you might be Doc Nelson," he said.

"He's on his way," Kathryn told him. "I just talked to him on the car phone. What have we got, Walt? Another fire bomb?"

"Uh-huh. Looks like a ringer for the Hanlon killing," Earheart said. "Some sort of incendiary device on the lower body, the bomb squad says. Burned hotter'n hell. Set the whole apartment on fire. Victim is probably a Peter Valenzuela, age forty-eight, worked for a downtown construction and drafting service, lived alone."

"Anyone see anything?"

Earheart shrugged a massive shoulder. "I've got a team out now knocking on doors," he said. "But this is a busy area. Lots of people coming and going all the time."

"Building have a doorman?"

Earheart shook his head. "Buzz-in."

"Who phoned it in?"

"Neighbor in the next apartment over, name of Thorn. He said one of his neighbors was out in the hall, told him there was a fire. He called 911."

"Anyone talked to the neighbor yet?" Dave asked.

"He's at the hospital," Earheart said, checking his notebook. "Smoke inhalation and first-degree burns. I've got a detective up there waiting to talk to him. Name is Edward Hatch, sixty-eight, widower, lives alone. He tried to put out the fire; it damned near extinguished him. He's going to be okay, though."

"You said a ringer for the Hanlon killing. How was the body found?" Kathryn asked. "Was he restrained?"

Earheart nodded. "Yep. Cuffed to the bed, hands and feet. Buck naked."

"So this isn't just another homicide," said Dave, "unless we have a copycat."

"Yeah, great," Earheart said sourly. "Listen, Purington has set up a briefing for four o'clock this afternoon."

"Damn," Kathryn said. "Sunday afternoon? I promised Emma I'd take her to the movies."

"You'll probably be able to make the early evening show," Earheart said dourly. "Let's face it, we're not gonna have a hell of a lot to discuss. No suspects, no motive, no leads. Jesus, it makes me angry we can't get a handle on this guy."

"We're all angry, Walt," Kathryn said. "And feeling helpless and stupid because people are being murdered and we can't stop it."

"At least we've got one thing going for us," Dave said. "Nobody can commit this kind of murder and not screw up sooner or later."

Earheart shrugged again. "You know that," he said. "I know that. The question is, does the sonofabitch who's doing it know that?"

The elevator shaft was still clogged by drifting smoke, so Kathryn and Dave took the stairs to the third floor. Along the unlit hall, the carpets were waterlogged and slippery. A huge black burn mark encircled the carbonized doorway of the apartment like an obscene nimbus. As they entered, a deputy at the door logged them in and handed them face masks to filter out some of the stink of smoke, burned wood, and burned flesh. They didn't help much. The walls were black with soot. Flakes of ash stirred and floated about them, and charred floorboards crunched beneath their feet as they crossed the room.

It was a small apartment, two bedrooms and one bath. The living room was almost entirely gutted, the windows facing into the light blown out. Inside the demolished bedroom, the bright flare of halogen-arc lights lent a movie-set atmosphere to the crime scene. Investigator Charlie Yamamoto's flashgun bounced light off the greasy black walls. He looked up and acknowledged Kathryn and Dave with a slight nod as they entered but otherwise went about his work as if he were alone in the room. At crime scenes, Charlie didn't miss a thing.

The dead man, if you could call the grotesque cadaver a man, lay stretched in the X position in which he had died, a bloody froth around his mouth, head flung back as if still in agony, blind eyes staring wildly at the ceiling. Two investigators methodically measured, diagrammed, and dusted every smooth surface that remained intact for patent and latent fingerprint impressions, unfazed by the ghastly chaos around them.

"Looks like the same MO," Dave said, bending over the body for a closer look. "Any sign of forced entry?"

"Door locks appear to be intact," said Walt Earheart, who had followed them into the room.

"So the victim knew his killer. Or, anyway, let him in," Kathryn observed.

"That's the way it reads to me," Earheart said. "CSI found remnants of a wine bottle and glasses on the floor in the living room. He might have been entertaining someone. But with the place and the body in this kind of shape, we can't be certain about anything."

As with the earlier victim, Patrick Hanlon, some sort of incendiary device had devastated the lower center of the trunk, burning a hole the size of a plate through the abdomen. The flesh beneath the hand-cuffed wrists was mangled and bloody where the victim had wrestled with his unyielding restraints, and the ropes anchoring his feet to the bed were soaked with blood. Both arms appeared to have been dislocated, probably as the victim struggled to free himself.

"Neighbor who called it in said he thought he heard screaming," Walt Earheart told them.

"Was it the same kind of device as last time?" asked Kathryn.

"Everything points to it," Walt replied. "The bomb squad seized what may be remnants of the contraption and took them to the lab for analysis."

"Dave, check with the lab later, would you?" Kathryn suggested. "Odd the fire did so much damage outside the bedroom," she observed. "And so little in here."

The fire had marched across the floor from the bed to the chest of drawers, ignited a nonstructural partition wall, and burst into full flame in the adjoining living room, leaving the far side of the bedroom relatively untouched.

"The fire chief confirmed the origin of the fire was right here." Earheart gestured at the body. "Like you say, Kathryn, a freaky burn pattern."

"Every one's different," Dave said. "Draughts,

open windows, even drains can affect the way the fire runs."

"Lucky for us," Earheart answered. "If it had gone the other way, it probably would've burned down the house. At least we've got something to work with."

"Doesn't look like a hell of a lot to me," Dave observed sourly. "What about this guy's family?"

"I've got detectives working on that," Walt said.

"Any signs of theft?" Kathryn asked.

"In a mess like this," Earheart observed from years of experience with similar scenes, "it's gonna be tough to know whether anything was taken or not."

"He's not wearing a watch," Kathryn said.

"I noticed. We haven't found one. Yet."

"What about his wallet? House keys, car keys?"

Walt shook his head. Kathryn turned to Yamamoto, who was still taking pictures.

"Have your investigators photograph anything valuable that's still intact, please, Charlie," she asked.

His head moved in acknowledgment. He knew she was thinking out loud rather than issuing directions, and he wasn't offended.

"What about the handcuffs?" Kathryn asked. "And the rope?"

"Look like the ones found on Hanlon," Earheart replied.

"Valenzuela was forty-eight years old," Dave observed. "He could have been in Vietnam. I'll get a fax off to St. Louis on that one. Then I'll run his DMV, get his telephone and utility records."

"Good idea." Kathryn turned to Walt Earheart. "Anything on his answering machine?"

Earheart shrugged. "Sorry. It melted."

"What about the medicine cabinet? Anything there?"

"Just drugstore stuff. Doesn't look like he was taking any prescription medications."

"We need to know if Valenzuela knew Hanlon," Kathryn said. "Or if they had anything in common. Anything at all."

"Walt, can you have your detectives take care of that?" Dave asked. "I'm right in the middle of my investigation of Hanlon."

Everyone turned as they heard Morgan Nelson's familiar voice in the hallway outside.

"Hi, Doc," Charlie Yamamoto said. "The patient's over here."

"You're not much on the bedside manner, Charlie." Morgan Nelson grinned back at the investigator. "And I got to tell you, your patient doesn't look too chipper, either."

Dave Granz glanced at Kathryn and raised his eyebrows in silent question: *Are you finished?* She nodded in the affirmative.

"No point in us taking up valuable space," Dave said to Walt Earheart as Morgan prepared to conduct his preliminary examination. "We'll get out from underfoot."

"Morgan, call me with your preliminary results when you're through," said Kathryn.

"Gotcha," Morgan said.

With a final glance over her shoulder, Kathryn headed out into the ruined corridor and down the stairs to the street, Dave Granz close behind. The afternoon sun was welcome after the dank stench of the murder scene, the difference between the warmth of life and the chill of death.

Death.

Conjured up by sight of the contorted thing on the charred bed, the finality of the word hung in her mind like a hawk in an empty sky, always there, wheeling, watching, waiting to swoop.

"Let's get out of here," she said, and walked purposefully toward her car, shrugging her shoulders to expunge the image from her mind.

# 21

Kathryn chose the freeway route, accelerating into the number two traffic lane as Dave settled comfortably into the passenger seat. He switched on the tape deck, and the soundtrack of *The Big Chill* blasted out. How appropriate, she thought as she threaded the Audi into noonday tourist traffic. How perfectly appropriate.

Her reaction confirmed the tentative decision she had made earlier. *Now is as good as time as any,* she thought. *But what do I say? And how exactly do I say it?*

There was only one way, she decided: just come right out with it. She switched off the tape deck and drew in a long, deep breath.

"Dave, listen," she said, getting it all out fast. "There's something I need to tell you, and I don't know how, so I'm just going to come right out and say it. Please don't say anything until I'm finished. Okay?"

He turned slightly in his seat, frowning. "Sounds serious. Did I do something?"

"No, it's nothing like that. Listen, now, please don't interrupt. Last Sunday, I found a lump in my right breast. JoAnn Ota arranged for me to have a mammogram and ultrasound at the Breast Center. That's where I was on Friday. They confirmed there's a small lump. They can't tell if it's cancerous, so they want me to have it biopsied right away."

Dave hadn't moved since she began. Now he just stared at her in shock. "Kathryn, why—" he began.

"Not yet, let me finish," she said. It was easier to talk now that it was out in the open, now that it had been said aloud. "I knew I ought to tell you, but I didn't want to say anything until I was sure there was something to tell you about. I'm not sure, but I may need you to drive me to the surgery center for the biopsy. I haven't scheduled it yet, but it'll be sometime next week."

Dave let out his breath in a long sigh. "Ah, Jesus, Kathryn," he said, and she heard the agonies in his voice. "Why didn't you tell me?"

"I don't know. I honestly don't know. I was waiting for it to be the right time. And it never was, till now."

"I knew there was something. But I couldn't figure out what. Now I understand."

"I think . . . what I'm trying to say is, I've been going through so many different emotions, it was all I could do just to cope. I have such a strong feeling for you, I want us to have a long time together. And then there was Emma. She's just about gotten over dealing with her father's death, and I didn't want to, I can't . . . oh, Dave, I'm so damned mixed up and scared and angry."

Dave sighed audibly. "Kathryn, listen to me, you aren't in this by yourself. We've gotten through bad things together before, and we'll get through this, too, whatever it turns out to be. Just tell me what I can do to help, and I'll do it."

She looked at him. "You've already done it. More than you can imagine. Just by being there when I needed you to be. And by not saying something stupid like 'Don't worry' or 'Everything will work out fine.' And Dave—I don't want to talk about it anymore until the biopsy is done, okay?"

He nodded. "But what about Emma? Are you going to tell her?"

"Not unless I have to."

"You're sure that's how you want it?"

She nodded. "I'm sure."

Everything that needed to be said had been said. Although she knew Dave would need a while to deal with what she had told him, Kathryn felt better knowing he knew. They crossed the bridge over the yacht harbor and drove along the Esplanade toward Espanola. The beaches on Shelter Island were crowded, and out on the ocean sailboats scudded before the wind. Hot dogs and ice cream and not a care in the world. Just another bright, sunshiny California day.

# 22

The task force—Kathryn, Dave, Walt Earheart, George Purington, now expanded to include Morgan Nelson—assembled around the tables in the Sheriff's conference room a few minutes after four. Through the windows on the west side of the County Building overlooking San Patricio Park, Kathryn could see children playing on the swings. Although it was near the beach, boardwalk, fishing wharf, and other tourist attractions, the park was used mostly by locals. On Sundays, young families gathered there to picnic, feed the fat ducks in the pond, or just lie in the cool grass. Joggers and teenagers on rollerblades moved along the running track beside the river.

On such a beautiful afternoon, Kathryn would have infinitely preferred being out in the open with Emma and Dave instead of cooped up in the stuffy little room inside the Sheriff's office. But when a task force meeting was called on a case she could eventually

175

prosecute, her presence was mandatory. She made herself concentrate.

". . . DOJ found no physical evidence to link the courtroom bomb and the incendiary devices used to kill Hanlon and Valenzuela," George Purington was saying. "The construction methods and the materials used were completely different. In addition, the courtroom bombing appears to have been a random act, whereas Hanlon and Valenzuela were specifically targeted. My conclusion is that the courtroom bombing and the incendiary homicides are probably not connected."

"What if you're wrong?" Dave said. "What if there is a connection between them?"

"What makes you think there might be?" Earheart asked, leaning forward, brows knitted.

Dave shrugged. "Nothing I could put in a report. Just a gut feeling."

"Come on, Dave," Earheart said heavily. "Don't wish a serial bomber on us."

"We may have one anyway," Purington said heavily. "There are marked similarities in the MO used in both the incendiary homicides."

"In that case, we better concentrate on that," Earheart said. "Dave, where are you at with Patrick Hanlon?"

"I've interviewed family members, neighbors in the immediate vicinity of his home, and his business associates," Dave said, opening a thick manila folder. "Patrick James Hanlon, born in Fullerton, California, February 22, 1949. Only child, parents reside in Westwood, California. They don't know much about his private life; I gathered they weren't very close. He was in business for himself—an industrial designer.

Checked with his creditors. He paid his bills on time. Never been arrested."

"What about his sex life?" Earheart asked. "CSI seized a whole stack of S&M and bondage magazines from the spare bedroom."

"One of his business associates admitted to frequenting a popular gay bar on The Strip with him. Neighbors said he brought women home from time to time," Dave replied. "So maybe he swung both ways."

"Neighbors tell you anything else?" Walt asked.

"Nothing specific, just he was no trouble, sort of quiet, kept mostly to himself."

"What about his work?" Kathryn asked.

"Business associates, everybody I talked to, said he was a first-class designer and a really nice guy, but they didn't know him very well. I ran registration checks on his car, a '90 Miata. I'm waiting on medical, telephone, insurance, and utility records."

"Anything to add on Hanlon, Doc?" Earheart asked.

Morgan Nelson shrugged. "You've got my autopsy protocol," Nelson said. "And before you ask, I can't tell you much about his sex life," he added with a glint in his eye, "because there wasn't anything left of that part of his body to draw any conclusions from."

"Could that be significant, Doc?" Dave asked. "Is the killer burning out that part of the bodies to cover something up?"

"Possibly," Nelson said. "There's something almost biblical about it. It could even be a very specific form of punishment. The killer could be saying, 'You used that on me. But you'll never use it on anyone else.'"

"You mean revenge?" Kathryn asked. "For what?"

Morgan shrugged. "Whoever did this wasn't a passing acquaintance, male *or* female. Casual relationships don't stir up that kind of emotion. This was someone who really hated him."

"You mean, maybe someone Hanlon threw over for somebody else?" Dave said. "You think we should be looking for a lover or ex-lover?"

Nelson shrugged again. "It's a possibility, that's all. I was just thinking out loud."

"What about the Valenzuela homicide, Doc?" Earheart asked. "You got anything for us there?"

"I can't give you much yet, because I've only done a preliminary examination at the scene," Morgan said. "I'll know more after I've completed the autopsy. It's scheduled for Tuesday evening."

"George?" asked Earheart, looking at Purington.

"I've got DOJ's examination report on the Valenzuela bomb's components," Purington said. "As I said earlier, there are a number of similarities in the MO. DOJ's findings tend to confirm the homicides of Hanlon and Valenzuela are linked."

"How so?" asked Kathryn.

"The device that killed Valenzuela was homemade and thermite-based, consistent with the one that killed Hanlon. There was one major difference, though," Purington added. "CSI found a small bottle beside Valenzuela's bed. It contained traces of sulfuric acid and rubber."

"Which means what?" Earheart asked.

"It could mean the killer used a delay mechanism, something that took a long time to set off the fire bomb," replied Purington.

"That might explain why Valenzuela's body was in such bad shape," Nelson said. "Arms dislocated, flesh torn from the wrists and ankles. He put himself through hell trying to dislodge the thing from his body. He knew he was going to die, and about as painfully as possible, a long time before it happened."

"How long was the delay?" asked Kathryn.

"In real time, it could have been as much as fifteen minutes from the time the device was activated until it triggered the bomb," said Purington. "For Valenzuela, an eternity. The rest of his life."

"My God," Kathryn whispered. "We have got to find some way to stop this madman."

"Look, Kathryn, we all feel bad," Earheart said. "We've all had sleepless nights over this. But we can't work miracles."

"George, you think the Bomb Data Center could help us any?" Morgan Nelson asked.

"Can't see how," Purington replied. "They don't do direct investigative work. They're a great resource for information—technical research, bombing incident summaries, and statistics, that kind of thing. But field work . . ." He ended the sentence with a shrug.

"Could they tell us how our bombings fit in statistically with the national picture?" Kathryn asked.

"I can tell you that myself," Purington replied. "In 1993, BDC received reports on 2,980 bombing incidents. The total number of casualties involved was 1,372, forty-nine of whom died from their injuries. That includes 1,042 persons injured when a bomb went off in the World Trade Center building in New York City on February 26."

"Nearly three thousand a year," Kathryn murmured. "That's what, sixty a week, ten a day countrywide. But not many fatalities. So our bomber is scoring unusually high."

"That's because he's not run-of-the-mill, which most of the cases George has cited would have been," Morgan pointed out. "Most bombings are random. Even when they're targeted, the target represents something—a corporation or a government office, something the bomber can't reach. These killings aren't like that. These are personal."

"How, personal?" Purington said.

"Look at the scenario," Morgan said. "Hanlon—and Valenzuela, too, probably—invites a partner to his home for sex. Disregard the evidence of forced entry at the Hanlon crime scene; assume it's the killer's attempt to throw us off course. Straight or gay, it makes no difference, people who are into S&M and bondage don't take chances on their sex partners. Hanlon knew his killer and invited him into his home, just as Valenzuela did. I'd bet on it."

"You said . . . when you were autopsying Hanlon, you said whoever killed him, it had to be someone who hated him very much," Kathryn recalled. "Someone who wanted him to suffer very badly."

"Right," Morgan said. "And it looks like he wanted Valenzuela to suffer even more."

"Okay," Dave said. "Let's say you're right. Valenzuela knew his killer. Hanlon knew his killer, too. That being so, they probably had some kind of sexual connection before. So here's my question. Why didn't the guy kill them the first time?"

"Something happened," Kathryn said. "Something triggered him. But what?"

"I could give you a dozen reasons, Katie," Morgan said. "And every one of them a perfectly logical motive. Fear. Blackmail. Religious mania. Homophobia. Jealousy. Revenge. Abandonment. Take your pick. It could be any of them, all of them."

By the window, Kathryn rested her chin pensively in her hands, elbows on the conference table. Off to the south side of the County Building was a lawn bowling field, where every Sunday afternoon during the spring and summer, elderly men and women clad in white participated in a city-county sponsored tournament. Many of them lived in three large retirement complexes on crooked Cayuga Street, which delineated the park's western boundary. An animated exchange was taking place between two groups of white-haired bowlers, and Kathryn smiled. You didn't stop wanting to win just because you got old.

"Well, I guess we're not going to accomplish much more today," Earheart said, confirming what everyone already knew, that they were still a very long way from identifying the killer of Peter Valenzuela and Patrick Hanlon. "Thanks for coming in, all of you. And hey, Kathryn?"

Kathryn turned at the door. "Did you forget something?"

Earheart grinned. "Get a move on. You and Emma can probably still make the late-afternoon matinee," he said.

She did; and they did.

# 23

Court reconvened in the case of the State of California versus Richard Hudson in Department Eight of Santa Rita Superior Court at precisely ten A.M. Following the usual opening formalities, Kathryn's third witness, Marian Browning, was seated, sworn, and settled into her chair behind the bulletproof plexiglass shield protecting the witness stand.

Kathryn had scheduled Browning last for two reasons. First, she preferred to proceed chronologically before the jury; Browning had been Hudson's final victim. Second, strategically, Browning was by far Kathryn's most impressive—albeit also most unpredictable—weapon. A part of Kathryn's mind grappled with the problem even as she prepared to begin her direct examination.

She had to get Marian Browning to admit to the jury and the entire world that she had let herself be persuaded to transgress against her own rigidly observed credo of clean living and because of it became

182

HIV-positive. The element of unpredictability—and it was not inconsiderable—came from the fact that Browning was bitterly distressed and angry about it and might well express that anger as forcefully in court as she had in some of their earlier meetings.

Kathryn approached the witness from one side, so the plexiglass did not impair her view and so that the witness would be facing the jury as she spoke. Neatly dressed, short and sturdy, with close-cropped brown hair and wearing no makeup, Marian Browning had the sinewy physique of an athlete.

"Where do you work, Marian?"

"At the People's Clinic, downtown. There's another in Espanola, but I never work at that one."

"And what do you do there?"

"I'm a nurse's aide."

"Tell me," Kathryn prompted, "as a nurse's aide, do you ever have direct contact with patients who come in for medical care?"

"Sure. I take their medical histories, make notes for the doctor or physician's assistant, prep them, and so on. A lot of times they don't even have insurance, that's why they come there. If they're scared or worried, I try to reassure them before they see the doctor. It's the most satisfying part of my job."

"Okay. You said you often work nights. Why is that?"

"The clinic is open in the evenings for patients who work or can't come in during the day. I prefer nights so I'm free to work out at the fitness center during the day when there aren't so many people."

"I understand you train with weights. Would you tell us why?"

"I believe physical conditioning and a healthy lifestyle are the key to good health. Working out with weights is one of my means of achieving it."

"How many nights a week do you work at the clinic?" Kathryn asked.

"Five, but not necessarily the same nights each week. It's a walk-in clinic. We're open seven days a week, eighteen hours a day, from six in the morning until midnight. My shifts rotate. Sometimes it's Monday through Friday, the next week Tuesday through Saturday, and so on. So there's always cover."

Further questioning elicited the information that Marian Browning lived with her sister and brother-in-law. In exchange for caring for her niece and two nephews and doing light housework, she paid no rent. She lived in a spare bedroom with its own private bath. Each morning, after helping to get the children off to school, she stacked the breakfast dishes in the dishwasher, did a load of wash, and tidied up around the house. Then she would catch a bus to the Midtown Fitness Center, spending much of the late morning and early afternoon pumping iron and working out on the rowing machine. By the time she got through, took the bus home, and showered, the children were home from school. She helped with their homework until their parents arrived home from work. By then, there was barely enough time for a quick bite to eat before she went to work.

"Would you describe your lifestyle as hectic, Marian?" Kathryn asked.

"Yes, I would. I have very little free time."

"I agree. I'm worn out just talking about it." Kathryn smiled and switched subjects. "Do you have a boyfriend, Marian?"

"No, I do not."

Kathryn picked up a copy of the *Coastal Times* which had been premarked with a people's exhibit red sticker and handed it to the witness.

"Marian, please read to the jury the ad circled in that paper," Kathryn told her.

"'I'm not looking for a dream woman,'" Marian read, her diction clipped and precise, "'just a good friend for conversations, movies, cuddling, and quiet times. You are strong, educated and mature, twenty-seven to thirty-seven. Please reply with a photograph to Box 4834.'"

"Did you reply to this ad?"

"Yes. I sent a photograph. Head and shoulders."

Kathryn walked across to stand near the jury box, taking her time. It was a well-tried technique. It required the witness to look at her, and in doing so to look at the jury. The space between them required them both to project their voices. If the witness could hear her, and vice versa, then so could the jury. Standing next to the jury also enabled her to watch them as well as Marian Browning, to determine when they were paying attention and when they were not.

"Will you tell the jury why you felt it necessary to find a partner through a connection ad?"

"As I told you, I work nights, and it's hard to meet people. I have friends who met people through the ads, and it worked out fine. I thought I'd try it."

"Can you tell us what it was about that ad that motivated you to respond?"

Marian Browning gave a self-conscious shrug. "Look, I know I'm not a beauty queen. But it said he wasn't looking for a dream girl. Someone to share more important things. I guess I replied because it sounded sincere. Sincere," she spat, her voice suddenly cold with rage as she turned to glare at Richard Hudson. "What a joke. Richard Hudson is about as sincere as a rattlesnake, and twice as deadly."

Belker was on his feet before she had finished speaking.

"Your Honor, this is unacceptable! Ms. Mackay is provoking this witness, trying to poison the jury against my client."

"Sit down, Mr. Belker," Judge Woods snapped back. "The prosecution did nothing improper here." He turned to face the witness, leaning forward so she could see his face. "Ms. Browning, I know this is difficult for you, but you must only answer the prosecutor's questions. You must not add personal remarks of any kind. Is that understood?"

"Yes, Your Honor," Marian Browning said. She didn't sound particularly chastened, Kathryn thought.

"So it was through the ad you've just read that you met the defendant?" Kathryn continued. Although she had not precipitated Marian's emotional response, and would never condone it, it certainly had not hurt her case.

"He called and suggested we meet."

Browning's testimony describing the sequence of events following her initial meeting with the defendant was substantially the same as that of Mitten and Sorensen. He told her he worked in computers. She didn't understand much of it but found it fascinating. They met a few times at the Coffee Roasting Company, usually in the early evening before she went to work. Movies and pizza on her nights off, two weeks in a row; another night when—admitting it to the jury clearly embarrassed her—she called in sick so she could spend the evening with him.

Finally, one Saturday night, he invited her to his condominium for a home-cooked seafood dinner. Like the earlier witnesses, she remarked on what a fastidious housekeeper he was, and on his culinary skills. They spent a long, leisurely evening eating, talking, listening to music, and drinking wine—she rarely drank alcohol but under the circumstances allowed herself to be persuaded.

"He said it was to keep him company, so he could loosen up," she said. "He said he found it hard to talk about himself."

"And did he?"

Marian nodded. "It was really late, and we'd been talking for hours. Then right out of the blue, he told me when he was a kid, nine years old, they put him in a home, his father had been . . . he was sexually abused. He never saw his parents again."

"Were you shocked by that?"

"No, just the opposite. I knew it must be difficult for him to talk about. I felt he must really trust me to be telling me this."

Later still, he told her he had become a disciple of the Maharishi Mahesh Yogi, and for nine years he had been celibate, doing transcendental meditation.

"He said that was why he placed the ad. He'd forgotten what to do, how to talk to women. Then he suggested we get to know each other better—intimately. He asked me if I knew what he meant."

"And what did you reply?"

"I said yes, I knew what he meant." She glared at the defendant.

"And did you have sexual intercourse with the defendant that night?"

"Yes, I did."

"And did Richard Hudson use a condom?"

Marian Browning shook her head. "I told him he should. He said, 'I told you, I've been celibate for nine years.' And he'd had a blood test in conjunction with minor surgery a few months before and tested negative for HIV. I was drunk. I believed him. What a fool! I should have just shot myself, it would have been quicker. And more fun."

Martin Belker was already on his feet again, but Judge Woods motioned him to sit. The judge turned once more to Marian Browning and frowned down at her sternly.

"Ms. Browning, I've admonished you once already. You will confine yourself to answering the prosecutor's questions. Do I make myself perfectly clear?"

Marian Browning, who was glaring at the defendant, apparently did not hear—or chose to ignore—the judge.

"Ms. *Browning!*" Woods boomed. "Answer me immediately! Do you understand?"

"Yes, Your Honor," Marian Browning said tonelessly, her eyes never leaving Richard Hudson's face. "I understand."

Only partially mollified, Judge Woods nodded at Kathryn to continue.

"And was that occasion the only time you had sexual intercourse together?"

Although Kathryn would never have admitted it, her witness's outburst had been more than she could have ever hoped for. One of the unwritten laws of the courtroom was that no matter what the judge told them to disregard, a jury never forgot anything that was said in its presence.

"No. It happened twice more. At his place."

"And after that first time, did the defendant wear a condom when you made love?"

"We didn't *make love,* Ms. Mackay, we had *sex,*" Marian Browning snapped. "And, yes, he wore a condom both times. I insisted."

"How could you be certain he always wore a condom, Marian?" Kathryn asked.

"Because I took them with me. I made sure he never touched me after that without wearing a condom."

Kathryn put a look of incredulity on her face. "Marian, let me get this straight. Are you saying you only had unprotected sex with the defendant once, and that after that he always used a condom?"

"That's right. And he got real angry about it. Said he couldn't '*feel* it,' and kept saying if I cared about him at all, I would trust him. But I told him no condom, no sex."

"How long did your relationship with the defendant last?"

"About two months in all. But we were only intimate for a couple of weeks. He seemed to lose interest after I insisted that he use a condom."

"Then what happened?"

"I hadn't talked to him for a couple of days after the last time we had sex, then he called. He said it was all over between us, he didn't want to see me anymore."

"Were those his exact words?"

"Pretty much. He called me a tight-assed bitch and said I deserved everything that was going to happen to me. I didn't know what he meant at first. He said, 'I've got AIDS, Marian. I've had it for a year.'"

"What was your reaction to that?"

Marian glared at the defendant, then at Judge Woods, who cautioned her with a silent arch of his eyebrow and a tilt of his head. Marian made a visible effort to control her emotions.

"There was such hate in the way he said it, at first I thought it was some kind of sick joke. But it wasn't. It was like he was glad he'd done it. I tried to call him a dozen times, but all I ever got was an answering machine. So I didn't bother going to his place to see him—I knew it would be pointless."

"Did you tell your sister?"

Marian Browning shook her head. "I couldn't."

"So what did you do?"

"I went to another walk-in clinic in San Jose, where nobody knew me. The aide there did what she could to help, but even though I knew I'd only had unprotected sex once and the odds were in my favor, I was still afraid. I felt like one of those poor people who come into my clinic—scared and alone."

"And what was the result of that test?"

"It was positive. I have HIV."

Now, as sudden tears filled her eyes, the vulnerable young woman behind the confident facade became visible. She fumbled in her purse and found a tissue, dabbing them away.

"I'm sorry," she whispered. "I didn't mean to cry."

Kathryn waited, sharing Marian Browning's distress, knowing the jury would be as deeply moved as she had been by this strong yet sensitive young woman's story. When she was satisfied the witness was composed, she stepped back.

"I have no further questions for this witness, Your Honor," she said.

Almost two hours had elapsed since Marian Browning had taken an oath to tell the truth. With a glance at the wall clock, Judge Woods said, "Thank you, Ms. Mackay. At this point, the court will recess for lunch and reconvene at one-thirty."

"All rise!" the bailiff called.

As the judge left the courtroom, Kathryn walked across to the witness stand and touched Marian Browning's arm. "That was just fine, Marian," she said. "Thank you. When court reconvenes, the defense attorney will have some questions for you, then you'll be finished."

Marian Browning nodded her understanding. "I'm ready."

"I know you are. Just remember what I told you. He may try to confuse you, get you to contradict things you've already said. Don't let him. Just answer the question, tell the truth, but don't volunteer any information that isn't asked for. Don't guess. If you don't know something, say, 'I don't know.' If he asks you a question you don't understand, say so. Give yourself time to think, to formulate your answer before you reply. And, Marian, be careful. I understand your anger, and I share it. But this is not the place to show it."

"I'll try," Marian Browning said, and Kathryn

knew she would. Excusing herself, she left Marian with the victim-witness advocate and went across to where Dave was standing. There was only so much preparation you could give witnesses, only so many caveats they could remember. After that, you just had to cross your fingers and hope for the best.

# 24

"Walt Earheart's come up with a connection between Valenzuela and Hanlon," Dave said. He was sitting in one of the leather chairs in Kathryn's office on the second floor of the County Building. "Apparently, they both frequented the same gay clubs."

"Where does that get us?"

"It means we now have to at least consider the possibility we could be dealing with a homophobic killer," Dave said. "They often mutilate the bodies of their victims."

"If this guy could be a homophobic murderer, it would certainly put a different spin on things," Kathryn mused. "Maybe it's time to bring in a profiler to help us."

The State of California had its own mind hunter, a Supervising Special Agent of the Department of Justice's Criminal Investigation Response Team who had completed a ten-month fellowship at Quantico, one of only twenty-four graduates of the Criminal Investigative Analysis Program nationwide. But he was in constant demand, and often unavailable.

"Time's too precious in a case like this, Kathryn. By the time we get a request processed through the bureaucracy, and the profiler is assigned and up to speed, two or three more people could be dead. This psycho's moving too fast. Why don't you work up the profile? You're as good as what's-his-name in Sacramento, anyway."

Before Hal Benton had appointed her his Senior Trial Attorney, Kathryn had written and published a comprehensive research paper that proposed that although profilers were available on request to all law enforcement agencies, there was a case for each county having at least one prosecutor on its staff capable of constructing a basic criminal profile. Her recommendations had been implemented all over the state, including Santa Rita County. As a result, she had spent six weeks studying the techniques of criminal profiling with the "mind hunters" of the Behavioral Science Unit—now the Investigative Support Unit—at the FBI Academy in Quantico, Virginia, near Washington, D.C. For better or worse, she was the resident expert.

"I don't have the expertise to profile homophobic incendiary bombers, Dave. We really should ask DOJ for their assistance."

Dave shook his head stubbornly, and she knew why. Quite apart from his innate mistrust of mind hunters in general, uppermost in his mind was the fact that if they requested one, the profiler DOJ would send down was Steve Giordano, with whom he knew Kathryn had once had a brief but intense relationship.

"You underestimate yourself," he said. "Look, why don't you talk to Doc Nelson about it? He's autopsying Valenzuela tonight."

"Maybe I will," she said. "You going to be there?"

"I'm going to have to pass," Dave told her. "Would you brief me tomorrow?"

"Where are you going?"

"Jim Field is being discharged from County," he said. "I'm bringing him home."

# 25

Court reconvened exactly on schedule, the way Judge Woods liked it. He made himself comfortable, took a brief moment to look at the jury and the crowded public benches, then nodded to Marian Browning.

"You're still under oath, Ms. Browning," he reminded her. "Go ahead, Mr. Belker."

Defense counsel walked toward the witness stand and stopped well short of the witness, as if he preferred not to be too close to her. She stared at him impassively, and Kathryn hid a smile; among professional athletes, it was called a "game face."

"Miss Browning," Belker began, "you stated you only had sex with Mr. Hudson three times, and only once when he didn't use a condom. Is that correct?"

"Yes."

"Are you sure about that?"

"Absolutely certain, sir. I can count."

"I'm sure you can, but that wasn't the question. Isn't it possible that you had unprotected sex with my

196

client more than once, maybe as many as a half-dozen times?"

"No, sir, it is not possible. I am not promiscuous. I know exactly how many times I had sex with your *client.*"

"Of course." Belker sneered. "I forgot your infallible memory. Let me ask you another question. How many glasses of wine did you drink that night—the night you told us you had unprotected sex with Mr. Hudson?"

"Two or three. I'm not certain. I wasn't counting."

"You don't know how many glasses of wine you drank, but you're certain how many times you made love with my client without a condom. Do you always get drunk on two glasses of wine?"

"I resent your implication, sir," Marian Browning snapped. "I don't normally drink wine at all. And I can assure you that if I had not been drunk, I would never have agreed to anything so unsafe. I—"

"That's not what I asked you, Ms. Browning!" Belker snapped, anxious to interrupt her testimony, which was obviously not going his way.

"Objection, Your Honor," Kathryn said. "The witness hasn't finished her answer."

"I agree," the judge said. "You may complete your answer, Ms. Browning."

"Thank you, Your Honor," Marian Browning said politely, clearly enjoying being the cause of Belker's scowl. "As I was saying, I am unaccustomed to wine, and I was drunk. But while it's possible I might not recall how many glasses of wine I drank, I would most certainly remember how many times I had sex. Maybe you see it the other way around."

"I see, very well, let's move on."

Martin Belker looked and sounded uncomfortable, as if he felt the witness was proving to be more than he could handle. Kathryn watched him as he walked across to take a position near the jury box similar to the one she had occupied earlier. And for the same reasons, she thought.

"You told this jury you work as a nurse's aide, is that correct?"

"That's right, Mr. Belker."

"You've been a nurse's aide for, what, eight years?"

"Correct."

"And during those eight years, you have come into direct contact with hundreds, if not thousands of patients, would you agree, Ms. Browning?"

"I couldn't give you the exact number."

"Is it possible, Ms. Browning, that in the last eight years, you could have been bitten by a patient who, unbeknownst to you, was infected with the HIV virus or AIDS?"

"It's possible, but I don't have any recollection of being bitten."

"You have from time to time performed cardiopulmonary resuscitation on patients, correct, Ms. Browning?"

"Yes," Marian replied hesitantly.

"Then it's possible you could have been exposed to the HIV virus while performing cardiopulmonary resuscitation on a patient who, again, unbeknownst to you, was positive for HIV or AIDS."

"I—I don't know."

"In the course of your work as a nurse's aide, you come into contact with bodily fluids such as blood, isn't that so, Ms. Browning?"

"Yes, but I wear latex gloves," replied Marian.

"Isn't it possible that on one or more occasions you neglected to wear gloves and came into contact with a body fluid that carried the HIV virus or was infected by AIDS?"

"No, Mr. Belker," Marian shot back. "I always wear gloves."

"Always, Ms. Browning? You're sure?" Belker said, putting theatrical disbelief into his voice.

"Objection, asked and answered," said Kathryn, rising from her seat."

"Withdrawn," replied Belker. He moved away from the jury now and back to face Marian Browning. "One final question in this area, and we'll move on. You have from time to time during the course of your work as a nurse's aide been stuck accidentally by needles, isn't that so?"

"From time to time," replied Marian warily.

"Could you estimate for this jury how many times this might have happened?" asked Belker.

"No," replied Marian resignedly.

"Would I be correct in saying you consider yourself a knowledgeable and competent health-care professional?"

"Yes, I do. I take pride in my work."

"Of course you do," Belker said smoothly. "I can see that. So, it would be fair to presume you stay current on health-care issues—for instance, before you met my client, you were aware that certain diseases, serious and sometimes deadly, can be transmitted through unprotected sex?"

"Of course I was."

"You were aware before you made love to my client

that if a person is HIV-positive, he or she could transmit the virus to a sexual partner through unprotected sexual intercourse—correct, Miss Browning?"

"I prefer to be addressed as 'Ms.' not 'Miss,'" Marian Browning said coolly. "And, once again, I did not *make love* to your client, I *had sex* with him. But to answer your question, yes, I was aware that a single unprotected sex act is all that's necessary to transmit the HIV virus."

"Thank you. I'll try to remember your fine distinction between 'love' and 'sex,'" Belker said sourly. "Now, *Mizzz* Browning, wouldn't you agree with me that you knowingly and consciously chose to engage in sexual intercourse with my client without using a condom understanding fully the risks involved, ignoring all you knew, and thereby voluntarily assumed the risk of contracting HIV?"

For a long, long moment, Marian Browning glared at Martin Belker, and Kathryn could see her trembling visibly with anger.

"That, sir, is absurd!" she rasped. "No, I did not voluntarily assume the risk of contracting AIDS. I could not assume a risk I did not know existed. Your client lied to me. He invented a sick story about having surgery and being tested negative for HIV for the sole purpose of convincing me to have sex with him, then he got me drunk to make it easier. And it worked, sir—once. However, to answer your question more fully," she said, rising in the witness box as she pointed at Richard Hudson, "your client—*that man!*—infected me with the HIV virus, and he did it intentionally. And I hope he rots in hell!"

A stunned silence enveloped the courtroom as she

collapsed into her chair, exhausted by her own anger. It lasted only a moment, until Judge Woods reacted angrily to Marian Browning's denunciation.

"Ms. Browning, you have tried this court's patience enough!" he snapped. "I can, I will tolerate no further outbursts. If you are so misguided as to make another, I will be forced to hold you in contempt of court and order you confined to jail until such time as you can control yourself. Do you understand me?"

The last four words were almost fired like separate shots from between his clenched teeth. If the judge expected Marian Browning to be intimidated, he was immediately disappointed. She looked him unflinchingly in the eye before she replied.

"Your Honor," she said, "it was not my intention to be disrespectful to you or the jury or to anyone else in this courtroom. But I feel as if I am being treated as the criminal here rather than as a victim. Since I am already under a sentence of death, and for no other crime except that of being extremely imprudent, you will appreciate the threat of a few nights in jail arouses no fear in me. In fact, it would be a distinct improvement over the hell I'm living in."

Kathryn felt like cheering. In one simple speech, Marian Browning had summed up the frailties of the judicial system and, in the process, done more to enhance the prosecution's case and destroy the defense's than the combined testimony of every other witness who would be called upon. It came as no surprise to her when Martin Belker elected not to put any further questions to the witness.

"Thank you, Mr. Belker," Judge Woods said heavily. "I think that will be more than enough for today. Ladies and gentlemen of the jury, thank you for your attention, and once again please keep in mind my admonition that you are not to discuss this case among yourselves or with anyone else."

"All rise!" Bailiff Chris Taylor called as the judge left the bench. Kathryn sat quietly, still stirred by her witness's testimony. Only rarely, perhaps no more than once in a career, if one was lucky, did a prosecutor get a witness who had such a powerful effect upon a courtroom as Marian Browning. She stood up as Marian came across to the table.

"I just wanted to thank you, Kathryn," she said with a glance at Belker. "That man tried to make me sound . . . loose and stupid."

"No way could he ever have done that," Kathryn told her.

"That's good to hear," she said. "Would you . . . could I buy you a cup of coffee sometime? After this is . . . all over?"

"I'd love that." Kathryn smiled. "I'll walk you outside. I've arranged for an inspector to give you a ride home."

"No need, the bus is fine," Marian said.

Kathryn watched her as she pushed out through the barrier and left the courtroom, a stocky, plainly dressed woman whom yesterday one might have passed on the street without even noticing. Yesterday, perhaps, but not today. Today Marian Browning had made everyone notice her: a decent, brave, and honest woman who had had the courage to stand up in front of the whole world and tell Richard Hudson—and all the other Richard Hudsons out there—that she refused to be a victim.

# 26

By the time Morgan Nelson was ready to begin the autopsy on Peter Valenzuela, Kathryn had been in the autopsy suite for almost half an hour. Each time Nelson appeared ready to begin, the phone rang. Finally, with a muttered curse, he switched it off and vowed to ignore it the rest of the night. Except for the constant soft murmur of running water, the morgue was empty and still; along the corridor somewhere, the sullen drip of a tap into an empty steel sink sounded like the far-off echo of a slowly beaten drum.

"Something bothering you, Katie?" Morgan asked as he readied the devastated body of Peter Valenzuela for examination.

"Nothing special." She fenced. "Why do you ask?"

"You seem . . . preoccupied," Morgan said. "I don't quite know how to put it. Like you have something on your mind you want to talk about, but can't."

Surprised by his insight, Kathryn avoided the implicit question.

"You know me, Morgan. I'm always on edge while I'm in trial."

He nodded agreement, but she sensed he was not entirely convinced.

"You sure you really want to tough this out, Katie?" he said. "You don't have to, you know. It looks like it might be pretty much a rerun of the Hanlon autopsy."

"Let me sit in for a while anyway," Kathryn said. "I'd like to understand what happened to Valenzuela and Hanlon. So far, I haven't been able to."

"Scott Fitzgerald once wrote something about the rich being different from you and me," Morgan said, working on his knives with steady concentration. "The same might be said of people like our friend Valenzuela here. Sexual masochists are different from you and me."

"How so?" asked Kathryn.

"Cast your mind back to last summer. The autoerotic deaths. Remember?"

"I remember," Kathryn said feelingly. *Will I ever forget?*

The long hunt for a vigilante who killed rapists and duplicated autoerotic death scenes to conceal his murders had ended in the tragic death of a DA's Inspector named Michael Gaines. She never passed the stairwell outside her condominium without hearing again the echo of the shot that had ended his life. And remembering Dave Granz, his face like iron, telling her it was over. As if it would ever be over.

"Then you'll recall autoerotic sexual behavior is just having fun without a sexual partner. And that when it goes wrong, the majority of autoerotic deaths are caused by asphyxiation."

"Risk-taking is the thrill, right?" said Kathryn. "The closer you go to the edge, the bigger the charge."

"That's it exactly," replied Nelson.

"I seem to remember you telling me how important it was in such cases that investigators carefully check knots and other restraints."

"Very important. In a fatality, the way knots are tied, the way handcuffs are fastened, can often indicate quite conclusively whether the victim placed the physical restraints himself, or whether someone else did."

"And here?"

"No question about it, someone else put them on."

"How can you tell?"

"You saw the body."

"You mean the way he struggled?"

Morgan nodded approvingly. "Right. If he'd been alone, put them on himself, he'd have tied slip knots on the ropes, had the key to the handcuffs close by where he could reach it when he wanted it."

"So what kind of sex games was he playing?"

"The common terminology used to describe this range of sexual behavior is 'bondage and domination.' Bondage refers to the use of physically restraining materials or devices that have special sexual significance for the user—ropes, chains, handcuffs, hoods, blindfolds, gags—even bandages. Different degrees of restraint, different associations. It's all very individualistic."

"And domination?"

"It takes a variety of forms, from gentle sadism—

say, being caress-whipped with a silk dressing gown cord or slapped around a little—escalating to the infliction of, and willing submission to, serious injury and sexual humiliation."

In addition to whatever pain might be induced by the restraints used, the recipient might also invite the infliction of pain on erogenous zones such as the nipples, anus, or scrotum, or on the actual genitalia themselves, Morgan told her. Usually the 'game' was ended by an agreed signal between the dominator and the subject, a code word or a physical sign if speech was not possible.

"There are as many varieties of sexual behavior as there are people," Morgan said. "Your normal is someone else's anathema, and vice versa. Whatever your imagination can conjure up, no matter how bizarre, no matter how disgusting it might seem to you, someone somewhere has already done it—in spades. And got a sexual kick out of it."

"What about Valenzuela?"

"The cuffs on Valenzuela were lined with lamb's wool, Katie. They were for holding but not for hurting. CSI found some burned remnants of what might have been rubber foam insulation on the floor of the apartment. My guess is there was something between his skin and the ropes on his ankles when the game started, too."

"Padding?"

Morgan nodded confirmation. "Some of these sadomasochistic games can mark you up pretty badly," he said. "Generally speaking, the people who play them don't want their friends or relatives to know how they get their kicks, so they use padding to prevent abrasions or bruising that might trigger embarrassing questions."

"So what did his partner do to him?"

"That's what we're about to find out," Morgan said, switching on his mini-cassette recorder. "Okay, it's eleven twenty-one P.M., June 26. The body under examination is that of a well-nourished Hispanic male, apparent age forty to forty-five, identified as Peter Charles—we'll probably find he was born Pedro Carlos—Valenzuela by a coroner's ID band present on the right ankle."

He fished in the pocket of his surgical robe and brought out a flexible tape measure with which he quickly checked and called out the dead man's height, five feet ten inches. Kathryn jotted it down on the clipboarded autopsy form Morgan had handed to her earlier. Later she would make notes of the weights of various organs as Morgan extracted them—lungs, liver, heart, brain.

"Right," he said. "Let's swab some of this soot off him, and maybe we'll be able to see something."

With long, strong strokes of his powerful forearms, he swabbed the encrusted soot and detritus off the dead man's upper torso. The wet flesh gleamed fishbelly-white in the bright overhead lights.

"Ah," she heard him say as he bent over the body. "Interesting. Come here, Katie."

She put down the clipboard and went across to stand beside the tilted table on which the body lay. Morgan Nelson handed her the six-inch-diameter magnifying glass he had in his hand.

"Here," he said, pointing to the right side of the dead man's chest just above the nipple. "See?"

Squinting through the magnifying glass, Kathryn could see three dark purple parallel lines, each perhaps half an inch across. They ran downward into the ghastly hole that had been burned through the body by the incendiary device.

"What are they?" she asked.

"Wait," Morgan said.

Going around to the other side of the table, he lifted the dead man's right arm with his left hand, holding out his own right hand and wiggling the fingers, *gimme*. Kathryn slapped the magnifying glass into his palm.

"More here," he said. "Come see."

She walked around the table and looked over his shoulder. Around the little run of muscle beneath the armpit was a similar set of marks.

"Couldn't see these at the death scene," he said. "Parallel bruises and subcutaneous tissue damage on the left pectoralis major and right serratus anterior. Both consistent with the body having been struck with something whippy, perhaps a split cane switch or a whip with leather thongs, probably the latter. Before he was killed, our friend here was flagellated."

He straightened up and beamed at Kathryn as if he had just done a clever conjuring trick. "The skin isn't broken, so I'd say it wasn't serious, just hard enough to arouse. In other words, sexual foreplay, not punishment whipping."

"What was that thing they used to say, different strokes for different folks? This puts kind of a new spin on it, doesn't it?"

"If nothing else, it narrows down the field a tad," Morgan said. "It suggests the killer could be a sadist, or at the very least what they call a dominator,

someone who specializes in dishing out punishment
sex."

"Sexual intercourse?"

Nelson shrugged. "No way of knowing," he said.
"If any sex took place, the fire destroyed any traces
there might have been on the body."

"What now?"

Morgan picked up his large surgical knife. "I'll get
started on the cutting," he said. "Katie, you look
tired. Why don't you go home, and I'll call you with
my findings."

Kathryn nodded. "Maybe I will at that," she said.
"By the way, I talked to Dave about calling in a
profiler. He said I ought to take a shot at it."

"It's a good idea. You've got the training."

Profiling was not an art, it was a skill. A crime scene
processed through an experienced investigative brain.
Although Kathryn was not an investigator, her close
association over the years with the processes of law
enforcement and investigation, enhanced by the
training she had received at Quantico, had given her a
comprehensive overview of criminal behavior.

The questions you wanted answered were not why
someone had been killed but how it had been done
and what kind of person might have done it. Why
didn't matter. Cops weren't interested in why. They
were interested in how old the guy was, was he black
or white, was he married or single.

"You want to talk it through while I'm getting our
friend here ready?" Morgan said, interrupting her
reverie.

"You know how it works, Morgan, it's a step-by-
step thing," she said. "First, evaluate the acts. Then
the crime scenes. Then analyze the victims."

"Okay," Morgan said. "Start with the murders."

"Our killer is a planner. We know he manufactures portable incendiary devices and takes them with him to the scene of the killings. Leaves us nothing—no prints, no physical evidence. That says organized and intelligent to me."

"Agreed."

"There's a . . . ferocity about the killings. You remarked on it. You said whoever was doing this really hated his victims, wanted them to suffer. Could he be homophobic?"

"He could be, but I don't think so."

"Why not?"

"The whipping. If the killer was genuinely homophobic, he probably wouldn't be able to control himself. Whoever put those marks on Valenzuela knew exactly how hard he was hitting him."

"Then why kill them?"

"Something that happened to him?" Morgan guessed. "Something he holds them responsible for? Something they don't know they did, but he does?"

"The victims have only one thing in common," Kathryn pointed out. "They had sex with the killer."

"No," Morgan corrected her. "That's the only thing we *know* they had in common. There could be a dozen other things we don't know about."

"Okay, accepted. The killer knows his victims. He has probably been intimate with them before."

"Agreed."

"The victims are ethnically mixed: white and Hispanic. Which means, on statistical probability, the killer is white."

"And probably younger than his victims," Morgan added.

Kathryn nodded agreement. The fact that the murders had been carried out so methodically supported that proposition. Which meant he would be less than forty years old, quite possibly in his late twenties or early thirties.

"And if he has multiple partners, that militates against his having a live-in lover, so he either lives alone, in the parental home, or with some undemanding other. Given the age bracket, I'd go for alone," Kathryn decided.

"Don't forget the different social strata," Morgan reminded her. "Our killer is as comfortable in Valenzuela's little apartment as he is in Patrick Hanlon's nice old Victorian house."

"So he'd be of a social class superior to Valenzuela but at least equal to Hanlon?"

"Too easy," Morgan said. "It would have more to do with background, education, wouldn't it?"

"You're right," Kathryn said. "Someone used to dealing with people of all types. A good education. Maybe he speaks other languages. Remind me to check with Walt Earhcart to see if Valenzuela spoke Spanish. Could he be someone in the public sector, perhaps?"

"Good, Katie," Morgan said. "Very good indeed. But he could just as easily work in the theater, music, the arts."

Kathryn shook her head. "I don't think so. This guy is too . . . feral."

"Interesting choice of words," Morgan observed. "You think he's crazy?"

"Like a fox, maybe. Which leads to the next question: How did he treat the bodies of his victims?"

"With contempt, I'd say," Morgan replied. "Even

loathing. He just lit the fuse, walked away, and left them to burn."

"You see the anomaly? Here is a man who has just played sadistic sexual games which we can probably assume culminated in sexual intercourse, then almost immediately afterward sets up his partners' deaths. Not only that, he knowingly leaves them to suffer agonizing mental and physical torture before the firebomb kills them."

"It's not an anomaly if he feels they deserve it for whatever they did to him. Don't lose sight of the fact this is a person who enjoys inflicting pain, Katie. Someone who *thinks* punishment."

"An abuse victim?" Kathryn said, with a quick flash of inspiration. "Someone who was punished, perhaps unjustly, as a child or young adult?"

"It's a truism abusers are frequently themselves the victims of abuse." Morgan nodded. "A history of physical abuse might certainly have influenced his own sexual preferences."

"Okay, what have we got?" Kathryn said, counting on her fingers. "An organized killer, a coldblooded sadist who sets up and triggers the deaths of his victims with considerable care. A gay white man, in his late twenties or early thirties, with a working knowledge of chemicals and explosives, living alone, possibly abused as a child or young adult. Intelligent, good with people, may speak Spanish, possibly works as a public servant. He'd have to be a car owner; the crime scenes are a long way apart."

"It's a good start," Morgan told her. "Keep working on it."

"I will," Kathryn said, encouraged by her progress.

"Just tell me one thing: could Valenzuela have been murdered by a woman?"

Morgan paused, one rubber-gloved hand on the dead man's chest, and stuck out a meditative lower lip.

"Yes, a woman could easily have done this. Dominatrix women frequently figure in the kind of sexual activities we're talking about here," Morgan said. "Why do you ask?"

"Just a thought. Nobody asked the question before. But everything we've said so far about the killer could apply to a woman."

"Try it out on the task force," Morgan told her. "Or run it past Dave. Where is he, by the way?"

"Jim Field was being discharged from the hospital this evening," Kathryn told him. "Dave brought him home."

Morgan nodded. "I saw him this morning. Jim, I mean."

"How was he?"

Morgan shook his head. "Not good. Nobody seems to be able to get through to him. He's convinced himself he's going to be a useless cripple for the rest of his life."

"And is he?"

"Not at all. The stump's healing nicely. In fact, one of the reasons I went up there was to tell him I got him an appointment to see a prosthetic specialist in San Francisco."

"And . . ."

Morgan shook his head. "An artificial hand isn't going to cure what's ailing him. What's wrong with Jim is he really doesn't want to be alive."

*Or he's scared to be,* Kathryn thought, with a sudden flash of intuition that came from what she herself was experiencing right now. *It's easier to opt out than to face it.*

"You've gone very quiet," she heard Morgan say, and she realized she had lapsed into silence.

"Just thinking about Jim," she said, hoping she was making it sound reflective. "Would it help if I talked to him?"

Morgan shrugged. "Might be worth a try. But it's going to take him a long time to work all that bitterness out of his system."

"Yes," Kathryn said thoughtfully. "I think right now I can understand that."

Poised to make the big Y incision in the body on the table, Morgan stopped as he saw her turn away from the sight of the blade going through the flesh. After gently laying down the big knife, he came around the table and looked her straight in the eyes.

"What is it, Katie?" he said softly.

She shook her head and looked away. "It's something I . . . something I have to deal with on my own."

"Don't try to lock me out, Katie," he said, his voice almost sharp. "I know you too well. Something's been troubling you all night. I saw it the minute you came in here. Not work, something else. Something bad."

She felt her resolve not to talk about herself crumbling. Besides Dave, Morgan was the best, most sympathetic friend she had, a dear, good man who was closer to her in many ways than the father she had hardly known. For nearly a decade, he had been her supporter and confidant. If anyone could ease her through this, it was Morgan.

"Talk to me, Katie," he urged her. "Maybe I can help."

"Maybe you can at that," she said. "Tell me about biopsies."

# 27

"Your Honor, the prosecution calls Dr. Ronald Freeman," Kathryn said, and waited as her witness took his place on the stand.

Ronald Freeman was a tall, thin man with deep-set dark eyes and thinning hair combed back from a center part. His face was long and narrow, with deep lines running from a prominent hooked nose to his thin-lipped mouth. His charcoal-gray suit and formal manner made him look like an accountant.

With doctors, however, as with accountants, what you saw wasn't always what you got. Kathryn had once dated a CPA who had served in the United States Navy's Submarine Service—definitely no place for the faint of heart—and rode Harley-Davidsons in his spare time, yet showed up each day at his office in a three-piece suit very much like the one her expert witness was wearing.

She watched the jury discreetly as Dr. Freeman swore his oath to the court clerk. She could see they

216

already approved of him, as she had intended they should.

"Good morning, Doctor," she said. "Please tell the jury your profession."

"I am a doctor of medicine."

"And where are you currently employed?"

"I am the Director of Health Services for Santa Rita County."

Kathryn had thought carefully before summoning an expert witness on AIDS. She had concluded that although most people, no doubt including some if not all of the jurors, believed they knew everything there was to know about AIDS, few people actually did. It was her job now, through Dr. Freeman's expert testimony, to walk the jury through the extremely complex nature of the disease, how it was transmitted, and what effect it had on the human body, so that by the end of the trial, they would understand well enough to arrive at a guilty verdict.

"As the Director of Health Services, Doctor, can you briefly describe your duties for the jury?"

"Certainly. I administer all aspects of the county's medical services. We provide a wide range of health-care services, many to indigent patients, and we also interface with and advise the private medical community on many health-care issues. For instance, at our clinics—we have six in various parts of the county—we provide alcohol, drug testing, and counseling programs; environmental and mental health services; and routine ongoing public and private health-care delivery. The difference between us and other health-care providers is that we're vastly larger than most private clinics, and we minister to a more diverse patient base. In addition, we provide certain health services that are unavailable in the private sector. For example, we have specialized teams of health-care experts devoted strictly to the disease of AIDS—an HIV testing program, HIV Early Intervention Program, an HIV Care Team, and an AIDS treatment and counseling program. We are the only provider of such services in the county."

"Thank you. Doctor, are you primarily an administrator, or do you personally treat patients?"

"My administrative managers run the department. I personally am heavily involved in the treatment of patients, especially HIV-positive and AIDS patients. My area of specialty is the prevention and treatment of AIDS."

"Would you please tell the court how and where you received your medical training."

"Certainly. I graduated from Harvard University with a degree in medicine, performed my residency at Beth Israel Hospital in New York, then trained for several years at the Centers for Disease Control and Prevention in Atlanta, Georgia. I returned several years ago to Johns Hopkins University and earned a degree from the Program on Law and Public Health. I accepted the position of Director of Health Services here in Santa Rita four years ago because this area of the country is one of those most affected by AIDS. I believed I could do something to help."

"Have you served as a consultant and published any articles in your field of specialty, Doctor?"

"Yes. My research in the areas of HIV transmission and AIDS treatment has been published in the *New England Journal of Medicine,* the *American Journal of Public Health,* and the *European Journal of Epidemiology,* among others. I have served as a consultant to the California Prisons Authority in connection with its AIDS-in-prison project; I am adviser to the president's National Gay Task Force, the San Francisco AIDS Foundation, and the American Foundation for AIDS Research."

The process Kathryn was obliged to walk the doctor through was called *voir dire,* literally, "to see/to say," a means of demonstrating to the judge that the witness was suitably qualified as an expert, and to the jury that his opinions were valid. An expert witness is the only witness permitted by law to offer opinions rather than facts, to respond to hypothetical questions, and tell the jury what he or she *thinks* rather than *knows.*

Of course, both Judge Woods and Martin Belker were perfectly well aware of Dr. Freeman's qualifications; he was one of the state's most highly respected experts on AIDS and other infectious diseases. That wasn't the point. Kathryn knew the defense would gladly stipulate to the doctor's impressive qualifications, but she preferred the jury to hear them for themselves.

"Doctor, would I be correct in saying that today, thanks to movies, TV, and newspaper coverage, everyone knows what AIDS is?"

Dr. Freeman allowed himself a thin smile. "Most people think they do. But in point of fact, the average person knows surprisingly little about the disease."

"I see," Kathryn said, looking at the jury. "In that case, Doctor, perhaps you could tell us exactly what AIDS is."

She felt the jury's eyes on her, knew their expectations. One of the things she had learned long ago about juries was that the way she dressed, the way she applied her makeup, the way she conducted herself in court, all had a profound effect on their perception of her, and of the People's case. The court was not a theater, but it was nevertheless like being onstage. Clothes were a statement. If she dressed too casually, the jury might conclude that the case was unimportant; This morning, as she did each morning she was in trial, Kathryn had given careful thought to her choice of clothing, striving to look formal but not stuffy, businesslike but not unapproachable.

"The acronym A-I-D-S stands for acquired immunodeficiency syndrome. It is a disease caused by a virus."

"And the name of this virus?"

"Its full name is human T-cell lymphotropic virus type three, or HTLV-3. It is better known as the human immunodeficiency virus, HIV for short, and it is extremely contagious."

"Can it be spread in the same manner as a common cold or chicken pox?"

"No. It is contagious in the same way sexually transmitted diseases such as syphilis and gonorrhea are spread."

"Can it be spread by everyday social contact?"

"No, it cannot. Shaking hands, hugging, social kissing, crying, coughing, and sneezing will not transmit the AIDS virus. Nor—popular misconception to the contrary—can it be caught in a swimming pool, or by eating food touched by someone with the virus, or from sharing bed linen or towels or cups or straws, or from doorknobs or telephones or toilet seats."

"What about saliva?"

"The virus has been found in saliva, and also in tears. However, since the first case of AIDS was diagnosed in 1979, no instance of transmission from these bodily fluids has ever been reported."

"What about more intimate contact, Doctor? Body massage, say?"

Dr. Freeman shook his head. "As long as the contact is nonsexual," he explained patiently, "there is no risk of contracting AIDS. The same applies to masturbation. Most nonsexual behavior is safe."

"But some behavior is not. Can you give us an example?"

"High-risk behavior—such as sex between homosexual and bisexual men. About seventy percent of AIDS victims throughout the country are in this category. The other most common source of infection is from needles shared between intravenous drug users."

"Can AIDS be contracted from heterosexual sex? Sex between a man and a woman?"

"There is no risk of AIDS between two mutually exclusive or monogamous partners in a long-standing relationship," Dr. Freeman said.

In spite of his somewhat forbidding appearance, he was a good witness. Decisive, clearly spoken, authoritative. Kathryn's job now was to take him step by step through every aspect of the disease without making it sound like he was reading from a medical journal and losing the jury's attention.

Taking him through it a step at a time, she had him first describe how the virus infects the body and then how it destroys the immune system by attacking the T-lymphocytes, replicating itself faster than the body can replace its T-cells.

"What happens when the immune system is destroyed?"

"Without a functioning immune system to ward off other germs, the infected person becomes increasingly vulnerable to infection by bacteria, protozoa, fungi, and other viruses and malignancies such as *Pneumocystis carinii* pneumonia, tuberculosis, and meningitis."

"And cancer?"

"Yes," Freeman said. "And cancer."

Kathryn paused to let the words sink into the jury's consciousness. She wanted them to realize the implications of what Richard Hudson had done to the three victims whose stories they had heard.

One by one, the questions came and were answered: the incubation period, the symptoms, the various types of cancer that could be triggered by the disease. Without appearing to, Kathryn watched the jury closely throughout the witness's exposition. If she had detected the slightest sign of apathy or boredom on their faces, she would have cut Dr. Freeman's testimony short, but there was none. Now just a few more questions would nail it down and make the point.

"Tell me, Doctor, is there a cure for AIDS?" she asked guilelessly.

"No."

"Is any such vaccine in development?"

"Not to my knowledge."

"Is there any vaccine that would prevent uninfected persons from contracting the disease?"

"No, there is not."

"Is there any vaccine or drug that will halt the progress of the disease once infection has taken place?"

"No, there is not."

"So if someone deliberately infected two persons

with AIDS, he would effectively be condemning them to death?"

"Objection!" Belker shouted, scrambling to his feet. "Argumentative!"

"Withdrawn. Thank you, Dr. Freeman. I have no further questions."

Belker was still on his feet, his face a study in frustration.

"Mr. Belker, do you have anything for this witness?" Judge Woods asked.

"No, Your Honor," Belker said, still fuming. "The defense will call its own expert on AIDS later."

"That being the case, this would seem an appropriate point at which to adjourn," Woods said. "Thank you, Dr. Freeman, you may step down." He paused a moment and then addressed the general audience.

"As presiding judge, I am required to attend an important meeting scheduled for tomorrow morning. You are therefore advised that court will not reconvene until tomorrow afternoon at two P.M. I will again remind the jury to keep my earlier admonitions in mind."

As the judge left the courtroom, Kathryn glanced around. Most of the media people had trickled out before or during Dr. Freeman's testimony. Nothing sensational today, nothing gory, nothing anybody would be interested in reading in the newspaper or seeing on TV. Dave Granz's voice broke in on her reverie.

"You okay, Kathryn? Anything you need?"

His solicitude touched her. "Right now, no, I'm fine," she said. *It's later I'm not so sure about*, she thought to herself. "Where are you off to?"

"I need to check in with Walt Earheart," Dave told

her. "And I've got a couple of things of my own I need to take care of."

"Anything breaking on the bomber?"

"Only our heads," he said, vexed. "Sonofabitch hasn't left us much to work with."

She watched him as he walked out of the courtroom, wishing they had more time to talk. Both for herself and for him. She wanted to know how he felt about what was happening to her, how he was dealing with the possibilities it conjured up. But there was always something that took priority at work and then at home. An old Helen Reddy song threaded through her mind. *I am strong. I am invincible. I am woman.* She smiled to herself. *You better believe it.*

# 28

"Anything breaking on the Hanlon and Valenzuela homicides?" Dave asked Walt Earheart.

Earheart made a wry face. He took a cigarette out of the pack and put it in his mouth without lighting it. They were sitting in his cluttered office opposite the conference room in the Sheriff's Office.

"Not a damned thing," he said sourly. "In fact, this whole mess is like shoveling stainless steel ball bearings up a stainless steel hill and trying to make them stick."

"What did your people come up with on Valenzuela?" asked Dave.

"Age forty-eight, born in Portland, Oregon, lived in the county since 1984. Moved to Laguna del Mar about six months ago. Kept pretty much to himself at work, doesn't seem to have made many friends, although his colleagues spoke highly of him."

"We need a connection," Dave said. "Something

more than the fact that Hanlon and Valenzuela both frequented gay clubs."

"We did find one thing," Earheart told him. "When we checked their phone records, it turned out both of them had made calls to a number listed for an astrologer named Angel Flores with an address in Mission Hills. I've sent detectives up there two or three times, but they've never found anyone home. Neighbors say they hardly ever see anyone about the place. We ran the name through the computer and came up with nothing. No criminal history, nothing—she doesn't even own a car."

"She?" Dave mused. "Angel's a Hispanic man's name. A woman would be Angela, Angelica, Angelina."

"Come on, Dave, the computer—"

"Checks automatically, I know, I was just thinking out loud. How many calls were made?" Dave asked.

"Two for Hanlon, three for Valenzuela."

"Why? What's the connection?"

"Jesus, Dave, who the hell knows? Maybe they were consulting her for financial advice. I read someplace at least three hundred of the companies in the *Fortune* 500 use astrologers." The big man grinned.

"What about Jim Field?" Dave said. "Did you find anything to connect him to Hanlon or Valenzuela?"

"Not a thing," Earheart said.

"Did you ask him if the name Angel Flores means anything?"

"Not yet. I'll send a detective over to talk to him."

"Skip it," Dave told him. "I'm on my way up there now. I'll ask him myself." He pointed at the unlit cigarette in Earheart's mouth. "You ever going to light that thing?"

Earheart took the unlit cigarette out of his mouth, looked at it, and put it back into the pack.

"I'm trying to quit," he said. "So I don't carry matches. Listen, if Jim comes up with anything on Flores, give me a call, okay?"

"You got it," Dave said.

# 29

Kathryn arrived at the Center a little after four-thirty and sat leafing through a magazine in the waiting room until it was time for her consultation. At precisely four forty-five, Dr. Marie Snyder appeared and ushered Kathryn into her office.

It was a warm room, a window with wooden blinds looking out onto the narrow street, off-white painted walls, wine-colored carpeting, and dark cherry office furniture.

"I've been reading about your trial," Dr. Snyder said as they sat down. "How much longer do you think it will last?"

"We should present closing arguments next week sometime," Kathryn told her.

"So it's almost over."

Kathryn smiled. "You know what they say: 'It ain't over until the fat lady sings.' For me, that means until the jury brings in a guilty verdict."

"Think they'll find Hudson guilty?"

228

"That's a tough one to call," Kathryn confessed. "All the defense has to do is convince one juror there's reasonable doubt."

While they were talking, Dr. Snyder had taken out Kathryn's file and opened it on the desk in front of her.

"I've talked to a good friend of mine who's a pathologist. About cancer in general and breast cancer in particular," said Kathryn.

"Did you find that helpful?" Dr. Snyder asked.

"In a way, yes," Kathryn said. "I feel better having it out in the open where I can deal with it, instead of lurking inside me like an assassin waiting for his moment."

"Interesting analogy," Dr. Snyder said. "Did you ask your friend about biopsies?"

"Yes, I did," Kathryn said. "He suggested I discuss stereotactic biopsies with you."

"Your friend is right on the money," she said. "We think it's the wave of the future."

"He said it's very new."

"It is. It's ninety-six percent as accurate as surgery in detecting cancer. It's also quicker, less expensive, and easier. Most important of all, we get the answers fast. No more waiting weeks for test results—they're back in twenty-four hours."

"What exactly is involved?"

"Okay, start at the beginning. It's called a stereotactic automated large-core biopsy."

"Large-core?" Kathryn said warily.

Dr. Snyder smiled. "Only in microscopic terms," she said reassuringly. "Here's what happens. You lie facedown on a table that is lifted up in the air, something like a car hoist. The radiologist sits underneath while the breast pokes through a hole in the table and is held by a clear plastic screen. Several stereoscopic mammograms are taken which gives the radiologist a three-dimensional picture of the suspect area of the breast on the computer screen."

"Would I be under anesthetic?"

"Local only. There's no pain. The whole procedure takes less than half an hour."

"Does it leave a scar?"

Dr. Snyder shook her head. "No, and here's why. The radiologist slips a hollow needle into the breast, stopping just before the area to be tested. She uses the computer to lock onto the coordinates of the lump. These are fed into a sort of gun that fires a smaller cutting sleeve up through the needle, taking a minute core sample from the lump in a fraction of a second."

"And that's it?"

"That's it."

"Will I have to be hospitalized afterward?"

"Not at all. You'll only be here a couple of hours."

"Then what happens?"

"The radiologist sends the excised tissue to a pathologist. The pathologist runs a series of tests, then calls the radiologist to discuss the results, positive or negative. Then the radiologist calls you."

"Would you perform the procedure?" asked Kathryn.

"If you wish."

"How soon can you do it?"

"You don't beat about the bush, do you?" Dr. Snyder smiled. "There's no rush, you know. A couple of days won't make any difference."

"They'll make lot of difference to me," Kathryn

said fiercely. "I need this settled. I want to get on with my life."

Marie Snyder shook her head, smiling. "Kathryn, how did you ever become such a *balleboosteh?*"

"A what?"

"It's Yiddish," the doctor explained. "It means something like career-woman housewife."

"And it's obviously the origin of the word *ball-buster*. Is that how you see me?"

"I see a tough lady. Or maybe it's a lady who found out she needs to be tough."

"Tough?" Kathryn smiled. "I'm not so sure about that. I remember when I first moved up here, I called a friend and confessed that I didn't know if I could do it all—single mother, full-time job. And she laughed and said, 'Kathryn, you'd *better* be able to do it all.' So I learned to be a fighter, Marie. Once I identify the enemy, I step up and take it on. Maybe it's the Irish in me."

"Whatever it is," Dr. Snyder said, "just make sure you never lose it."

"I don't have the luxury of choosing," Kathryn said, standing up. "Thanks, Marie."

They walked to the exit together. "Something tells me you've already pretty much decided what you're going to do," the doctor said as they reached the door.

"You're right." Kathryn smiled. "I just need to make a few arrangements. I'll call you in the morning to confirm."

# 30

Dr. James Axler looked like everyone's idea of a benevolent and loving grandfather. Medium height, late fifties, slightly pudgy, with a full head of white hair, he had beautiful brown eyes and one of the most endearingly warm smiles Kathryn had ever seen.

Kathryn had heard of Axler before. He was one of the very few expert witnesses whose professional credentials and stature lent him a credibility comparable with that of Kathryn's witness, Dr. Ronald Freeman. She was therefore not surprised when Belker called him to testify.

After swearing the oath administered by the court clerk, Dr. Axler settled himself comfortably in the witness chair and smiled pleasantly at Martin Belker as he replied that, yes, his profession was that of a practicing medical doctor.

"Doctor, would you please tell the Court where you received your medical training?"

"I earned my doctorate of medicine at Princeton

University and completed my residency at New York University Hospital. It was in New York where AIDS was initially diagnosed in the United States, and as a result of my work at NYG, I commenced a study of epidemiology at Miami University Hospital in Florida. After being board-certified as a specialist in epidemiology, I accepted a position as director of the AIDS Health Project at the University of California, San Francisco Medical School, where I served both as director of the project and as a member of the medical school faculty."

"And where are you currently employed?"

"I am presently dean of the School of Public Health at the University of California, Berkeley," Axler replied, his diction impeccable. "As you may be aware, Berkeley's School of Public Health is generally considered to be among the United States' leading HIV and AIDS research facilities."

"Do you specialize in any one particular area of epidemiological research and practice, Doctor?"

"Yes, I do. I specialize in HIV and AIDS."

Kathryn watched and listened patiently as Belker took his time showing the jury just how expert an expert Dr. Axler was. Now, as Belker began examining his witness, Kathryn leaned forward attentively, concentrating on not just the questions but the intent behind them.

"Doctor, was it because of your experiences with AIDS patients while in New York that you became interested in that disease and decided to devote your entire professional life to the research and the treatment of AIDS-affected persons?"

"Yes, that was one reason. But there was another."

"Oh? And can you tell the jury what that was?"

233

"Certainly. I myself am HIV-positive."

Martin Belker looked at the jury in well-rehearsed surprise; of course, he already knew the doctor's medical condition, as did Kathryn.

"I'm sorry to hear that, Doctor," Belker said.

"Forgive me, Mr. Belker, but pity is the last thing either I or anyone infected with the HIV virus needs. Great strides are being made in AIDS research, and we will eventually develop a cure. There is hope, Mr. Belker. Being HIV-positive is by no means a death sentence."

"Thank you, Doctor," Belker said smoothly. "I am sure our awareness of your condition will help us all appreciate the legitimacy of your testimony. I'd like to now ask you a few questions about the HIV virus and AIDS."

Axler nodded and folded his hands together in his lap, leaning forward with his lips slightly pursed. When Belker's next question turned to how the disease was spread, Kathryn realized where he was heading. His intent, reinforced by Dr. Axler's testimony, was to show that AIDS could be contracted even in the most carefully regulated environments— by exposure to blood through accidental spills, by failure of protective gear, by accidental needle pricks—laying the groundwork for suggesting, in his closing, that the victims might have contracted the disease from some source other than the defendant. She bet herself his next platform would be the reliability—or otherwise—of condoms, and she was right.

"Is the use of a condom a one hundred percent effective way to avoid contracting AIDS?" Belker asked.

"No, nothing is one hundred percent safe," Dr. Axler said, "except abstinence, which, as I remarked earlier, we humans seem loath to practice." Dr. Axler permitted himself a small smile, and Kathryn noticed one or two of the jury returning it. He was a good witness.

"No, there is a small but quantifiable risk of contracting HIV even between sexual partners who use a condom all the time," he continued. "Studies have determined a measurable failure rate among condoms, varying from one or two percent to as high as twelve percent for certain well-known commercially available brands."

"Twelve percent," Belker repeated, laying surprise on with a trowel. "That's twelve failures in every hundred. That would mean anyone who engages in *any* form of unprotected sex risks contracting AIDS and that even when a condom is used, there is still a slight but recognized possibility that it may fail."

"That's correct."

"And would you say that almost everyone is or should be aware of these facts?"

"I most certainly would."

"Thank you, Doctor. Now, assuming that a person having negligently—strike that—having consciously chosen to engage in risky sexual behavior, becomes infected with the HIV virus. Does that mean they will inevitably develop AIDS?"

"No. Someone can be HIV-positive for many years without developing AIDS and, in fact, may never develop AIDS at all. In my own case, for example, I tested HIV-positive more than ten years ago, and I do not have AIDS."

"Let me be quite sure I understand you, Doctor.

235

You're saying that even if one tests positive for HIV, it may never develop into AIDS, is that correct?"

Dr. Axler smiled his genial smile. "Well, Mr. Belker, you are both correct and incorrect. Correct in summarizing my previous response. Testing HIV-positive certainly does not invariably lead to AIDS."

"And the incorrect part?"

"AIDS is not a fatal disease. AIDS affects the body's immune system, making the body susceptible to other diseases, but it does not itself directly cause death. The most frequent cause of death among AIDS victims is pneumonia."

"So . . . AIDS is not a fatal disease in and of itself?" Belker repeated, turning again to make eye contact with the jury.

"That's correct."

Belker nodded. He had made his point, and he was happy, Kathryn thought. Even though two of Hudson's victims had contracted AIDS, he was telling the jury, it didn't mean it would kill them. Knowing Belker, she knew there would be another half-dozen questions that had Axler more or less say the same thing. He wasn't taking any chances on the jury missing the point.

"One final question, if I may, Doctor," Belker concluded. "Taking into account the risks of unprotected sex, and the demonstrable failure rate of protective devices such as condoms, knowing as you do the extent, nature, and wide availability of literature on HIV and AIDS, would it be your expert opinion today that anyone—*anyone*—who engages in sex with a new partner knowingly assumes some risk, however small, of becoming infected by HIV?"

"Yes, that would be my expert opinion."

"Thank you, Doctor." Belker turned triumphantly to Judge Woods. "No further questions for Dr. Axler, Your Honor."

"Ms. Mackay?" Judge Woods inquired.

Kathryn sat at counsel table for several moments before rising. She stood and approached the witness, a perplexed look on her face.

"Dr. Axler, I hope you'll forgive me, but I'm a little confused by one of your answers to Mr. Belker's questions. I wonder if you could clear it up for me and the jury?"

The perplexed look and the hesitant approach were a technique Kathryn frequently used, identifying with the jury, who were often confused by expert testimony.

Dr. Axler smiled his ingratiating smile. "Of course, Ms. Mackay."

"Fine. Now, you stated that in your expert opinion, information about AIDS is so readily available to the general public that virtually anyone ought to be aware of it, and that engaging in behavior similar to that discussed in the literature, if such behavior is risky, constitutes a knowing and willing acceptance of that risk. Is that correct?"

Dr. Axler smiled, this time a little less genially. She saw him playing back the tape of what he had said inside his head and deciding he was on unassailable ground.

"Yes," he said stiffly. "I believe that's the substance of my testimony."

"Thank you. Doctor, you told us you work in Berkeley. Do you live there?" Kathryn inquired. In fact, she knew exactly where he lived, in San Francisco, in the neighborhood known to natives as "the Avenues."

Axler was puzzled by the change of direction. "No," he responded cautiously. "I live in San Francisco,"

"And how do you get to and from work each day, Doctor? Do you take public transportation?"

"No, I drive."

"I see. And when you commute to and from work, do you ever have occasion to use Gough and Franklin streets?"

She saw Martin Belker get to his feet. He had no idea where she was headed, but wherever it was, he clearly didn't like it.

"Objection, Your Honor!" Belker brayed. "The route Dr. Axler takes to and from work is irrelevant, as is his mode of transportation."

Kathryn smiled up at the judge. "Your Honor, if I may be permitted to proceed, I think the court will see the relevance of my questions," she said smoothly.

Judge Woods deliberated only momentarily. "Very well, Ms. Mackay, but make your point, please. Objection overruled. The witness will answer the question."

Like Belker, Dr. Axler sensed that this line of questioning was taking him somewhere he didn't want to go, but he had no choice but to answer.

"Yes, I drive Gough and Franklin streets almost every day."

"And, Doctor, are those streets—Gough and Franklin—very steep?"

Axler glanced at Belker, who was poised to object but knew it was too soon for him to do so again.

"Yes, they are among the steepest streets in San Francisco," he replied grudgingly.

"They certainly are. I have driven them myself, and I remember thinking, God help anyone whose brakes fail on *those* hills. Now, Doctor, are you aware that there is a small but quantifiable failure rate in the mechanical parts of automobiles—brake systems, for example?" Kathryn asked.

Belker was on his feet again. "Irrelevant, Your Honor! Besides, this witness isn't an expert on automobiles or mechanics. He's a doctor. Ms. Mackay should be instructed to restrict her inquiries to the area of Dr. Axler's expertise."

"Your Honor, the defense opened the door to this line of questioning by inviting Dr. Axler to comment on matters of common knowledge," Kathryn reasoned. "I merely wish to further expand Dr. Axler's testimony in that regard."

Woods looked at Belker without too much sympathy.

"She's right, Mr. Belker," he said gravely. "You asked Dr. Axler his opinion on matters of common knowledge. Now Ms. Mackay has the same right. Objection overruled."

"Doctor?" Kathryn said, moving a little closer to the witness. "Are you aware that mechanical systems on automobiles—brake systems, for instance—can fail from time to time? Please answer the question."

"Yes," Dr. Axler said testily. "Of course I am."

"And *how* do you know that, Doctor?"

"The fact that machines aren't perfect is a matter of common knowledge. Everyone knows that."

"Very good. Then, Doctor, doesn't that mean that each time you—or, for that matter, anyone else—

drive your car, you are knowingly and voluntarily accepting the risk that someone's brakes might fail? Do you believe, sir, that if a car's brakes failed on Gough Street, killing or injuring you or someone else, that because you are aware of and have accepted this extremely small risk, no action should be taken against the car's owner, *even if that person knew the brakes were faulty and failed to do anything about it and failed to tell you?*"

Too late, Martin Belker realized the trap Kathryn had led his witness into. He started to rise to object, but before he could open his mouth, Judge Woods waved him back to his seat.

"Well, that's . . . that's not exactly the same thing . . . that's not what I meant at all," James Axler stammered. "There's always some risk, but . . ."

"You're absolutely right, Doctor," Kathryn said. "There's always some risk in anything we do. So I ask you again, when the owner of that defective car gets into it and drives over Gough or Franklin streets, knowing those streets are extremely unsafe for cars with faulty brakes, and then injures or kills someone when the brakes do fail, do you advocate that the driver not be held accountable for his reckless, despicably antisocial behavior? That people may be exempted from advising persons whom they may knowingly endanger so that those persons may choose for themselves the level of risk they wish to assume? Would you, sir, knowingly drive your own car over those same streets knowing the brakes were about to fail, or would you—like any other decent, responsible person—take all reasonable precautions to avoid endangering innocent and unsuspecting passersby?"

Without waiting for Dr. Axler's response, Kathryn

turned and stalked back to her table. Even if he had made one, the doctor's answer would have been superfluous. She knew by looking at them that the jury had already taken her point.

Time to move on, she thought. The twin objects of cross-examination were first to discredit adverse witnesses and second to draw out from them, if possible, evidence favorable to your own case. That was where she was going now. She turned around to face the witness.

"Dr. Axler, you must be aware that statistics released at the 1995 White House conference on HIV and AIDS revealed that about five hundred thousand cases of AIDS have been diagnosed nationwide?"

"Yes, I am."

"And are you also aware of the fact that more than three hundred thousand people have died of the disease?"

"Of course."

"The toll has been heavy in California, hasn't it? Do you know the figures, Doctor?"

Dr. Axler's eyes were wary, but he had to answer. "I believe there have been approximately fifty-two thousand deaths."

"You're absolutely right," Kathryn said. "And isn't it also a fact that Santa Rita County has the seventh highest per capita incidence of AIDS in the State of California, that the epidemic has claimed the lives of more than three hundred and twenty-five county residents, and that officials estimate about one thousand more carry the virus?"

"I believe your statistics are substantially correct," the doctor replied.

Kathryn swooped. "You testified on direct that

contracting the HIV virus does not inevitably lead to AIDS. Tell me, Doctor, how do you reconcile your testimony with these frightening figures?"

"Objection, argumentative!" Belker shouted.

"Withdrawn," Kathryn said smoothly. "Dr. Axler, are you saying here you know *for certain* that a person who becomes infected with HIV will never contract AIDS?"

"No, I am not. I do not know. No one could know any such thing for certain," Axler replied edgily.

"In fact, Doctor, doesn't the undeniable fact that three hundred thousand people have died from AIDS if anything suggest the very reverse—the probability that a person who contracts HIV will die from AIDS?"

Belker was on his feet again. "Objection, calls for speculation!"

"Withdrawn," Kathryn said. "No further questions."

She smiled politely at the witness. He didn't smile back.

## 31

Angel's sanctum sanctorum was a three-room, one-and-a-half-bath apartment in a modern building on a hillside near the Mission Heights Mall. All of the rooms were neat almost to the point of austerity. Except for the bedroom.

The boudoir, as Angel preferred to think of it.

It was the largest room in the apartment, dominated by a four-poster bed with velvet draw curtains that actually worked and matching red velvet drapes on the windows. On one wall hung a full-length antique mirror with an ormolu frame, flanked by two full-sized framed Mucha prints.

This was where Angel came to life. No one had ever seen that. No one ever would. It was a ceremony as personal, as meaningful, as that of a matador donning the traje de luces, the suit of lights, before the corrida to come.

And tonight, what would it be?

Tonight, the sexy underthings chosen with such

*loving care from the Victoria's Secret catalog. Tonight, the clinging black silk dress with the cutaway that swooped almost to the coccyx, the tight halter top that emphasized the proud breasts. Tonight, the pure silk panties from Bloomie's, the stiletto heels, the diamante ear studs.*

*Simplicity. Elegance.*

*Tonight, the Estee Lauder makeup, the Chanel lip gloss and perfume, the Lancôme eyeshadow and lash thickener. The blond tresses combed and teased just so. Then the tan cashmere coat from Saks, the little black purse.*

*And hidden beneath them, the hatred.*

*None of them ever saw that. Angel was far too clever to let any of them see the rage burning behind the mask, the clothes, and the makeup, under the skin. Until it was too late. Until it was time for them to pay for what they had done, the way Patrick Hanlon had paid, the way Peter Valenzuela had paid.*

*Tonight, it would be Gray's turn to pay.*

*Gray was a Pisces, and gullible as a fish. All of them were. And, like all of them, Gray had swallowed Angel's astrological bait. It was hard to believe that men with otherwise lively, critical minds could believe in something discredited by scientific discoveries as long ago as the seventeenth century, but they did. They wanted to believe the heavens ruled their destiny, exercising impersonal sway over mere humans through cosmic energy, that in some mysterious way at birth they had been given a kind of blueprint that decreed the course they took through life.*

*Like wicked, wealthy, sybaritic Gray with his Dom Perignon and his inexhaustible supply of pot. He was waiting now in his beautiful Cathedral Heights home.*

*Waiting for Angel to tell him that with Mercury moving forward again and Mars boosting his energy, he could become tonight the real Gray instead of all the roles he played for others, bringing him celestial permission to embark again with Angel on the long, exquisitely excruciating voyage of sexual exploration they had shared before, each increment choreographed, expected. The breathless urgency of foreknowledge, the stormy sea of chastisement, the long, slow, lingering pirouettes of reward.*

*Angel knew exactly which delicately perverted little games Gray liked best, which little nuances excited him, which goads aroused him. And tonight, he would have them all, whatever depravities his iniquitous heart desired. Except for one thing, Angel thought, smiling. Tonight, one thing would be different.*

*Tonight, the climax would be . . . unique.*

# 32

Turning north off Alameda, Dave followed the climbing curve of North Laguna Drive around to Coronado Avenue and pulled to a stop outside the Field house, a three-bedroom ranch-style home with a patch of lawn in front in need of cutting. Rochelle Field answered the door, wiping her hands on a dish towel. Without makeup, her hair untidy and straggling, she looked wan and tired.

"I was just cleaning up after dinner," she said. "Did you eat? You want me to fix you something?"

"It's okay, I ate already," Dave lied. "How are you, 'Chelle?"

She lifted a shoulder and gave him a smile that didn't part her lips. "You know," she said. "Okay."

"Kids in bed?"

She nodded. "And don't even think about going up there to say good night," she said firmly. "Or they'll still be running around at ten o'clock."

246

"Anything you say, boss." Dave grinned. "Jim inside?"

"Go on in," Rochelle said. "You want a beer?"

"Thanks, 'Chelle, I'm fine," Dave told her, and went into the living room.

Jim Field was sitting on the sofa, apathetically watching TV. He looked up as Dave came in. "Thought I recognized that voice," he said, pointing the remote at the set.

"Leave it on if you're watching something," Dave said.

Field shook his head and switched the set off. "Crap," he said. "One thing you find out real quick if you're home all day, there's nothing but crap on TV."

"Oh, I don't know," Dave grinned. "All those soap operas. Just like real life."

"Crap," Field repeated. His face looked puffy, and his color was bad. There were coffee stains on his shirt, and he needed a shave. "So what brings you out here?"

"Just touching base," Dave said. "And one thing I wanted to check out with you."

"Shoot," Field said. "You want a beer?"

"'Chelle already offered me one," Dave said.

"Hell, have one. Gives me an excuse," Field said. "Hey, 'Chelle, how about a couple of Coors?"

"Sure, coming up," Rochelle called from the kitchen.

"Anything new on the bombing?" Jim asked as Rochelle came in and handed them their beer. She put a bowl of Doritos on the coffee table in front of the couch and went back into the kitchen.

"I just came from the Sheriff's Office," Dave said,

247

choosing not to notice Jim's use of the singular. "Walt Earheart says, and I quote, it's like shoveling stainless steel balls up a stainless steel hill and expecting them to stick."

"I know that feeling."

"Turns out, apart from being gay, Hanlon and Valenzuela had something else in common," Dave continued. "An astrologer in Mission Hills, a woman called Angel Flores. That name mean anything to you?"

"Angel Flores, Angel Flores," Field said, looking at the ceiling. "Sounds stagey, doesn't it? Angel Flowers."

"You ever hear it before?"

Field shook his head. "Sorry. Doesn't ring any bells with me."

Dave shrugged. "Just thought I'd check. It was always a long shot."

"Okay, Granz," Jim said. "What did you really come up here for? Out with it."

Dave held up his hands, palms out. "You got me wrong," he protested. "I came by to ask you about Angel Flores."

"Yeah, and check how the cripple is doing, right?" Field said sourly, lifting his bandaged arm.

"Hal Benton said to say hello," Dave said, ignoring the remark. "Wants to know when you're coming back to work."

"Good question," Field said. "*¿Quien sabe?* as they say in Chihuahua."

"Chill out, Jim, it's never that bad. You're just feeling down."

"You'd know."

"Listen to me, Jim," Dave said, his voice hard.

248

"I've been all the way down that road. I've had all the nightmares you're having, all the bogeymen crawling around in your skull. Looking at the woman you love and wondering if she shudders when she looks at you. Listening to that little green worm in your brain that keeps telling you you'll never be a whole man again, nothing will ever be the same, the tears and the self-pity. Lying in bed in the morning and wondering what's the fucking point of getting up, and lying in bed at four A.M. wondering if it wouldn't be a lot easier to just be dead. How am I doing, Jim? How am I doing?"

Field shook his head. "You—I never knew."

"There was a psychopath out there. We called him the Gingerbread Man, a bastard who was killing young women and mutilating their bodies. One night, I got a call from a guy who said he'd seen our man dumping the body of a girl, and I arranged to meet him in a parking lot. It turned out it was the killer. He fractured my skull with a wrench and then went to work on me with a surgical scalpel. Like a butcher slicing pork chops."

His voice was harsh. He touched the hairline scars that ran down the side of his face, a faraway look in his pale blue eyes.

"At first they thought I'd just die, but I pulled through. And then they told me the good news, Jim: maybe my face would heal, but my right hand was so badly chopped up they doubted I'd ever get back more than about thirty percent mobility. When I heard that, I thought, 'Shit, it's finished, just take me outside and shoot me.'"

"You never talked about . . . your hand," Jim Field said.

Dave held up his right hand, stretched the fingers wide, then made a fist.

"Four operations, physical therapy, you name it. And I worked. Jesus, how I worked at it. But that wasn't what got me out of the hole. What got me out of the hole was a lady by the name of Mackay."

Field frowned. "Kathryn?"

"See, she believed in me, Jim. Every time I gave up on myself—and there were quite a few times I did— she was there. She made me believe I could do it."

"Why are you telling me this?"

"Kathryn was my someone to keep trying for, Jim," Dave said. "She still is. You've got someone, too. Rochelle, the kids. Make a fight of it, Jim. Don't quit on them, okay?"

Jim Field looked at him eye to eye for a long, silent moment. Then he shook his head and smiled wryly. "Never figured you for a shrink," he said.

"And such reasonable consultation fees."

Jim held up the beer can in his left hand. "That mean you want another of these?"

Granz shook his head. "I'd better get going. Give me a rain check?"

"Sure," Jim said. "And Dave? I hear you."

"Knew you would," Dave said.

As he stood up, his pager began beeping. Rochelle Field heard it, too, and came in with a portable phone.

"I knew it would be County Comm," she said. "I already dialed them for you."

Dave took the phone and spoke into it. "County Comm, this is Inspector Granz," he said. He listened for a moment, nodded. "Cathedral Heights Drive,

8144, got it," he said. "Tell Ms. Mackay I'm in Alameda Heights, and I'll meet her at the scene."

He put down the phone and looked up to find Rochelle and Jim watching him intently.

"Bad?" Field said.

Dave nodded, his face grim. "We've got another one," he said. "Another fire bomb."

## 33

Cathedral Heights was up in the mountains about ten miles out of town in what its residents liked to call redwood country. With few homes in the area selling at less than a million dollars, it was one of those places where they just didn't have crime.

Well, Kathryn thought as she picked her way through the tangle of fire hoses lying on the wet gravel, they had it now. The CSI van was drawn up outside the house, the area cordoned off with yellow tape to ensure the integrity of the chain of evidence, investigators already at work checking for tire and shoe tracks. Kathryn saw Dave Granz's Jeep easing past the fire appliances and waited till he came across to join her. He didn't waste time on pleasantries.

"County Comm said a fire bomb," he said. "Same as the others?"

"Looks like, from what I read in the affidavit," Kathryn replied. As in the Hanlon and Valenzuela investigations, she had reviewed and approved the affidavit for the search warrant. "Let's go inside and take a look before they move the body to the morgue. Morgan should be in there already."

Dave nodded in agreement. "Does the SO have an ID on the victim yet?"

"Tentative one. Graham Carter," she told him as they ducked under the yellow tape and walked up the drive to the house. "You may remember there were a lot of news features on him sometime back. He made a serious fortune reissuing radio nostalgia on CD. As you can see from the home he built."

"Any witnesses, anyone see anything?"

"I talked to Walt on the cellular on the way over. Carter employs a Filipino cook-housekeeper, but she only works till seven. He's got detectives out checking the neighborhood, but the houses are so far apart up here . . ."

She shrugged and left the rest unsaid. Dave didn't need an explanation. The Carter house stood on almost an acre of wooded land, reached by a semicircular graveled drive that curved gently between the trees and was almost invisible from the road. It was the sort of home nobody ever goes into by mistake.

"Here comes Doc now," Dave said as the familiar figure of Morgan Nelson appeared backlit in the open doorway. He lifted a hand as he saw them.

"Katie," he said. "Dave. Looks like we've got another one. Body handcuffed to the bed, incendiary device ignited on the groin. Same kind of damage as last time, burned right through the body and the bed. Luckily, the bedroom has stone floors, so this time the place is in better shape."

"Same MO as before?" Dave said. "Naked? Feet tied, handcuffed? Indications of S&M?"

"Looks like. I won't be able to tell you for sure until I get him on the table."

"Who's the IO, Morgan?" Kathryn said.

"Harry di Stefano caught the call," Morgan said. "But Walt Earheart's taken over."

"There's Walt now," she said, and raised a hand. Earheart saw the signal and came over to join them. He appeared disgruntled and out of sorts, as if he was looking for someone he could blame for being called out on this.

"Boy," he said, exhaling gustily. "What a mess. It's good to breathe fresh air."

"How bad is it inside?" Dave asked.

"The bedroom's gutted," Earheart told him. "But apart from smoke damage, the rest of the house is pretty much okay. Maybe this time CSI will find something that gives us a handle on the bastard who's doing this."

"What about the housekeeper, Walt?" Kathryn asked. "Has she been located yet?"

"She lives in Prospect Heights. I sent Coughlin and Silvero down to interview her."

Kathryn nodded. The two SO detectives were one of the best teams on the force.

"If there's not much damage inside, maybe we'll be able to build up a better picture of the victim's lifestyle this time," Kathryn said. "Dave, check in with CSI. The warrant's 'wish list' includes Carter's business and personal records. Be sure they seize his address books, correspondence, computer files, e-mail, you know the drill."

"Got it," Dave said.

"Walt, my office can obtain Carter's medical, telephone, and utility records. We'll contact his bank. Seize his bank records and search any safe deposit boxes that turn up."

Earheart nodded automatically. They'd done all this before. As Kathryn finished speaking, a large white van with a dish antenna on its roof swung into the parking lot, and a young woman with blond hair that shone in the lights got out and looked around expectantly. She was followed by crew with cameras and mike booms.

"Shit," Walt Earheart said, his voice aggrieved. "Channel Eight. Just what we need." He shrugged his massive shoulders as if readying himself for combat and went across to talk to the TV people.

"You got any idea when you'll autopsy, Doc?" Dave asked Morgan.

"I imagine you guys'll want my protocol on this one sooner rather than later," Morgan said. It was a tenet of homicide investigation that you got your best chances of coming up with a suspect in the first forty-eight hours. Every day after that, the odds against finding the killer mounted. "How about tomorrow morning?"

"Sounds good to me," Dave said. "But Kathryn won't be—"

He stopped abruptly, his face stricken, realizing he had spoken out of turn. Kathryn touched his arm and smiled reassuringly.

"It's okay, Dave. Morgan knows."

"That so?" Dave said, and Kathryn thought she heard a thin thread of displeasure behind the words. It wasn't jealousy—pique, maybe. Dave had never really come to terms with her close relationship with

Morgan, maybe never would. She gave a mental shrug. Men were from Mars, Dave more than most. She loved him for what he was, not what she might be able to turn him into.

"You call me tomorrow, let me know how it went, Katie," Morgan said. "Dave, eleven A.M. in Siberia, okay?"

"Got it," Dave said again.

As Nelson hurried away, Kathryn glanced back toward the brightly lit area behind her. The bombings were beginning to attract as much media attention as her AIDS prosecution. Two more TV vans had arrived now, and another couple of cars. The blond reporter was talking to Walt Earheart. *He'll love that,* she thought.

"Let's go see what happened in there," she said, and led the way across to the house. Logging in with the cop on the door, they found themselves in a spacious tiled hall with a curved staircase, a coating of soot marring its paintwork. At the top of the stairwell was a hall with beige carpeting. A starkly modern painting hung askew on a wall above a soot-covered sofa and glass-topped table. Triple doors and a huge picture window looked out onto a deck that encircled the front of the house. Every flat surface was greasy to the touch. The carpets were soaked with water and blackened with stamped-down soot.

It was almost impossible to imagine what the interior of the master bedroom had originally looked like. Burned sticks that had been furniture, charcoal underfoot that had been carpet, charred remnants of drapes on the shattered windows formed a ghastly backdrop for the ruined bed on which the contorted body of Graham Carter lay, the pale whiteness of his upper body contrasting bizarrely with the seared and blackened flesh around his devastated groin.

As they came in, Charlie Yamamoto was taking overall and detailed color photographs and Polaroids of the scene. The zip and buzz of the camera drives and the bright flicker of the flash gun lit the room like a scene from Dante.

"Charlie, when you can, get some photos and video we can use in court, okay?" she said. "Like last time. Nothing too specific, you know what to do."

Charlie nodded. Witnesses and jurors in a trial were rarely as hardened to crime-scene photographs as cops. A set of pictures and video that minimized gore, genitals, and distracting background material was often very useful in both investigation and trial.

"Did Doc Nelson fix a time of death?" Dave asked Les Dougherty, who was standing outside the room with a gurney, waiting for clearance to take the body away.

"He said he couldn't be precise, but around nine."

Kathryn leaned over to examine the handcuffs shackling the dead man's wrists to the twisted brass headboard. As before, they were lined with lamb's wool.

"They look like the same kind as before," she said. "Are these things widely available?"

"They don't sell them in Safeway." Dougherty grinned. "But if you know where to shop . . ."

"Would that be somewhere to start? Specialty places, sex shops?"

"SO has already covered that angle," Dave said. "Anyway, most of the people who use this sort of stuff usually buy mail-order. But you're right, it might be worth another shot."

They went back down to the ground floor and out into the cool night air. Walt Earheart was standing outside talking into his squawk box.

"Do you need me for anything else?" she asked when he was through. Earheart gave her a negative head shake.

"We're closing it down as soon as the TV people have got what they want."

"Ten seconds on the local news," she said. "Not much to get burned alive for, is it?"

"Some people will do anything to get into the movies," Walt said with a tired smile.

"Okay, I'm outta here," Kathryn said. "Dave, see you later."

She walked to her car around the outside of the crowd, avoiding the TV reporters. One of them recognized her and waved, but Kathryn pretended not to notice. She needed time alone now. Time to psych herself up for tomorrow. Time to think about consequences.

Time.

It was the most precious commodity in the world. You spent it from a purse that could never be refilled and never thought of what you were spending.

She drove back to Espanola, up the hill to her condo, and parked the car outside. Like closing a door, she put the awful sights she had seen out of her mind. The air was summer-soft and balmy. It was good to be alive. She looked up at the sky. The stars were coming out.

*Waiting, waiting, how I hate waiting.*

# 34

Ed Hatch looked slightly taken aback when he opened his apartment door and saw Dave Granz standing in the hall outside. Granz showed him his badge.

"Like to ask you a few questions, Mr. Hatch," he said. "Could you spare me a minute?"

"Police?" the old man said. "I already talked —"

"I'm an inspector from the District Attorney's office, Mr. Hatch," Dave told him. "How are you feeling?"

Hatch shook his head irritably. "Had the damnedest hacking cough ever since that fire," he complained. "Feels as if the damn smoke got stuck inside my throat. Can't seem to cough it up."

He was wearing a baggy, stained white polo shirt over grubby slacks, with carpet slippers on his feet. His eyes were rheumy, and his hair was uncombed; he needed a shave.

"May I come in, sir?"

"What?" Hatch looked surprised. "Oh, sure, sure. Place is a bit of a mess, you know how it is."

The layout of the apartment was almost exactly the same as Peter Valenzuela's: a sort of hallway, with the kitchen on the right, opened up into the living room with the bedroom on the left. The air was stale, and Dave was conscious of a persistent smell, somewhere between unwashed clothing and cooked cabbage.

The wood-block floor was badly in need of sanding and polishing, Dave noticed, with a frayed carpet at its center. Beneath the two windows looking out onto the street was a table and four ladderback chairs. In the center of the table lay a big, battered, leatherette-bound Bible. In one corner, two sagging armchairs were arranged in front of a twenty-seven-inch Motorola TV that was probably the most valuable thing in the apartment. On one wall was a bookcase with what looked like family photos on top, on the other a glass-fronted cabinet containing dozens of miniature liquor bottles. Hatch followed Dave's gaze.

"Collected them for years," he said. "Me and the wife. We'd go to Mexico, get tequila, go to Canada, get whiskey."

"Are you a widower, sir?" Dave asked.

"Ellie died six years ago," Hatch told him. "Fifty-seven. Cancer of the esophagus."

"I'm sorry."

"The Lord giveth, and the Lord taketh away," Hatch said philosophically. "I was just making coffee. It's only instant, you want some?"

"Instant's fine."

"Comin' up," Hatch said, and bustled off. While he was in the kitchen, Dave glanced at the framed pictures on top of the bookcase. One was a wedding photograph, its colors faded by age. The young man in Army uniform was clearly Edward Hatch. His bride was dark-haired, plump, cheerful-looking. In a silver frame next to it, a smiling young couple stood outside a frame house, proprietorial pride on their faces. Son, perhaps, or daughter, he decided. There were a number of smaller photographs, most of them of a young tow-headed boy and a little girl with long blond hair at different ages. Grandchildren, he guessed.

"How do you take it?" the old man called from the kitchen.

"Black, no sugar," Dave said. "You were in the service, Mr. Hatch?"

"Right," Hatch said as he reappeared from the kitchen carrying two cups. He handed one to Dave. "How'd you know?"

"Just looking at your pictures," Dave said. "World War Two, right?"

"Volunteered in 'forty-four," Hatch said. "Feet never touched the ground. We shipped out to England right after D-Day. I was assigned to the Third Army, activated August first. You know who commanded the Third Army?"

"No, sir, I don't."

"General George S. Patton. Old Blood and Guts, we called him. Ever hear of him?"

"Yes, sir. There was a movie—"

"Movies!" the old man said contemptuously. "It wasn't like in the movies, son. Two hundred and eighty-one days we fought, all the way from France to Czechoslovakia. They gave me the Silver Star. My boy Teddy has it, that's his photo there."

"Rough times," Dave observed.

"'I will say of the Lord, He is my refuge and my fortress: my God; in Him will I trust.' Psalm 91. You can sit down if you want to."

"This is fine," Dave said, leaning against the door-jamb. Time to move the conversation into the present, he thought. "How about we go over what happened the day of the fire together?"

"You people found out who done that yet?"

"Not yet, sir. Look, why don't I just ask you a few questions, okay? Maybe jog your memory."

"I talked to all those police downtown. Told them everything."

"I saw the reports, sir. I'd just like to go over what you remember, if you don't mind."

Edward Hatch shrugged and sat down in one of the armchairs. *Please yourself,* his body language said.

"What was the weather like that day, Mr. Hatch?" Dave asked.

The question clearly wasn't what Hatch had expected. He canted his head to one side so he looked like a curious rooster.

"Weather?" he said.

"Nice day?"

"It was a real nice morning. No mist, warm."

"You'd gone out to do what?"

"I went over to the Seven-Eleven, I was out of milk for breakfast."

"Can you remember what time you left, Mr. Hatch?"

Hatch shrugged his bony shoulders. "Nine-thirty, quarter of ten, something like that."

"Lot of traffic about?"

"Traffic?" Hatch said, his voice querulous. "What's traffic got to do with it?"

"Just trying to put you back there that day in your mind, Mr. Hatch," Dave said disarmingly. "Now,

262

why don't you tell me what happened? Don't leave anything out, no matter how unimportant."

One of the newer techniques of interrogation was what was known as the cognitive interview. In typical police interviews, detectives basically asked the witness to tell what happened, which resulted in a narrative response followed by a series of questions about detail. Then they went over it again from the top. In the cognitive interview, the questioner tried to trigger memory by taking the witness back to the crime scene and asking the witness to tell what he or she saw and not to hold back any detail, however trivial. When the account was finished, the questioner then asked follow-up questions in reverse order, starting at the end of the story and working back. Although it took a little longer, the technique produced not only more pertinent detail but often as much as a third more facts than before. Kathryn and Dave had used the technique together many times.

"Easy enough," Edward Hatch said, pulling on an earlobe. "You want s'more coffee?"

"No, thanks," Dave said. "So you were on your way back from the Seven-Eleven. Then what happened?"

"I had the sack in my arms, milk, I bought some English muffins. I crossed over the street, said hello to Bill Miner, the old gray ghost we call him, plays pool all day down there in Duffy's bar. When I got to the door, I had to back in, the door's got a strong spring on it. That was when I saw the woman, and I sort of—"

"Woman?" Dave said sharply. "You never mentioned a woman when you talked to the sheriff's detectives."

Edward Hatch frowned. "Sure I did. I told them. Sure I did."

"No, sir, you did not."

"Well, hell, it was just some woman, couldn't be that important, could it?"

"Let me decide that, Mr. Hatch," Dave said urgently. "Okay, here it is, you're coming back from the Seven-Eleven, you come into the foyer of the building, and you see a woman. What was she doing?"

"Leaving, I guess. I didn't pay her too much mind."

"Can you remember what she was wearing?"

"Sure. She had on a tan coat, she kind of pulled up the lapels, ducked her head down as she passed me. And I thought, funny that, why would she care if I saw her or not?"

"You didn't speak to her?"

"Apocrypha 3:23," Hatch intoned. " 'Be not curious in unnecessary matters: for more things are showed unto thee than men understand.' "

"Sure, sure. So the woman—she went out of the building. Did she go up the hill or down?"

"Down, toward Altamira. I seen her through the window as I got in the elevator."

"Okay, you're in the elevator. What happened next?"

"I thought I heard something on the way up, but you know how it is these days, every place you go they play that damn rinky-tink music. Soon's the elevator doors opened, I smelled smoke. And I heard someone screaming."

"You said it was a man's voice—are you sure?"

"Sounded like it. I ran along the hall to my door. I was going to call the police. Then I saw smoke coming out of 3B. Old Henry Thorn come out his door, and I yelled at him, 'Call the fire department!'"

"Had the screaming stopped?" Dave asked.

"Far as I remember, yes."

"The building doesn't have smoke alarms?"

Hatch made a contemptuous sound. "Cheapskate who owns this place? You must be kidding."

"How bad was the fire by then?"

"Smoke everywhere, couldn't see a hand in front of your face," Ed Hatch said pridefully. "Then the door blew out into the hall, *whoomph!* Darn near got me, but someone pulled me back, I don't know who. I heard sirens, and then I guess I blacked out. When I woke up, I was in the ambulance on my way to the hospital."

"Thank you, Mr. Hatch," Dave said. "That's fine. Just a few more questions, then I'll get out of your hair."

"I'm not going anyplace," the old man said with a shrug.

"Does the name Patrick Hanlon mean anything to you, Mr. Hatch?"

Hatch shook his head. "Nope."

"Graham Carter?"

"Nope."

"These are their photographs. You ever see either of them, visiting Valenzuela, maybe?"

Ed Hatch stared at the photographs, then shook his head a third time.

"Not as I recall."

"Okay. This friend of yours, Bill Miner," Dave said. "Where would I find him?"

"Now? Your best bet is Duffy's, down the hill and

265

around the corner of Altamira. He hangs out there all the time."

"Can you remember what you said to him that morning? On your way back from the Seven-Eleven?"

Hatch frowned. "Something about the weather. Gonna be another hot one, gonna get hot today, something like that."

"Then you came into the building."

"Like I told you. I had the shopping sack in both my hands, so I had to push the door open with my butt."

"And that was when you saw the woman?" Dave said.

"She was just coming out the elevator."

"You said she was wearing a tan coat. What kind of coat? Long? Short?

"Long. Midcalf."

"What kind of material? Close your eyes, think."

"Wool, maybe. Good quality."

"Did it have a belt?" Dave asked.

"No. It was loose, full. Like it was more for evening wear."

"Good, good. What kind of collar?"

"I don't recall."

"You said she tried to hide her face," Dave said. "How?"

"With the coat col—oh, I get it. Yeah. Yeah. A big turnup collar, right? Right."

"Okay, we're doing great," Dave said. "Tan coat, no belt, big turnup collar. What kind of shoes?"

Hatch furrowed his brow again. "I didn't notice."

"What's the floor in the hall made of?"

"Tiled, sort of imitation marble."

"Did she make a noise as she walked?"

Hatch's brow cleared. "Yeah. Sure she did. *Click click click.* Heels, she had on heels."

"How tall?"

Hatch shrugged. "Medium. Five-eight, like that?"

"What about her hair?"

"Long, blond."

"Straight or curled?"

"Oh, curled. Real stylish."

"What color eyes?"

"I told you, she kind of ducked her head. I couldn't really see."

"Was she carrying anything? Purse? Shoulder bag?"

"No purse. Just a sort of briefcase."

"A leather briefcase?"

Hatch shook his head. "Just one of those black webbed plastic things with the Velcro handles, you know, ten bucks in Woolworth."

"You said she wore heavy makeup. What did you mean?"

"It was like, you know, piled on. Overdone."

"You mean thickly applied?"

"Yeah. And a lot of lipstick. That shiny stuff."

"Lip gloss? Red, pink, what?"

"Red. Like a wound."

"Why'd you think she hid her face?"

"I figured she didn't want to be recognized."

"You ever see her before?"

"No."

"You're certain?"

"Sure."

"Then why would she be afraid of you recognizing her?"

The frown reappeared on Ed Hatch's forehead. "Good question, son," he said. "I never thought of that. I just figured, you know, maybe she was someone else's wife, or a call girl, or maybe she was peddling drugs."

"That happen a lot in this building?"

"Well, no. I just figured."

"Why?"

"You know. The way she looked. Overdone. Tarty."

"Mr. Hatch," Dave said. "You're terrific."

Ed Hatch looked at him in astonishment. "What?"

"Your buddy Bill Miner," Dave said, standing up. "You said I'd find him at Duffy's, right?"

"What you want to talk with him for?" Hatch said querulously.

"So he can help us catch the lunatic who killed Peter Valenzuela and put him in prison," Dave told him.

"Remember Saint Paul to the Romans," the old man said sententiously. " 'Vengeance is mine; I will repay, saith the Lord.' "

"Not if I get there first, he won't," Dave told him.

# 35

"I've been trying to reach you," Walt Earheart said as Dave Granz walked into his office. "I think we've finally got a break. Take a look."

Fanned out on his desk was a pile of color photographs, not the usual police eight-by-tens but standard 35-millimeter snapshots. Groups of men in casual clothes, some at the beach, others standing by a car, somewhere in San Francisco by the look of it.

"Where did you get these from?"

"CSI seized them at Carter's house," Walt said. "Recognize anyone?"

Dave shrugged. "Can't say I do."

Earheart grinned. "When you saw them, they weren't looking their best," he said. He laid a finger on one of the shots that showed a slender man in his late forties standing beside another shorter, thicker-set man with dark curly hair.

"The one on the left is Carter," Earheart said. "The guy on the right is Peter Valenzuela."

269

Dave looked up sharply. "They knew each other?"

"Pretty well, by the look of it," Walt said. "Here they are again. And here."

"What about these others? This is Valenzuela again, right? But who's this guy in the other photograph?"

Earheart smiled. "Thought you'd have guessed," he said. "It's Hanlon."

"That means—"

"Wait," Earheart said, holding up a hand. "There's more."

"Tell me."

"We submitted incident summaries of our bombing homicides to the FBI Bomb Data Center. Turns out Santa Clara County Sheriff's Office had submitted an incident report that matched the MO of the Hanlon, Valenzuela, and Carter homicides. The BDC faxed us a copy of their report. A guy by the name of Lawrence Sutterfield was found burned to death on June ninth in Saratoga. As I said, same MO, same bomb materials, but the narrative statement of the report puts Sutterfield in the company of a young woman in the early afternoon hours preceding his death."

"I'll be damned," Dave said. "That's what I came up here to tell you, Walt. There was a woman at the Valenzuela scene. She was seen leaving the apartment building just a few minutes after the fire started."

Earheart raised his eyebrows. "Where did this come from?"

"The old boy who fought the fire, Ed Hatch."

Earheart frowned. "How come he never told us when we interviewed him?"

"He didn't think it was important, just some woman he passed in the hall."

"She didn't live there?"

"He said he never saw her before," Dave said. "But here's the kicker, Walt. Someone saw her on the street after she left the building, a guy named Bill Miner. He swears what he saw was a man dressed up as a woman."

Earheart stared at Dave without speaking for a long moment. "Jesus, Dave, are you sure?" he said finally, and sat down. "A transvestite?"

"Walt, remember what Doc Nelson said about the dominatrix? It all fits together, the S&M, the bondage, the whip marks . . ."

"Okay, suppose you're right," Earheart said. "Where do we start looking for the wom—the guy?"

"CSI seized an address book from Carter's home, correct?" Dave asked.

Earheart nodded. "Bingo," he said, and tossed a slim leather-bound indexed book onto the desk.

"You going to tell me, or do I have to look myself?" Dave said.

"Hanlon, Valenzuela, they're both in there. And so is our old friend Angel Flores."

"Angel Flores. Jesus, yes, of course!" Dave said. "That's it, Walt! Don't you see? That's our mystery cross-dresser. It's got to be. Your detectives thought she was a woman because they saw the word *astrologer*. But probably that's just a cover. That's how she—he—makes his sexual contacts."

"You saying you think this Angel Flores could be the bomber?"

"Make me a better offer."

"Say you're right. Then who was the target in the courtroom?"

"I've been wondering about that, too. Then something Rochelle Field said popped up in my mind. She

271

said, 'Why is it always good people who get hurt—why don't they bomb the bad guys?' And I thought, what if the target of the courtroom bombing was Hudson?"

"But . . . Hudson's straight," said Walt. "Isn't he?"

"You thought so. We all thought so. But what if we're wrong? What if he's bisexual? Walt, if he's somehow connected to Hudson, Valenzuela, or Carter, all this would start to make some sense."

"What do you want to do?" Earheart said. "Go over to the jail and ask him?"

Dave shook his head. "He's got a lawyer, Walt, which complicates things. Besides, there's someone else we need to talk to first."

"You mean Angel Flores?" Earheart said. "I told you, we already tried to locate her half a dozen times, how do you—?"

He was talking to himself. Dave was already on his way.

# 36

Dave didn't say a word as they came into the condo, just took Emma's hands in his and adopted the conspiratorial adult-to-adult tone of voice that virtually guaranteed she would do anything he asked.

"Listen, Em, your mom needs a couple of hours to herself," Kathryn heard him telling her daughter. "How about you and I take Sam for a walk on the beach?"

"Cool," Kathryn heard Emma reply.

"Does cool mean you want to go?" Dave asked her with a smile, remembering when "hot" meant yes.

"Of *course* it does, Dave," Emma said with more than a hint of impatience.

Kathryn smiled as she heard the door close behind them. It was uncanny the way Dave read her moods, always a surprise to find such sensitivity under that brusque, no-shit exterior. Very few people were privileged to see that side of Dave, and she considered herself lucky to be one of them. She knew exactly

273

when he picked up on her unspoken message—as they were entering the Breast Center parking lot after her biopsy, she had kind of leaned into him as they got to the car, her head on his shoulder.

"You know what, Dave?" she said. "I'm tired."

"Is that a fact?" he responded with heavy irony. "You damn near got killed in a bombing, you've been putting in sixteen hours a day with the Hudson trial and the bomb investigation, and you top it all off with a biopsy, then what do you do? You complain you're *tired!* Boy, what a wimp!" He kissed her on top of her head. He loved the smell of her hair.

They had driven over to pick up Emma in silence, not needing to talk, and as soon as they walked through the door, he had whisked Em and Sam off to the beach, Sam's tail wagging happily as they strolled down the hill. And, the truth was, Kathryn was glad to get the time alone, some space in which to organize her thoughts.

Before she went to the Breast Center, she had decided that the best way to put the medical rituals out of her mind would be to concentrate on something else. So, as the white-gowned nurse prepped her for the procedure, Kathryn directed her thoughts away from what was happening to her body, concentrating instead on the closing argument she would make the following day in the Hudson case. And, to her mild surprise, it had worked. By the time the doctor was finished, she had decided on the points she needed to make and how to make them.

The local anesthetic ensured that the operation itself was painless, as Dr. Snyder had promised, but Kathryn found the experience of being conscious of everything that was happening to her body without the appropriate accompanying sensations oddly unsettling.

"You can take the bandage off tomorrow," Dr. Snyder told her afterward. "Shower, if you like."

"Will I feel pain after the anesthetic wears off?" asked Kathryn.

"Not significant pain. Take a couple of Tylenol if it keeps you awake. Go home, take it easy. I'll call you tomorrow with your test results."

"Thanks, Doctor. For everything."

"No thanks necessary, Kathryn," Dr. Snyder replied, giving Kathryn a small hug.

And now the waiting began, and the questions that would not go away stalked through her mind like jungle cats. *Is it cancer? Will I lose my breast? Worse, my life?*

Who'd look after Emma?

She knew what Dave would say if she put the question into words. And he would mean it, too. There was no one in the world better for Emma—providing Kathryn was there as well. But could Dave handle Emma alone? Could he be her father, mother, teacher, and confidant as well as chauffeur, cook, cheering section, and support team?

No matter how many times she chased it around inside her head, Kathryn couldn't come to an acceptable conclusion. She sighed and opened her laptop, trying to concentrate on her closing argument. *Try not to worry about tomorrow,* Marie Snyder had said. The unspoken question lurking in the deep recesses of her mind would not go away so easily.

*What will I do if it's cancer?*

\* \* \*

The evening was warm and windless, the ocean flat and calm and the sky the color of blueberries. Down below, the Shelter Island lighthouse beamed its bright signal toward unseen ships on an unseeable horizon.

"Finished your closing?" Dave asked as Kathryn walked out onto the balcony and sat down in the lounge chair beside his.

"I think so," she said. "I can run through it again before court tomorrow morning."

*Tomorrow. Don't think about it.*

"You ought to get an early night," Dave suggested gently.

"Yes, Mother," she said, sipping the hot cup of tea Dave had brewed for her, glad of the warmth it put inside her.

"You're preoccupied, I can tell. What is it, the bombings?"

Kathryn could read Dave's moods almost as well as he read hers. *Does that make us soul mates?* she wondered.

"It can wait," Dave said. "Dr. Snyder told you to take it easy."

"She meant my body, not my mind. Come on, what is it?"

"Angel Flores."

Dave told her about his interview with Ed Hatch earlier that day, his discovery that the woman who had been seen leaving the building where Peter Valenzuela had been torched might have been a man, and his later conversation with Walt Earheart.

By running Angel Flores's telephone number through the cross-directory, he told her, detectives had speedily determined that Flores lived in a ground-floor apartment in Mission Hills, not far from the Hillside Shopping Center.

"Earheart had sent deputies up there a few times trying to locate Flores, but they never found anybody home. I checked with neighbors, and one of them, a Mrs. Marina Blythc, said Flores only comes up there occasionally. I contacted the property management company that manages the apartment complex, and they told me the rent is always paid by a Bank of America check card."

"Did you contact B of A?" asked Kathryn.

"I went up to the Mission Hills branch this morning. Right after I talked with Walt. I spoke with the manager. He said all he is permitted to tell me is whether someone has an account with the bank and, if so, what the account number is. Government Code Section 7480 prohibits his giving out anything more without a court order."

"And?"

"And Angel Flores has a check card account with B of A. She, or he, simply presents the card number to the property management company to pay the apartment rent and signs an authorization slip. The rent amount is automatically deducted from the checking account into which the deposits are made. There aren't any checks written. Deposits are always made at ATMs. No face-to-face contact with anyone in any branch of B of A."

"Couldn't you get anything else on the account?"

"Not without a court order. So I got in touch with a guy I know. We worked on an embezzlement case a few years ago and recovered some money for the bank. He agreed to give me some information if I promised to forget where I heard it."

Kathryn made an angry exclamation, and he held up his hands in a mock surrender.

"I know, I know, you don't like me making deals like that, but we've got to have this stuff today."

"Damnit, Dave!" Kathryn's exasperation with his *fait accompli* was real. Even though she knew he had done the street-smart thing, it didn't mean she couldn't register her disapproval. "Okay, no questions about who told you—what did you find out?"

"Well, for openers, he said that on the application form opening the account, Flores gave the County Planning Department as employer."

"The Planning Department? Then we can easily—"

Dave held up a hand. "Uh-unh. Way ahead of you. The Planning Department personnel officer was my next stop. Nobody named Angel Flores has ever worked there."

"Damn. Where does that leave us?"

"I'm not sure. But something is weird. The apartment no one lives in. The bank account that's accessed by remote control. The telephone number with no long-distance or message-unit phone calls that can be traced. Everything's set up to give nothing away. It's like chasing a goddamn ghost." The tension in Dave's voice revealed his frustration.

"Well, we know Angel Flores exists," Kathryn insisted.

"Not necessarily," Dave answered. "It's a lot of work, but it's still possible to put together a false identity. Start in the Santa Rita cemetery. Find the grave of a child who was born about the same time you were, but died during infancy. Not uncommon at

278

all. Armed with the name, date of birth, name of the child's mother and father, apply for a replacement birth certificate from the County Clerk-Recorder's office. You'd have to swear out an affidavit of loss, but that's no problem. The certified birth record becomes the foundation of your new identity. Using the birth certificate, apply for a Social Security number. Take those two documents to the Department of Motor Vehicles and get a driver's license. From there on, it's a piece of cake. Credit cards and charge accounts are easy. Pretty soon, you've created a brand-new person—who doesn't exist."

"Okay, the next logical question is why? Why would someone go to all this trouble? Especially the apartment."

"That's a good question. Maybe she, or he, needs a place to change identities," Dave speculated. "To metamorphose. Or maybe . . ."

"Or maybe what?"

"Hey," Dave said very softly. "What if . . . suppose the apartment is where she—he—makes the bombs."

Kathryn stared at him incredulously. "Are you sure you don't read minds?"

"What?"

"I'll explain later," she said. "Go on, go on."

"My instincts say Angel Flores doesn't exist," Dave explained. "That nobody actually lives at the Mission Hills apartment, at least not full-time. And she— damnit, why do I keep saying *she*—whoever this Angel Flores is, I'm sure of one thing, it's not a woman—it's a man who cross-dresses as a woman. Sure as hell."

"Okay, let's say you're right," Kathryn said. She

wanted Dave to confirm her profile without any prompting. "Flores is a man, not a woman. Tell me what he's like."

"Young," Dave said, thinking out loud. "From what Hatch told me, he has to be. Young and good-looking, slim, medium to slight build. Intelligent, too, enough to be attractive to men of very different backgrounds. Those victims weren't dummies. Plenty of social skills, charm, sophistication. But behind that exterior there's a psychopath. Another bomb waiting to go off."

"Very good," Kathryn said.

Dave leaned forward. "What did you mean when you said did I read minds? Have you worked up a profile?"

Kathryn nodded confirmation. "It's preliminary and incomplete, but we definitely agree on the salient points. We see the same guy."

"Go on."

"I talked it through with Morgan Nelson. Our preliminary findings show that the bomber is most likely a white man, late twenties or early thirties, possibly abused as a child or young adult. He'll either be living alone or with someone who's very permissive and uncritical. He's intelligent, good with people, may speak Spanish, and probably works in the public sector or for a service-oriented company. And he has a compelling need for escape occasionally. Craves solitude when his mood regresses to childhood. A secret apartment would be perfect."

"Public sector." Dave knitted his brow in concentration and looked skyward. "That fits, Kathryn. Someone who knows his way around the County Building could have put that letter bomb on the counsel table without drawing attention to himself. And Flores pretended to be with the Planning Department on the bank application. Probably the first thing that came to mind at the time."

"It's promising," Kathryn said. "But it doesn't get us anywhere. What we need is a link between Flores and one of the bombings. Even a weak link would be enough. That would be enough probable cause to get a warrant to search the Mission Hills apartment."

"Richard Hudson," Dave said.

"What about him?"

"What if Hudson was the bomber's target?"

Kathryn frowned. "Hudson's not gay."

"That's what Walt said, too, but what if we're wrong? Suppose he's bisexual. Then it all starts to come together. It would explain his relationships with your victims but still connect him to Flores. Hell, Kathryn, maybe Hudson just isn't out of the closet."

Kathryn was silent for a long moment, assimilating the implications of what Dave just said. She had learned long ago never to dismiss even the most bizarre idea without full consideration. An old friend had once told her, "Always remember, when one door closes, another door opens." It was advice she never forgot. Was this a new door opening?

Dave interrupted. "We need to talk to Hudson, Kathryn. And sooner rather than later. Can you fix that?"

"It's pretty tricky," Kathryn told him. "The Sixth Amendment prohibits police-initiated questioning of a represented suspect regarding the crime he has a lawyer for. And Hudson's represented by counsel."

"I know that. But the prohibition only applies to those crimes he's charged with, doesn't it? I'm no lawyer, but I wouldn't have thought that prevents us from talking to him about other matters. Or does it?"

Kathryn shook her head. "The Sixth Amendment restriction doesn't apply if we only question Hudson about a crime other than the one he's charged with."

"Then let's go."

"Wait, wait," Kathryn said. "Hudson has previously invoked his Fifth Amendment Miranda rights to counsel. All police interrogation, no matter what it's about, is barred unless his lawyer is present. Which means there's only one way we can talk to him—with Belker there."

"Shit," Dave said angrily. "Well, it will have to do. We need to talk to this guy, Kathryn."

"I know," Kathryn said, making her decision. "And we're going to, right now. I'll call Ruth to come up and stay with Emma. You contact Belker, have him meet us at the jail right away. Tell him we need to talk with his client, and don't take no for an answer."

"Let him try," Dave said.

# 37

"What are you going to do?" Angel said.

"I don't know. I don't know."

"Granz is getting too close. You heard what Marina said. He's talked to the property manager. He's probably talked to the bank. You can't let him find out . about me. You have to stop him."

She was right, of course. She was always right. It had been a shock to learn from their Mission Hills neighbor that Granz had been poking around, the questions he had been asking. No one had asked those kinds of question before. It had all seemed foolproof. How much had he found out? How much had he guessed? How dangerous was he?

"He can't stop us," Angel said. "You mustn't let him jeopardize the plan. Richard Hudson has to die. You promised me."

"It's too dangerous, Angel. It's . . . this isn't the way I wanted it."

*"There's no choice. You know there's no choice."*
*"I know. But how, Angel? How?"*
*"You'll think of a way. You always do."*
*"His car? That big red Jeep he's so proud of?"*
*"Yes," Angel said fiercely. "Yes, good, yes."*

# 38

"You know who I am, Mr. Hudson," Kathryn said. "This is Inspector David Granz of the DA's office."

"I've seen him in court," Hudson said.

Dave said nothing but nodded his acknowledgment at Richard Hudson and his attorney, Martin Belker. They were sitting in the interview room of the Santa Rita County Jail, a matching single-story complex built at the same time and from the same uncompromising concrete as the County Building. Furnished with only the bare necessities: a rectangular, battleship-gray steel table bolted to the floor, four upright chairs, and a wall telephone to communicate with the jail officers outside, the room stank of stale tobacco smoke and sweat. Hudson and Belker sat together on one side of the table, Kathryn and Dave opposite, nearer the door.

"What do you people want?" Hudson asked.

It wasn't immediately apparent whether the ques-

285

tion was directed at Belker or Kathryn, but it was obvious Hudson wasn't happy.

"As I told Mr. Belker, we'd like to ask you a few questions. It won't take long. I'd like to record the interview, if I may."

When Belker signaled his approval, Dave placed a mini-cassette recorder on the table in front of Kathryn, punched the Record button, checked that the tape was turning, and nodded to Kathryn.

"For the record, it is June twenty-ninth, six forty-five P.M.," she began. "Present are myself, Kathryn Mackay, District Attorney Inspector David Granz, Richard Hudson, and Mr. Hudson's attorney, Martin Belker. Mr. Belker, you've consented to your client's interview, correct?"

"Contingent upon your assurance that this matter does not relate to the ongoing trial of my client."

"You have that assurance," Kathryn told him. "We wish to ask your client some questions about a totally different matter. A murder investigation."

"Wait a minute—" Hudson said.

"You're not a suspect, Mr. Hudson," Kathryn reassured him. "But we think you may have some information that may assist law enforcement in identifying the killer."

"Really?" Hudson said smoothly. "I can't imagine how. I feel like I've been in jail so long, I'm not sure I even remember who's president anymore."

He smiled at his own little joke. He was relaxed and self-assured, as if the shabby little room was his own apartment, Kathryn and Dave friends who had dropped in. It wasn't going to be easy to crack that confidence, Kathryn thought. His treatment of the women he had infected with HIV, everything she knew about him, told her Hudson was one of those men who consider themselves superior to the common herd and not bound by its rules.

"Well, why don't we ask you a few questions and see?" she proposed.

"Of course," Hudson said urbanely. "But let me ask you something before you begin. If I cooperate, if I come up with something that would help you, what's in it for me?"

Belker raised his hand palm outward to silence him. "Please let me handle this, Richard," he said firmly. "Ms. Mackay, I've advised my client that it may be in his interest to listen to what you have to say. So why don't you lay it out for us? If my client knows anything that would be helpful to you, then we can talk about what he can expect in return."

"Of course," Kathryn said. "Now, Mr. Hudson, have you been reading the newspaper while you've been in jail?"

Hudson frowned. "Sure. The *Gazette*. Why?"

"Then you'll have read about this series of bombings we've been having," Dave suggested.

"Oh, is that what this is all about? Yes, I saw the headlines. I didn't pay much attention, though. What I saw looked pretty gruesome." He gave a theatrical little shudder—an untypically feminine reaction, Kathryn thought.

"Mr. Hudson, the information I'm going to give you now is confidential; it has not been revealed in the press." Kathryn glanced at Belker and then back at Hudson for a reaction, but got none. "The media have reported these incidents as fire-bombings, but we have withheld the information that in each instance the victim was killed by an incendiary device that was placed directly on his genitals. They were literally burned alive."

Kathryn's intent was to shock both Hudson and Belker—and from the expressions on their faces, it had worked.

"Jesus, Mary, and Joseph," Hudson exclaimed softly. "On the genitals? What kind of lunatic would do a thing like that?"

"We believe the killings are related," Kathryn continued. "We believe the victims were all killed by one person, someone they were involved with sexually. And we believe the killer will strike again; there will be more victims unless you help us."

"I'm sorry, Ms. Mackay, but I don't see how my client could possibly have any information that would be of use to you," Belker protested. "He was in custody before the bombings began."

"We know that, Marty, and as I said, he obviously isn't a suspect." She turned her gaze fully on Hudson. "What we want to explore is the possibility he may have known one or more of the victims. Did you, Mr. Hudson?"

He frowned. "Know them? No, of course I didn't know them."

"You didn't know a Patrick Hanlon?"

"No." Hudson smiled disarmingly. "Look, I mean, I read his name in the paper. But that's all."

"What about Peter Valenzuela?"

"No."

"Graham Carter?"

Hudson made an impatient sound. "Look, I'm

trying to be helpful, but I don't know any of these men."

"You're quite certain?" Dave pressed. He was sure they were on the right track, but if Hudson was telling the truth, they were back at the beginning.

"Positive," Hudson said, pushing back his chair and standing up. "Are we through?"

"Sit down, please," Kathryn said, firmly but not unpleasantly. She needed his help. Hudson sat down, a frown creasing his forehead again. He looked at Belker, who just raised his eyebrows.

"Let's begin again," Kathryn suggested. "Maybe the names don't ring a bell, but if we told you more about them, perhaps it would help. Okay?"

Hudson shrugged. "If you insist."

"Once again," Dave chimed in. "Think carefully. Are you sure the name Patrick Hanlon doesn't mean anything to you? He was an industrial designer. Lived on Cabrillo Avenue in Alameda Heights."

"No. I don't know anyone in that part of town."

"Peter Valenzuela? Forty-eight years old, draftsman, lived in an apartment on Palmetto Drive? Small guy. Dark hair."

Hudson shook his head again. "Same again. No."

"Graham Carter, the record producer? Lived in a big house up in Cathedral Heights?"

"I told you, no. I read about them being killed in the paper, but that's all. The names don't mean a thing to me. Believe me, I'd be more than happy to tell you if I'd known them, but—"

"How about Angel Flores?" Kathryn asked offhandedly. The effect was electric. Hudson momentarily froze, mouth half-open, eyes wide with alarm.

289

Then he regained his composure. *He knows something,* Kathryn thought. She didn't have to look at Dave to know he'd seen it, too. His next words confirmed it.

"Come on," Dave urged. "You know who we're talking about. Angel Flores, lives in Mission Hills?"

Hudson shook his head. "No . . . look, that's the end of it, okay? I don't know any Angel Flores."

"I hope you're telling the truth," Kathryn said. "You see, we think Angel Flores killed those three men. Hanlon and Valenzuela. Graham Carter."

Hudson started to say something, then checked himself. He turned to look at Martin Belker, who realized something important had just gone down but had no idea what. Hudson got to his feet again.

"Look, you've asked me, and I've answered you," he said. "That's it. I have nothing more to say." He turned to his lawyer. "Marty, please advise the District Attorney that this interview is over."

Granz got up, too, and walked around the table to stand beside Belker's chair facing Hudson. "You're making a big mistake, Mr. Hudson," he said quietly. "A really big mistake. You should reconsider."

Hudson smiled and shook his head. "No, Mr. Granz," he replied confidently. "I told you I have nothing further to say, and I mean it. I don't know any of those men, and I don't know any woman named Angel Flores, either."

Dave's expression hardened. He stepped closer, his face not a foot away from the prisoner's. "Who said Angel Flores was a woman?" he snapped.

"It was . . . you said—"

"No, I didn't."

Hudson tried bravado and shrugged. "Well, I just assumed—"

"Angel is a man's name," Dave said.

"No more questions, please, Mr. Granz!" Belker snapped, rising from his chair and moving between his client and Dave Granz. He turned to Kathryn. "My client has nothing further to say. This interview is terminated."

Kathryn looked at Hudson for a long moment, then shrugged. "As you wish," she said, a lot more nonchalantly than she felt. She stood up and began putting items into her briefcase. "If that's the way you want it, Marty, that's fine with us. We were just trying to keep your client alive, that's all. Let's go, Dave."

"Wait a minute," Hudson said, holding up his hand like a traffic cop. "What do you mean, trying to keep me alive?"

"Someone's trying to kill you," Dave told him casually as he moved over to the phone.

"What?" Hudson said. "What?"

"You heard what the man said," Kathryn said curtly. "I told you we think Angel Flores killed Hanlon, Valenzuela, and Carter. We think it was also Angel Flores who bombed the courtroom last week. And we're pretty sure the bomb was intended for you, Mr. Hudson. You."

Hudson stared at them for a long moment, then disbelief curled his full lower lip. He shook his head pityingly. "You must be pretty desperate to try a stunt like that," he said. "Come on, Marty, get me out of here."

Belker rang the bell that summoned the detention officer to escort the prisoner back to his cell. As

Hudson walked past him, Dave tapped him on the shoulder.

"Think about this, asshole. He nearly got you last time. If we don't catch him, he'll probably try again."

Richard Hudson hesitated for a moment, as if he was going to say something, and then followed the guard out of the room. He didn't look back.

# 39

*They had made their decision.*

*He would kill Hudson when the jury brought in its verdict. That was the way Angel wanted it, and so that was how it would be. In a way, it was a better, a more appropriate finale, even though it hadn't been planned that way. He had originally intended it to be Lawrence first, then Richard. After that, Patrick and Peter and, last, the sybaritically epicene Graham. Then the bomb intended for Richard had gone off too soon and spoiled everything, and he told Angel they had to wait, they must, it was too dangerous to try again right away.*

*"You have to," Angel said. "He has to pay for what he did."*

*"You'll see," he said. "You'll see."*

*He imagined the scene, the foreperson handing over the verdict forms, the judge directing the clerk to announce the verdict, blissfully unaware that the whole procedure was totally irrelevant. Another court had already handed down its ruling.*

*That was how Angel wanted it. That was how it would be. And when it was over, the charade of his own life would be over, too. No more pretending. No more lying. They had gone over it again and again. Angel was right, it was the only thing to do. It was honesty. It was bravery. Then everyone would know, then they would understand.*

*He stood looking around. Court was in recess. The empty room was like a stage with the scenery still in place, barren without the presence of the actors who brought life onto it. The empty jury box, the court reporter's machine on its tripod pushed to one side, the unoccupied counsel tables, the vacant witness stand— all kindled a hint of sadness in him.*

*Such a waste. All through childhood, the thousands of times in those adolescent years spent trying to understand what it was about oneself that was different, desperate to sight others who felt the same way he felt, who were as he was. Them looking at him. Him looking at what they wanted him to be, wondering if that was what he really was, ignorant of his own life, making it up as he went along.*

*"He's so gifted," his aunt used to tell people. "So artistic. All the lovely things he makes for me to wear." Of course, she never knew, never even guessed. Those nights propping up some bar, "Strangers in the Night," on the jukebox, strangers rejecting him, him rejecting them. And all the rest of the time concealing it, acting the part life had given him, even though his heart was breaking. Until he found Angel, and release.*

*He sighed.*

*Today the jury in the Hudson case had heard both the prosecution's and the defense's closing arguments.*

*He had watched throughout with amused detachment, the only person in the court who knew nothing either of them said mattered. As the prosecutor led the jury through the maze of complex testimony they had heard, his mind was on the more important matter of how he was going to kill Hudson.*

*He had talked everything over with Angel, examining each option again and again, discarding one after the other until only one was left. The courtroom was by far the preferable theater. It would be televised. Everyone would see it. Everyone would know why. It was also the most dangerous, but he no longer cared about that. He was doing it for Angel. Nothing was more important.*

*The dialogue going on inside his head was so intense that he had to force himself to concentrate on what was going on in court. The prosecution spoke first. He liked Kathryn Mackay. She was bright and intelligent and tough when she had to be, but you knew there was sympathy there if you needed it. She always did a good job; today would be no exception.*

*The prosecutor had the burden of proving the defendant guilty beyond a reasonable doubt; therefore, the thrust of her argument was to convince the jury she had done so. He knew close cases were often won or lost in argument. Dead bang winners could be jeopardized by poor argument. Closing argument was the prosecution's opportunity to focus the jury's attention on the key issues, to get them to arrive at the desired verdict.*

*"As I told you at the beginning of this trial, ladies and gentlemen," she began, "attempted murder of the second degree is the attempted unlawful killing of a human being as the proximate result of an act involv-*

*ing a high degree of probability that it will result in death, an act committed for a base, antisocial purpose, with wanton disregard for human life."*

Throughout her long discourse, the prosecutor spoke to the jurors in a friendly, conversational tone, her manner methodical, her arguments logical and reasoned. She was sincere without being emotional, leaving all the theatrics, cute jokes, and humor to the defense. In her final remarks, she once more reminded the jury that for the defendant to be guilty of attempted murder, it was necessary only to show he had knowingly tried to infect his victims with the AIDS virus. Whether he had been successful in doing so mattered not at all.

It was a good argument, he thought. Crisp, logical, clear, simple. She had paid attention to her opponent's opening statement and the line of the questions he had directed at witnesses during trial, and now in her own closing anticipated his probable closing argument. He knew from experience that some prosecutors held back their best shots, sandbagged the defense attorney, and then pounced in what was called rebuttal. Not this one: Kathryn Mackay didn't appear to hold anything back. It would be interesting to see whether she had any tricks left in her bag when she got her second opportunity to argue her case to the jury.

He watched her as she came in smiling after the recess. She was noticeably brighter, happier, her eyes shining as if she had received good news. He wondered if she had, and if so, what it was.

Now it was defense lawyer Marty Belker's turn to address the jury for the last time. His closing was—perhaps predictably—more dramatic, more emotional than that of the prosecution. Good defense argument *wove in emotional elements in such a way as to move or motivate the jury. Shrewd and intense, Belker pulled out all the stops, pleading fervently for compassion, imploring the jury to see his client for the victim he really was.*

*"Here is a young man who began life disadvantaged, his parents religious zealots who denied him friends of his own age and abused him physically and sexually. Here is a young man who was placed in one foster home after another, who had never had the benefits of a normal home life. Yet in spite of these experiences, Richard Hudson put the past behind him. In spite of everything he suffered in his childhood, he became a hardworking, decent citizen. Then fate inflicted another cruel blow, making him a victim once again. He contracted AIDS."*

*He paused, sipped some water from the glass on his table, drew in a deep breath, and continued.*

*"Now, as if that were not enough, he is brought here before you on charges that never should have been brought. While my heart, while all our hearts ache for those infected with AIDS, the prosecution did not, cannot prove that Richard Hudson infected these women with the HIV virus."*

*He paused again and took another sip of water.*

*"The fact of the matter is, as we have shown, that one of these women could as easily have been infected by prior sexual partners, another by one of the patients at the walk-in clinic where she worked. And you will recall that one woman is not infected at all."*

*He went on to implore the jury, as he had done in his opening statement ten days earlier, not to further punish Richard Hudson, an innocent man who was a victim not only of AIDS but also of persecution by the*

*State of California and the Santa Rita District Attorney's office.*

*"Justice demands that you send a clear message to your community that victimization for political reasons is unacceptable," he told the jury, his forehead glazed with sweat. "Justice demands that you acquit Richard Hudson!"*

*It was hard to believe now, during this recess before the final act of the trial, with the dust motes spiraling in the shafts of sunlight coming through the window, that such highly charged drama had taken place here. Not that any of it mattered. All Kathryn Mackay's efforts to persuade the jury to find Hudson guilty, all Marty Belker's eloquent attempts to convince them Hudson was not guilty, weren't going to make the slightest difference. Hudson would neither serve time nor walk free.*

*"I want him to die," Angel had said. "And I want everyone to know why." So die he would, right here in this room. He looked around, visualizing how it would play the way a dance director looks at a stage to choreograph his dancers' movements. Him here, me there, thus and so, then tell them why, and end it. There was a sort of poetic justice to it. A pity there was no way of cleansing Richie with fire like the others, but it would be close enough. Close enough.*

*He smiled at the thought.*

# 40

"Rebuttal, Ms. Mackay?"

Kathryn stood up and smiled at the judge. "Thank you, Your Honor," she said.

He smiled back, and she wondered if he could sense the way she felt. Although her demeanor now was serious, inside she was still exhilarated, renewed, almost giddy. At twelve-thirty, earlier than she had expected, Marie Snyder had called her at her office.

"Good news, Kathryn," she'd said without preamble. "Your biopsy test results are negative. The lump was benign: there's no cancer."

It was like the sun coming out on a miserable winter day. A weight lifted off Kathryn's heart, and she found tears in her eyes. For a moment she was unable to speak.

"Thank you, Dr. Snyder," she heard herself say into the receiver. "Thank you."

She got up and looked at her face in the mirror. It seemed impossible that there was no change. Surely something should show, she thought. Excitement danced inside her. *No cancer, no cancer, no cancer.* She picked up the phone.

"Dave, could you come over to my office, please?"

"Sure," he said. "Anything special?"

"Just get over here."

She was smiling when he came in. It was no use, she just couldn't help it.

"You got your biopsy result," he said. It wasn't a question.

"I'm in the clear, Dave. There's no cancer."

A sudden unexpectedly overwhelming wave of relief swept through her, and she buried her face in his jacket so he would not see the tears. He held her close for a moment, not speaking.

"You know, Kathryn," he said softly. "I can say this now. When you first told me, I did something I haven't done for a long time. I went to church and prayed."

"And your prayers were answered."

He did not reply, and she looked up. He turned his head away so she could not see his eyes, his throat working.

"Yes," he said after a moment. Then, smiling, he took hold of her by her shoulders, holding her at arm's length. "We should celebrate. Dinner somewhere swell. Champagne."

"No," Kathryn said, almost fiercely. "We don't need any celebration. Nothing in the world could be better than this."

Now she stood to make her final argument to the jury. Strong, confident. She'd admired, even enjoyed, Martin Belker's closing argument. If she had been defending Hudson, she would probably have argued pretty much the same things, tried to evoke the same emotions, made the same plea. Out of the corner of her eye, she could see Belker watching her, a small frown creasing his forehead as if he could sense and was made uneasy by her visibly fresh vigor and certainty.

Like most good prosecutors, Kathryn believed that if you could not hit rebuttal paydirt in thirty minutes, you ought to sit down. Thirty minutes, then—half an hour to respond to the defense's summation and to make her most powerful and lasting impression on the jury before it retired to deliberate. She took a deep breath and turned her attention to the jury box.

"If it please the court," Kathryn began softly. "Ladies and gentlemen of the jury, the defense is right about one thing. Richard Hudson truly is a victim. A victim of the most frightening, the most deadly disease ever known to the human race. But as we were told by the defense's own expert witness Dr. Axler, himself infected with the HIV virus, we must not pity. Sympathize, certainly. Show compassion, by all means. We would be less than humane if we did not offer him that much.

"But we must not under any circumstances allow sympathy or compassion to blind us to the inhumanity and horror of the defendant's criminal behavior. Richard Hudson deliberately and with malicious intent set out to infect three young women with a disease he knew was certain to cause their deaths. Not during a passionate moment of exchanged love, not in an anguished cry for companionship or commiseration, not by an unfortunate but forgivable oversight.

No! These were pure, unmitigated, and intentional acts of attempted murder.

"Who better than someone himself infected and facing inevitable death could understand the despair, the sheer terror these three women would experience when they learned they might be infected with AIDS? Surely, knowing the depth, the extent of that fear, only a monster—a vile, despicable monster—would deliberately and with depraved intent transmit that unspeakable afflication to another human being?

"Yet that is exactly what Richard Hudson did. He deliberately and meticulously spun a web of deceit into which he lured three unsuspecting victims. He placed carefully composed relationship ads in a tabloid. He romanced his unsuspecting victims, wined them and dined them, won their confidence, and anesthetized them with lies about his celibacy. Then, like a spider with the fly trapped inescapably in its web, he injected each of them with a poison so deadly that everyone it touches is doomed to a slow and agonizing death.

"Did he allow his victims a choice? No more than the spider does the fly. How could they make a choice to assume a risk voluntarily when they did not even know that risk existed? He told them a vicious and plausible lie about having been tested negative for HIV, knowing, fully aware that inside his body a lethal time bomb was ticking, a time bomb he then planted inside these women's bodies without their knowledge and unquestionably without their consent.

"The defense attorney argued the prosecution failed to prove motive, that absence of motive establishes his client's innocence. The defense attorney is wrong. Motive is not an element of the crime charged. His Honor will instruct you that motive need not be shown by the prosecution for you to find the defendant guilty. Nevertheless, while I have no obligation to prove the defendant's motive, I'll take a few minutes to address what the evidence has shown motivated Richard Hudson to commit his crimes. The defendant became infected with the HIV virus, and that infection progressed irreversibly to AIDS. A rage, a consuming anger grew inside his heart, a cold and savage determination to revenge himself upon the same sex he believed infected him. This was revenge, pure and simple, an act born out of the rancor and self-loathing bitterness in his heart. He set out to deliberately and intentionally infect these women with AIDS, to make them suffer for the injury a woman had done to him. And he did so, without regret, without conscience, without remorse.

"I said earlier it would be inhumane not to feel compassion for the defendant, ladies and gentlemen, and that is true. But we must also feel revulsion. Here is a man who not only deprived his victims of the right to choose but deliberately resolved to deprive them of their right to live. Richard Hudson attempted to murder Victoria Mitten, Jane Sorsensen, and Marian Browning as surely as if he had placed a gun to their heads and pulled the trigger. And I ask you to convict Richard Hudson on those three counts of attempted murder. Thank you."

She returned to her seat and sat down, limp as a rag, totally drained. It wasn't enough to present your case well, to explain the evidence, to establish the facts. If you didn't put any passion into it, the jury didn't take any away with them. She had shown them she cared and wanted justice for the victims. If she didn't, why should they? That was her contribution, the extra something she had to give.

Through the fog of her sudden tiredness, she was conscious of Judge Woods's voice instructing the jury they must now retire and elect a foreperson. Court would recess until they had reached their verdict. It was all over. Kathryn turned to see Dave smiling at her.

"You were even better than I thought," he said.

"What does that mean?"

"Belker just slid me a note: Hudson wants to talk."

"Okay, let's do it," she said.

He nodded. "I'll just go get my tape recorder out of the Jeep. Meet you at the jail, okay?"

Whistling tunelessly, Dave walked briskly down Pacific and turned onto Alvarez. As he crossed the street toward the parked Jeep, he pressed the key button to disarm the alarm and release the central locking. There was a sudden orange glare, and a hard slam of sound flattened his eardrums. The front of the Jeep leaped upward two feet off the ground, and the hood, ripped off the vehicle by the force of the explosion, somersaulted over his head like some weird, lopsided bat, to land with a tinny crash against a wall behind him. He heard glass shattering, the sound of a man's hoarse shout. A ball of smoke rose from the wrecked Jeep, and a thin tongue of flame licked across the bodywork. It was only then Dave realized he was sitting in the middle of the street where the blast had blown him off his feet.

Rough hands helped him up, pulling him away

from the burning vehicle. Somewhere a siren wailed, coming nearer.

"That your car, buddy?" someone asked.

"Yes, it is, goddamnit!" Dave growled angrily and thought to himself, *What you don't know, buddy, is that bomb was meant for me.*

# 41

The interview room still stank of sweat and stale smoke. The graffiti on the walls were as obscene as ever. Kathryn and a still-shaken Dave Granz sat facing defense attorney Martin Belker and his client Richard Hudson across the interview table, exactly as they had the day before. Word of the attempt on Dave's life had traveled fast, and she could see the prisoner was scared now, really scared.

"I guess we don't need to tell you things have changed since we last talked, Mr. Hudson," Kathryn said. "Someone put a bomb in Inspector Granz's car. I'm confident when the bomb squad's report is in, it will confirm what we already suspect, that the bomber was Angel Flores."

Dave placed the jail's mini-cassette recorder on the table and started it.

"Start talking, Hudson," he said. "Time's running out."

Martin Belker held up a hand to tell Hudson not to speak and looked straight at Kathryn.

"My client has recalled certain information which might be helpful to your bombing investigation," Belker began. "He is willing to cooperate with you as far as possible, but we will require something in return."

It was standard bargaining procedure. Quid pro quo, Kathryn thought. The better you get, the better you give.

"What exactly did you have in mind?" she asked. "I'm sure your client isn't motivated solely by a desire to be a good citizen."

"Drop all charges against him," Belker demanded. "Your case is shaky, anyway. Drop all three counts, and maybe we can help."

Kathryn stood up. "You didn't beat about the bush, Marty, so neither will I. I won't do that. We wasted our time coming over here. Let's go, Dave." She began stuffing papers in her briefcase. Dave looked at Hudson and shook his head.

"You poor sad asshole," he said.

"Wait," Hudson said. Belker silenced him with a look.

"All right," he snapped. "Drop the Sorensen count. If my client goes down on the other two counts, you agree to recommend to Probation and the Court that the sentences run concurrent."

Kathryn kept her expression neutral, concealing her inward elation. She was tempted to grab the offer and run, but there was more to it than just that.

"You know I can't commit to a deal without the District Attorney's personal okay, Marty," she said.

"That's my offer," Belker said. "Take it or leave it."

"We need to hear the information first." Kathryn turned to look directly at Hudson. "How about it, Mr. Hudson?"

"I want to ask you something first." he said. "It's about this . . . these bombings. You said you thought . . . he might try to come after me again?"

"After what happened half an hour ago, I'd say it's gone from possible to probable," Kathryn said.

"Then I think you ought to give me round-the-clock protection, starting right now."

"We'll do everything we can to ensure your safety," Kathryn said. "But you've got to help us, too."

Belker shook his head and pointed at the cassette recorder. "He won't talk to you until we've cut a deal and it's on that machine."

Kathryn checked that the recorder was running. She didn't want there to be any confusion about what was said or promised. Then she looked directly into Hudson's eyes.

"Okay, here's the deal," she said. "You talk, and we listen. Tell us something that gets us to the bomber, something solid, not just guesswork, and I'll talk to my boss. I'll recommend we drop the Sorensen count and ask for concurrent sentencing on the other two. No guarantees. My boss can say no, and if he does, that's the end of it."

Hudson looked at Belker, uncertainty written all over his face.

"Take the deal before I change my mind," Kathryn told him. "Right now, or we're out of here. And we won't be back."

Belker looked at her, then at his client. "Can we have a couple of minutes alone?"

Kathryn grabbed her briefcase and stood. "Five minutes. And Mr. Hudson, while you're making up your mind, don't forget we believe you were the target of the courtroom bombing. We think Angel wants you dead."

Dave used the phone to have the detention officer let them out of the interview room. As the door closed behind them, Granz turned to raise his eyebrows at Kathryn.

"You're getting soft in your old age. I thought you'd be a rock."

"I'm being pragmatic," she said. "What with Sorensen testing negative for HIV, the jury may very well hang or acquit on that count alone. As for concurrent or consecutive, I can recommend concurrent sentencing to the judge till I'm blue in the face, but ultimately the sentence is up to him. And even if Hudson went down on all three counts and the judge maxed him out, the harsh reality is with AIDS he could be dead before he serves out his sentence."

No more than two minutes passed before Martin Belker swung the interview room door open and motioned Kathryn to come in.

"What are the chances Benton will go along with your recommendations?" he wanted to know.

Kathryn wasn't completely sure herself, but she didn't tell Belker that.

"He's never rejected a deal I've recommended before. And he wants the bomber caught. I think he'll go along, but I can't promise. If he doesn't, no deal, no matter how helpful your client has been."

"That's pretty iffy," Belker said, but he was wavering.

CHRISTINE MCGUIRE

"Fish or cut bait, Marty," Kathryn snapped. "We're not making a movie here. If your client has got anything to say, let's hear it."

Belker showed his exasperation for a moment but then shrugged philosophically. "Okay. You've got a deal. Do you understand what the deal is, Richard?"

"Yes, I understand."

"Go ahead, then. Tell them what you told me," Belker said. Hudson nodded and turned to face Kathryn and Dave.

"I lied when we talked yesterday," he began.

Dave looked up. "No shit?" he said with hugely fake amazement. Kathryn kicked him gently under the table. They needed this information, and she didn't want Dave's sarcasm to alienate Hudson.

"Are you saying you knew some of the men who were killed—Hanlon, Valenzuela, or Carter?" she asked.

"No, that was the truth. I didn't know any of those people." Hudson looked uncomfortable, trapped. The little silence lengthened as everyone waited.

"I . . . met someone called Angel once through a . . . a mutual friend," Hudson continued. "I'm not sure it's the same one you're talking about, but I think it could be. This was a while ago."

"This friend, was it a man or a woman?" Kathryn asked.

"A man."

"What's his name?" Dave asked.

Hudson shook his head, his body tense, his eyes wary. "That's not part of our deal," he said. "Knowing my friend's name won't help you catch your bomber. The only reason I'm telling you about this at all is that if Angel turns out to be the bomber, my

310

friend may be in danger. If you make me ID him, I'm not saying another word."

"We don't need to know his name. Go on, please," Kathryn said. It wasn't important right now to know the friend's identity, only Angel Flores's. If it proved necessary, she was confident she could get Hudson to reveal his friend's name later.

"We had a special relationship, my friend and I."

"A sexual relationship?" Kathryn asked.

He looked at her for another long moment, his eyes thoughtful, then shrugged. "Yes, a sexual relationship."

"You're telling us you're bisexual?"

Hudson was silent for a moment. He looked at Kathryn almost pleadingly. "What you said, in court. About me. It wasn't . . . that wasn't why. I don't blame women."

"Richard," Belker said sharply, "as your attorney, I must advise you not to continue discussing this matter with Ms. Mackay."

He shrugged. "It doesn't matter anymore. The jury is out."

"Go ahead," Kathryn said softly. "Tell me why. I'd like to know."

"I'm not sure I could tell you in a way you'd understand."

"Why don't you go ahead and try?"

"All those years," he said, his eyes blank with memory. "When I was a kid. The . . . things they did to me. And they were my parents. It's as if they burned something in my soul. It's not just . . . women. It's everyone. Anyone. All I have inside me is an emptiness. If you ate my heart, it would poison you."

"You can't punish everyone for what two people did to you," Kathryn said.

He shrugged. "I just thought I'd tell you. You seem to . . . understand."

"Let's get back to your friend," Belker said, cutting Hudson off.

"What was your relationship with him?" asked Dave.

"It wasn't exclusive. I didn't have exclusive relationships. But we had known each other a long time. My friend liked threesomes. Sometimes he would bring someone home and call me to come over. He was into S&M, too, you know what I mean? He liked to be tied up, then whipped before he had sex. I'm not into that sort of thing, so whenever he was in that mood, he had to see somebody else."

"Go on," Kathryn said encouragingly.

"Last time I saw him must have been over a year ago, maybe the end of March or early April of last year, something like that. He called me and asked me to come over. Said he had someone special he wanted me to meet. It was late, maybe nine o'clock, but I drove up there, and he let me in. He was wearing a silk robe, barefoot, a bottle of champagne in one hand, two glasses in the other. That told me this special someone else was already there."

"How did you know that?"

"My friend only drank when he was having what he called 'special sex.' Then it was always champagne, expensive champagne, and he never drank alone."

"Okay, so you went in. What then?" Dave asked.

"We went into what he called his den. A big room with a real fireplace, soft sofas, and cushions everywhere. There were no lights, only candles, and I could smell some kind of incense burning. He said, 'I've got a surprise for you. Come and meet Angel.'"

"Angel?" Dave's voice was tense. Kathryn touched his arm gently, and he relaxed, but only slightly.

"I saw this woman sitting on the sofa. Blond hair, a black silk dress, great body. When she said hello, she had this soft, sexy voice. I wondered what the hell was going on. My friend never brought women home. My friend said Angel was going to make tonight very special for us. So we drank some champagne, a lot of champagne, and we started fooling around. Then we were all together on the sofa, and it was, you know, getting steamy in there. And that was when I realized, I mean, there's some things you can't hide, right?"

"Angel wasn't a woman," Dave said.

Hudson looked surprised for a moment. Then he nodded confirmation. "That's right," he said. "But in that light, those clothes . . . you'd never guess."

"How old would you say Angel was?" Dave asked.

Hudson stuck out his lower lip. "Late twenties, mid-thirties?"

"Eyes?"

"Green."

"Natural hair color?"

"No idea."

"Height, weight?"

"Five-seven, five-eight, maybe a hundred and thirty, a hundred and forty pounds?"

"Did you hear your friend call her any other name? Only Angel?"

"Only Angel."

"Okay, go on, what happened then?"

"As I was saying, one thing led to another, and my friend and I were undressed with our hands cuffed behind our backs. Angel produced a leather whip out of a bag, a kind of cat-of-nine-tails thing, and then we—"

"You don't need to share the details of your sex life with us, Mr. Hudson," Kathryn interrupted, not unkindly. She turned to Martin Belker. "Is this all you've got, Marty?" she asked, unable to conceal her disappointment. "If it is, I have to tell you it's not enough."

"No, wait, there's more," Belker said anxiously. "Tell them about Angel, about following her home," he told Hudson.

"Afterwards . . . it was quite late. I followed her back to town when she left my friend's place. I was, well, to tell you the truth, it was curiosity. And it had been . . . I was intrigued, you know. I thought maybe I could call her sometime on my own."

"What kind of car was she driving?" Kathryn asked.

"White Nissan Sentra, late model, probably a year or two old."

"Did you get a license number?"

A head shake. "I wasn't interested. I just wanted to know where she lived."

"We know where she lives," Kathryn said patiently. "Mission Heights, off Highland Valley Drive. What we want to know is why she's—why he's never there."

"Okay, wait, maybe I can tell you that, too. See, I was curious who this Angel really was. After I followed her home, I checked the mailboxes. There was an A. Flores, so I figured that had to be her. I pushed the bell, but nobody answered. I thought, *strange.* I went back to my car and waited, I don't know, fifteen or twenty minutes. I was about ready to leave when I saw someone come out of the building, a man. It was raining, and he had on a three-quarter-length dark-colored raincoat and a rain hat. But it looked like he was wearing it more to disguise himself than to keep dry. You know, the brim of the hat was pulled down so it covered his face, and the coat was buttoned all the way up to the neck, and the collar was turned up. Looked weird as hell, especially in Santa Rita where hardly anyone wears a raincoat, no matter how hard it pours. It wasn't until he got into Angel's car that I realized it was, he was her. So I followed him."

"You know who he is?" There was no mistaking the tension in Dave's voice now.

"No, I never saw his face, only where he went. I meant to go back sometime, but then I was arrested before I got around to it. Like I said, I'm not into S&M, but I enjoyed myself that night. I guess I was trying to work up the courage to call him."

"All right, where did he go? What was the address?"

"South side, 282 28th Avenue."

Dave was on his feet in one lithe movement. "Let's get out of here," he said to Kathryn. "We've got to talk to Walt Earheart. Now."

# 42

After first contacting Judge Susan Barber by telephone, Dave faxed her his signed supporting affidavit and a search warrant to search Angel Flores's Mission Heights apartment and the 28th Avenue address. The judge confirmed receipt of the documents, swore Dave as the affiant, and once she was satisfied the affidavit demonstrated probable cause, signed the warrant and faxed it back. As soon as it was in his hands, Dave wrote "duplicate original" on the signed document, and they were ready to roll.

Deputies, detectives, and crime-scene investigators were dispatched to both locations simultaneously. Commander George Purington and specialists from the bomb squad accompanied the officers to the Mission Hills apartment on the likelihood they would find bombs or bomb-making equipment on the premises.

"Kathryn, you want to ride up to Mission Heights with me?" Walt asked.

"Thanks, Walt, but I'd better take my own car in case the Hudson jury comes back with a verdict," she told him. "I'll meet you up there."

By the time Kathryn reached the apartment block on the hillside west of Highland Valley Road, CSI had already begun its meticulous search and inventory of the contents of the apartment. Joe Coughlin, one of the SO detectives, confirmed there had been no sign of Flores.

"Go take a look in the bedroom," Coughlin told Kathryn, and pointed at a doorway. "Looks like Madonna used to sleep here."

Kathryn went in. The room was dominated by a king-sized four-poster bed with blood-red velvet drapes that matched the drapes on the windows. On the wall opposite the door hung an ornate full-length antique mirror with a gilded frame, flanked by framed prints of paintings by Alfonse Mucha. In front of the window was an antique dressing table littered with every conceivable kind of makeup. A velvet love seat stood against the side wall. A crime-scene investigator was going through rows of dresses in the walk-in closet. Another was examining drawer after drawer of flimsy underwear.

"Jesus," Earheart said, looking around. "You think maybe Flores brought tricks up here?"

"I don't think we're dealing with a prostitute here, Walt. It doesn't fit the profile," Kathryn said. "I'd say this is more likely to have been some sort of refuge, a place where he could 'become' Angel, the female. And enjoy it."

"Lieutenant!" someone called. "Take a look at this!"

With Kathryn following, Earheart went back to the

simply furnished living room where Joe Coughlin's partner, Tom Ney, was standing with a wastepaper basket in his hands.

"Just found these," he said. He turned the receptacle over, and a litter of torn photographs cascaded onto the table. It took only a matter of moments to fit them together; they were pictures of the fire-bomber's victims—Patrick Hanlon, Peter Valenzuela, Graham Carter—all angrily torn in half and discarded.

"In here," called George Purington.

Kathryn and Walt went through the adjoining room and into another fitted out as a brightly lit workshop. A long workbench with vises and clamps, rows of tools, retorts, and stainless steel mixing bowls stood next to a steel shelving unit holding labeled boxes of chemicals and gallon and half-gallon glass bottles containing sulfuric, nitric, hydrochloric, and other acids.

"Shit," Walt said. "This is where he made the bombs, right?"

"Right," Kathryn said. "The devil's workshop."

On a shelf above the bench between two stone bookends made of petrified wood were a dozen or so paperbacks, among them *The Anarchist's Cookbook, The Improvised Munitions Black Book, The Black Book Companion, Ragnar's Guide,* and *The CIA Field Expedient Incendiary Manual.* No need to guess where the bomber got his information.

George Purington was bent over the bench using a magnifying glass to study some materials one of the technicians had recovered from a wastebasket.

"Bad news," he said by way of greeting. "Our boy made a bomb in here, quite recently, maybe yesterday, maybe even this morning. We've got fresh traces of potassium chlorate, some smears of petroleum jelly, copper filings, and a couple of small pieces of piping."

"Which tells you what?" Earheart asked.

"Plastic explosive, copper tubing, my guess is he's made a pipe bomb," Purington said, straightening up. "And he's walking around with it right now."

# 43

He was not the slightest bit surprised when they told him the jury in the Hudson case had reached a verdict. Court would reconvene as soon as Judge Woods, prosecutor Kathryn Mackay, and defense attorney Martin Belker could be located and summoned to attend. It was as if it had been predetermined, inevitable.

Angel was pleased, too. Excited.

*Now they'll know. Now they'll all know.*

The pipe bomb he had made last night was beside him, snugly packed inside a layer of Play-Doh. The igniter was a simple device made from a book of matches and a strip of friction tape. One sharp tug would flame the matches and ignite the short fuse. Unstoppable, immediate, and lethal. Hudson would be dead before anyone could even react.

# 44

Twenty-eighth Avenue ran east-west through Little Italy, so called because some of the earliest residents of what had once been the little fishing village of Santa Rita had been Italians. Many of its houses featured Victorian-style bay windows, decorative glass vestibules, and gingerbread woodwork beneath the roof eaves.

As they approached the house, Charlie Yamamoto, who was driving, switched off the engine of his car and coasted to a stop outside. Detectives had established earlier that the owner was Madge Collins, a widow who had lived in the house most of her life. A metal plaque on the wall beside the front door announced the building had been declared a historic structure by the County of Santa Rita. Built in 1886, in the form of a cross with none of the rooms joining, it looked like a lot of work had been done on the place, and Dave bet himself it would feature handcarved woodwork, original hinges and door-knobs.

"Looks quiet enough," Dave observed.

"That's when to watch out," Yamamoto said grimly.

As Dave reached for the door handle, the car phone buzzed. He picked it up.

"Dave, it's Kathryn, where are you?"

"We're at 28th Avenue now. Just going in. What's up?"

"I just got a call the Hudson jury has a verdict. I'm heading for court now. Try and get back as soon as you can, okay? And Dave, be careful. Purington said Angel is carrying a bomb around with him."

"Do my best," he promised, and joined Charlie Yamamoto on the sidewalk. Charlie lifted his chin to SO detectives Ed Black and Merv Phy, whose car had slid to a stop behind theirs. They acknowledged the unspoken message with lifted hands and moved down adjacent Lucero Street to cover the back of the house. Dave led the way up the stone steps to the front door, knocked loudly, and said in a loud voice, "Police officers! Open up! We have a search warrant!"

No response.

"You want to force entry?" Charlie Yamamoto said.

Dave held up a hand as he heard a querulous female voice and the sound of soft shoes sliding on a stone floor.

"All right, all right, coming, coming."

The door swung back to reveal a stooped elderly woman in a shiny black dress with a frilly collar of white lace at the throat. Her hair, which was almost as white as the lace, was combed straight back and coiled in a bun at the nape of her neck. Her face was long and thin, with high cheekbones and deep-set dark eyes. Liver spots dotted her forehead and the backs of her hands.

"What is it, young man?" she said, a trifle irritably. "What is it?"

Late seventies, maybe eighty, Dave estimated. She looked as if she had stepped straight out of the pages of a Charles Dickens novel, and her accent made him wonder if as a younger woman she might have immigrated from Great Britain.

"Mrs. Collins?" Dave said. "Mrs. Madge Collins?"

"Yes?"

"My name is David Granz, ma'am. I'm an inspector with the District Attorney's office."

"Goodness," the old lady exclaimed. "Police? Is something wrong?"

"Are you alone in the house, ma'am?" Granz asked.

"Why, yes. Just now I am."

"We have a warrant to search your home, Mrs. Collins," Dave said, showing her the document. "May we come in, please?" Dave asked.

"Search warrant?" the old lady said. Although obviously taken aback, she nonetheless was as polite as she would have been to invited guests. "Yes, of course, please do come in."

She led them into what in another era would probably have been called a front parlor. Furnished in the Victorian style, with flocked wallpaper and patterned carpeting, it featured an ornate marble fireplace with a mantel clock, an upright piano with a Spanish shawl thrown across it, and a chaise longue that didn't look as if anyone had sat on it since 1812. The room smelled strongly of cats.

"May I ask what all this is about?" she inquired,

motioning Granz and Yamamoto to sit. She was so charming and innocent that Dave felt bad about violating the sanctity of her home.

He sat down on the sofa without answering her question, while Yamamoto remained standing. The old lady patted her chest with a bony hand.

"Would you young men like some tea?"

"I'm afraid this isn't a social call, ma'am," Yamamoto said. "We need to ask you some questions."

"Yes, yes, of course, oh, my goodness, how exciting," the old lady flapped. "How can I help you?"

"Does the name Angel Flores mean anything to you, Mrs. Collins?" Dave asked.

She frowned. "Flores? Flores? No, I don't think so. It sounds Hispanic. Is it Hispanic? I don't know any Hispanic people."

"You live alone, Mrs. Collins?" Dave asked her.

"Oh, no," she said. "My nephew Christopher stays with me from time to time."

"Is he here?"

"No, he's gone to work."

"Where does he work, Mrs. Collins?"

"I'm surprised you don't know, officer—what did you say your name was?"

"Granz," Dave said. "What do you mean, you're surprised I don't know?"

"Chris works for the Sheriff," she said brightly.

"I don't know any Christopher Collins working in the Sheriff's Office." Granz frowned. "You, Charlie?"

"No."

Old Mrs. Collins shook her head patiently. "He's not my son, Mr. Granz," she said, smiling forgivingly. "He's my nephew. My sister's boy. I was awarded custody of Chris when he was twelve. He had been . . . persecuted." She bit off the word as if it tasted bad.

"You mean abused?" Charlie Yamamoto asked.

Her chin came up proudly. "We put all that behind us," she said firmly. "I gave him a new home, a new life here."

"And a new name?"

"He didn't want that. He said he wasn't ashamed of who he was."

"You mean his name isn't Collins?" Charlie said.

"No, no." The old lady smiled. "It's Taylor. Chris Taylor."

"Chris Taylor?" Dave echoed. "Jesus, Charlie—he's one of the bailiffs in the Hudson trial!"

They stared at each other in horror. The bomber was in the courtroom. And Kathryn was in there with him.

# 45

Kathryn watched closely as Bailiff Chris Taylor led in the jury and then assumed his place at the table between the jury box and the barrier separating the well of the court from the spectator area. He looked pale and tense, and she wondered why.

As was often the case, the members of the jury wore somber expressions, as if each was feeling the burden of his or her responsibility. Kathryn wondered whether their solemnity was caused by the presence of the TV cameras. People—jurors were no exception—often put on what they thought was an appropriate face for TV.

The rasp of the buzzer tripped by the judge opening the door to enter the courtroom stilled the hum of conversation. Everyone stood as the bailiff snapped his command and Judge Woods took his place on the bench, a slight sheen of perspiration the only evidence of his high-speed drive back to the courtroom from the Cathedral Heights Golf Club.

326

"Please be seated," he said, and turned toward the jury. "Ladies and gentlemen of the jury, have you reached a verdict?"

The foreperson was a well-dressed man in his middle fifties whose name was Robert McCubbin. He worked, Kathryn remembered, for a public utility company. McCubbin stood up and cleared his throat.

"Yes, Your Honor, we have."

The phone on the bailiff's desk gave its muted shirr as Judge Woods nodded to Jack Kennedy, the second bailiff. As he started across the courtroom, the phone on Taylor's desk rang for a second time. *Odd,* Kathryn thought. *Why isn't he answering it?*

Kennedy took the verdict form from McCubbin and handed it to the judge, who read it with no visible sign of emotion before handing it down to the court clerk. The bailiff's phone shirred yet again, and Judge Woods's forehead creased into an irritated frown.

"Answer that phone, please, Deputy Taylor," he snapped. "I want silence in here while the clerk reads the verdict."

"The verdict is guilty."

At first, Kathryn wasn't quite sure what she had heard. The voice had come not from the court clerk but from behind and to her left. Judge Woods's mouth was set in an O of astonishment. A startled hum of conversation filled the courtroom. Every eye was now fixed on the bailiff, standing at his table. The phone rang again. Taylor ignored it as before.

"This court is now mine!" he announced. "And my sentence is death!"

Judge Woods's brows came together, anger suffusing his face.

"What the hell is going on?" he snapped. He

gestured to Jack Kennedy, standing stock still next to the court reporter. "Kennedy, remove Deputy Taylor from this courtroom immediately." Kennedy took two steps forward, his hand moving toward the butt of his holstered Glock automatic. Taylor lifted his right arm so everyone in the courtroom could see it. In his clenched fist was a length of metal piping perhaps a foot long.

"Don't, Kennedy!" he shouted. "This is a bomb. Do exactly as I say, or I'll detonate it!"

Somewhere in the courtroom, a woman screamed. Kennedy froze.

*Angel,* Kathryn thought, knowing without knowing how she knew. *Taylor is Angel.*

"Shut up!" Taylor yelled. "Silence!"

As if on his command, the telephone on the desk stopped ringing. The TV cameras had already swung around to zoom in on Taylor. Kathryn turned so she could see him, trying frantically to remember everything she had concluded about his personality as she continued to refine her profile. A planner, organized and in control. Intelligent, educated. Proud and vain. A punisher. Probably himself a victim of abuse. Schizoid? Multiple personality disorder? Was there a lever, a trigger anywhere in there?

"This court isn't under your control anymore, Judge Woods," Taylor was saying, his voice tense but calm. "The doors are secured. No one gets in and no one leaves until I have had my say."

"What . . . what do you want?" the judge said. His voice was muted, as if he was conscious of the need not to antagonize Taylor.

"Him!" Taylor said, pointing the steel tube toward Richard Hudson. The defendant and his counsel shrank back as if the thing might leap upon them.

"Are you Angel?" Kathryn said, standing up slowly, assuming control of the situation as naturally as she did the courtroom when in trial. "Are you Angel Flores?"

Taylor turned to stare at her, his eyes burning with rage.

"Shut up, shut up!" he shouted. "I'm doing the talking here, not you!"

"You are Angel."

"Be quiet!"

"Why did she kill them, Chris?" Kathryn asked, keeping her voice low, unthreatening. "What did they do to her? How did they hurt her?"

Her brain was turning like a dynamo. Maybe she could talk him down. If she could hold Taylor's attention long enough, there was a chance of outside intervention. How long would it take for someone to notice, for officers to respond?

"You want to know?" Taylor said. He moved across the room so he was standing next to the defense table. Hudson cowered back. Marty Belker's face was the color of putty. "I'll tell you! Angel was beautiful, she was caring. She gave them everything they wanted, everything! Made all their dirty little dreams come true. And what did they give her in return? One of them gave her AIDS! Maybe this one right here!"

He grabbed Hudson's sweater in his clenched left fist and pulled him toward him across the table, then jammed the pipe bomb under his chin, forcing his head back.

"Was it you?" he shouted. "Was it you, Richard? You bastard, was it you?"

"Jesus," Hudson croaked. "Jesus, listen—" His legs turned to jelly, a dark stain spreading across his pants as fear voided his bladder.

"They're all dead, Richard!" Taylor shouted, yanking him to his feet, dragging him away from the defense table and out into the center of the courtroom, the pipe bomb jammed under his chin. "You hear me? Cleansed with fire, all of them. Except you."

"Listen to me, Chris!" Kathryn said, her voice clear but devoid of threat. "You don't want to hurt any of these innocent people. Angel wouldn't want this!"

Taylor turned to face her, his face twisted in anger. "What do you know about it?" he said, the words sounding as if they were being wrenched from his throat. "How could you know?"

"Tell us what happened," Kathryn said. "Tell us what happened to Angel."

He hesitated momentarily, a faraway look in his eyes, and she knew he was listening to her now. Maybe there was still a chance, she thought.

"They all hated her," he said. "They hated her being so beautiful."

"She wouldn't want to end it like this," Kathryn said. "You know that."

"She would!" he said, a sob in his voice. "She does!"

"No, Chris," Kathryn said. "Not Angel. There is no Angel. There's only you. You're smart, you're clever. You know it's true."

"Sure," he said bitterly. "Smart, clever. Be the honor student, be the class president, be the wrestling champ. Be the All-American boy. Nobody knew. Nobody understood what I was going through. Except for Angel. She understood. And look what they did to her!"

"You heard the doctor, Chris. He said there was hope," Kathryn said very softly, taking a step forward. "Put down the bomb. We can get you help. I promise, just put the bomb down."

Taylor looked at her, and she could see the longing in his eyes. If she could just get another few metaphysical inches closer, she thought, there was a chance, a faint chance he might capitulate.

"No!" he said, his voice rising to a shout again. "It's too late! I'm already dead. Angel is dead!" He grabbed Hudson's jacket and dragged him back until they were close to the bench. "And so are you, Richard!"

With a thunderclap of sound that flattened the eardrums, the doors of the courtroom burst open inward, and a phalanx of officers in dark blue body armor surged into the narrow aisle, shouldering aside the television crews.

"Down, down down down!" they yelled. "Everybody down on the floor now now now!"

In the swirling smoke from the blinding, deafening flash-bang of the stun grenades, there were screams, shouts, pandemonium. Flat on the floor only six feet away, Kathryn saw Chris Taylor yank Richard Hudson's body around in front of his own, using him as a shield, heard the SWAT commander yell, "Hold your fire!"

Taylor moved backward crabwise around the bench, which Judge Woods had already abandoned for the safety of the floor. Keeping his hostage between them and himself as the SWAT team moved inexorably toward him, Taylor dragged Hudson behind the heavy security shield. He raised his right arm in the air, like an athlete punching the sky. Metal caught the light.

"Everybody get down, get down, get down!" one of the SWAT cops yelled. "Down down down down!"

As if time had frozen, as if the world was standing still, no one spoke, nothing moved, as Taylor ripped apart the igniter and stood up behind the bulletproof shield, his other arm around Richard Hudson's neck in deathly embrace.

"Cleansed!" he screeched, clutching the pipe bomb to his heart. "Cleansed with fire!"

A sudden bright orange and white flash and a simultaneous hard flat explosion rocked the room. There was hardly any blast, all of it contained behind the security screen. When she looked up, Kathryn saw the plexiglass was cracked like a shattered windshield and streaked with bright, crawling crimson. Smoke coiled upward as the SWAT team moved warily forward and around behind the bench.

"Jesus fucking Christ!" one of them said.

# EPILOGUE

"Nervous, sweetheart?" Kathryn asked.

"Oh, Mom!" Emma protested. "I'm not a beginner, you know."

She was very animated, her dark eyes alight with excitement. She had spent a good three-quarters of an hour before they left home lovingly polishing her violin and making sure she had plenty of rosin for her bow. Today was her big day, the Certificate of Merit evaluation and recital in the music auditorium of the University of California at Santa Rita, a beautiful enclave in University Heights, northwest of town.

"Mom, watch my violin, okay? I want to go talk to Mollie," she said. She looked very grown-up in her new black dress with the white stockings and black patent leather shoes.

"Don't be long," Kathryn told her. "They'll be starting anytime now."

"Oh, Mom," Emma said impatiently. "I'll just be over there."

333

The auditorium was crowded with parents. Today's recital was part of a program sponsored by the Music Teachers' Association of California, the annual evaluation at which students demonstrated their progress by playing solos of their own choice before their parents and friends. Emma had chosen *"Gavotte"* by Handel. It was a difficult piece, but she had practiced hard and was very confident.

Kathryn looked up as Dave edged along the row and sat down beside her.

"Dave, you're just in time. How'd the meeting go?"

"Good, I think," Dave said. "Jim is leaving for San Francisco tomorrow to be fitted with a prosthetic hand. He'll spend a few days up there breaking it in."

"That's good news."

"Hal told him he wants him back. Jim's agreed to come back a couple of days a week for starters."

"How's Rochelle?" Kathryn asked.

"Making plans for that trip to Cleveland." He smiled. "How about you? You recovered from the media blitz?"

"I never want to hear the word *reporter* again as long as I live," Kathryn said.

The last twenty-four hours had been a blur. In the wake of Friday's astonishing events, it seemed as if every TV station and newspaper in the country had descended on Santa Rita looking for exclusives. Hal Benton had wisely opted to mount a press conference at County. Being at the sharp end of it for two hours had been an ordeal Kathryn was happy to put behind her.

"Shhh," Emma said, sliding into her chair alongside Kathryn. "They're getting ready to start. I have to go."

"Good luck, Princess," Dave whispered. She pretended not to hear and joined the other young people mounting the rostrum to take their places. She sat down and stared straight ahead, as if furiously determined not to look at her mother or Dave.

The program consisted of seven solos and two ensemble pieces accompanied by Mrs. Hiscock, their teacher, on piano. When the teacher announced it was Emma's turn, she stood confidently before her music stand and began. She played well and without errors and smiled as the audience applauded.

Watching her daughter, Kathryn had a sudden awareness of loss, infinitesimal but acute, as she realized that the poised youngster on the stage was no longer just her little girl. Emma was growing up, taking her first confident steps toward a life in which Kathryn would play only a supporting role. Growing up, she thought. Growing away. It was simultaneously a sad and happy thought.

After the awards ceremony, they agreed to meet back at the condo. On the drive home, Emma clutched her certificate. Dave had promised her he'd have it framed so she could hang it in her room.

"I think a celebration is in order," Dave said when they met back at the condo. "How about Sophia's?"

"Yeah yeah yeah!" Emma said enthusiastically. "Burritos!"

"Chips and salsa," Dave added. "What do you say, Kathryn?"

"Sounds terrific so long as we're not too late. Tomorrow's a school day, and I have to be in court early," she said.

"What's a media blitz, Mom?" Emma asked unexpectedly, and for a moment Kathryn was taken aback. The astonishing scenes of Chris Taylor's final moments had been featured at the top of the news on every TV channel Friday night. Saturday and Sunday it was front-page news. Today Kathryn had hidden the newspaper before Emma could see it.

"When something very important is happening and all the TV stations and newspapers have stories about it," she said.

"Like the O. J. Simpson trial?"

"That's right."

"Or the one you were in?"

"Yes, that, too."

"I saw it one night on TV. You were talking to a doctor."

"You saw it on TV?"

"I didn't watch long," Emma said. "It was pretty boring, Mom."

Kathryn smiled. If that was the sum of Emma's exposure to the events of last week, fine.

"Dave?" Emma said. "Can I have frozen yogurt for dessert?"

"A brilliant musician like you can have anything she desires."

"Then can we take Sam?"

"Dogs and restaurants don't mix, Em," Kathryn said. "We'll take him for a walk later."

"We could sit outside," Emma pleaded. "He'll be good, Mom. I promise he'll be good. Won't you, Sammy?"

Sam lifted his head, gave her a mournful look, and thumped his tail on the floor.

"See?" Emma said proudly.

They all piled into Kathryn's Audi and drove up the hill to Laguna del Mar. They ordered their food and went outside to sit at a table beneath the trees on the little patio. Sam lay in the shadows watching hopefully for someone to throw a tidbit. When they were finished, Emma took in the paper plates and plastic forks and emerged with her frozen yogurt.

"What did you get, Em?" Dave asked.

"My favorite," she said. "Peanut butter with chocolate sprinkles."

"You sure you don't want something?" Dave asked Kathryn.

She shook her head. "I'm fine."

"I've wanted to ask, did Woods give you any hint what the verdict was?" Dave asked Kathryn.

"Not the blink of an eyelid," she said. "And even if he wanted to, the law precludes him from revealing the verdict. So we'll never know."

"One thing I couldn't figure out," Dave mused. "How come Hudson never realized Taylor was Angel?"

"He never saw Taylor up close. Only Angel. I imagine she looked a lot different."

"How do you think the verdict would have gone?"

"My gut feeling is the jury would have convicted on Mitten and Browning and hung on Sorensen. But now we'll never know. Taylor preempted them. All of us."

"I know you feel cheated," Dave said. "But there was nothing anyone could have done."

"Damnit, it doesn't seem like justice somehow," Kathryn said angrily. "I feel like I let everyone down.

The men who were murdered. And Hudson—I cut him a deal, and he got a death sentence instead."

"Think of it this way," Dave said quietly. "It was passed a long time ago."

She nodded. "I guess so. I just wish . . ."

"Let it be, Kathryn," Dave said. "Let it be. At least for this afternoon."

"You're right," she said. "This is Emma's day."

"Mine, too," he said lightly.

Kathryn feigned puzzlement. "Your day?"

"Sure," he said. "It's my birthday. You forgot, right?"

"Wrong." She smiled. "We didn't forget, did we, Em?"

Emma smiled conspiratorially as Kathryn laid the package on the table.

Dave picked it up, frowning. "Hmmm," he said thoughtfully. "Looks too small to be a new Jeep. So what can it be?"

"Open it, Dave, open it!" Emma said, wide-eyed with anticipation.

He tore open the gift paper and opened the box. The watch glinted, soft gold in the late sun. He took it out of the box and held it in the palm of his hand.

"Kathryn, it's beautiful," he said softly. "I—I don't know what to say."

"Happy birthday, Dave," Kathryn said.

"Yeah, happy birthday, Dave," Emma said, and kissed him on the cheek.

He looked at Kathryn, and she saw the emotion in his pale blue eyes. "How about we head home?" he said. "I know you want to make it an early night."

Kathryn smiled. "Not that early," she said, and kissed him.

"Well, well," Dave said. "What was that for?"

"Openers," Kathryn told him, and kissed him again. Emma grimaced and rolled her eyes skyward in pantomime embarrassment.

"You two," she said.